"You have th

Nancy teased, caressing his face, then the corner of his mouth. "I don't remember them from before."

Mark felt his body begin to stir. "Nancy...don't... please."

"Why not?"

Well, there was a very good reason why not. But one look at her moist, parted lips made him want to forget everything but the moment. "May I?" he murmured.

"I'd be disappointed if you didn't."

His mouth covered hers, and he savored the softness. His hands slid down her back, then up to the rounded sides of her full breasts. Softly, she moaned his name.

The sound brought him to his senses. "Nan...go easy," he whispered. "You don't want what you think you want."

She gazed up at him, her eyes dark with passion and need. "I know what I want, Mark...I want you...."

ABOUT THE AUTHOR

Since her first Superromance novel, published in 1983, Sally Garrett's touching stories of love, family and commitment have attracted a wide following of loyal fans. Sally herself has had a lot of love in her life. She raised four children and lives in rural Montana with her biggest fan—her husband, Montie.

STRING OF MIRACLES

Sally Garrett

Harlequin Books

TORONTO • NEW YORK • LONDON
AMSTERDAM • PARIS • SYDNEY • HAMBURG
STOCKHOLM • ATHENS • TOKYO • MILAN
MADRID • WARSAW • BUDAPEST • AUCKLAND

Published November 1992

ISBN 0-373-70524-7

STRING OF MIRACLES

With love and affection
to my special sister,
Linda Nell Garrett,
who lives in Phoenix, Arizona,
for enriching my life

Acknowledgments

The characters, setting and plot were different, but my husband, Montie, and I lived through many of the experiences shared by Mark and Nancy. Special thanks are extended to cardiologists James Cleveland, M.D., and George Reed, M.D., of Missoula, Montana, for their expertise and caring attitudes, and to Ronald V. Loge, M.D., of Dillon, whose devotion to rural health care, wisdom and dedication directed us to these other fine physicians.

A decade or more ago cardiac problems often meant a death sentence or semi-invalidism. Now these patients can live full, active and productive lives.

PROLOGUE

NANCY PRENTICE GAZED at the man sitting across the restaurant table from her. She'd always hoped Mark Bradford could be more than a special friend, but in spite of knowing him and working side by side with him for ten years, the unwritten ground rules of their relationship had never changed. Mark had shown no inclination to move their relationship beyond one of friendship. And she'd never found the confidence to initiate a romantic encounter.

Mark had first caught her eye when she joined the legal firm of Burnside, Bailey, Summerset and Zorn, one of the largest in Phoenix, Arizona. The list of partners on its corporate stationery filled the left margin from top to bottom. Mark had boasted early in their friendship that his name would be added to this "sacred" list before too long. And he'd been right.

Nancy would have liked to be in line for that list, too, but ten years earlier, as she'd approached graduation at Arizona State University, she had been forced to accept the reality of her financial plight. Too proud to ask for help from her parents or her sisters, she had reluctantly made a decision that would temporarily distract her from her chosen profession.

Ever since she'd first begun watching reruns of old black-and-white *Perry Mason* shows, she had wanted to be a lawyer. But even with a scholarship she could never afford graduate school. So, swallowing her disappointment but not her pride, she'd decided to become a legal assistant rather than a full-fledged attorney, and with her prelaw degree she'd had no trouble finding employment.

She'd been with Burnside, Bailey, Summerset and Zorn for six months when Mark Bradford first invited her to dinner and coaxed her into sharing her unfulfilled dreams. He'd offered to loan her the money to go to law school, and though she'd been touched by his incredibly generous offer, she'd declined it, of course.

From that first dinner together she'd been captivated by his good looks, intelligence and charm. But apparently the feeling was anything but mutual. Mark had never given her more than an affectionate brotherly hug or kiss, not even when he was named a junior partner two years earlier and she had shared in the celebration.

Perhaps it had been for the best. The legal profession wasn't known for long-term relationships.

Mark had helped her establish an investment plan and encouraged her to hold on tight to her aspirations. She also knew he'd gone to bat for her more than once and succeeded in getting her salary increases that had boosted the balance of her education fund.

Tonight she was saying goodbye to this special man. Two weeks earlier she'd given her notice to the firm and announced her acceptance into the school of law at Arizona State University in Tempe.

Mark laid his fork down on the plate. ''I know you can make it, Nancy,'' he said, reaching across the table to give her hand a squeeze. "You're intelligent and you're willing to work hard for what you want. You're bound to be a success. Someday we may be at opposing tables in a courtroom. God help us both." He grinned and squeezed her hand again.

Her heart skipped a beat at his lingering caress. His wheat-colored hair was short-cropped, accenting the strong lines of his cheekbones and jaw. Tonight his eyes reflected the sage-green of the shirt he wore, but she preferred him in rusty browns and earth tones to accent his golden tan and sun-bleached hair.

Smiling, she eased her hand out of his. "I know law school won't be easy but having worked in the business should give me an edge."

"Or make you cynical," he cautioned, his features too solemn for a man still in his early thirties. "What textbooks say about the legal profession is seldom the way it works in courtrooms. How often do the books discuss the 'Art of Compromise' or 'Maintaining a Poker Face While Negotiating Plea Bargains'? Did you see a course listed in the catalog on 'The Fine Art of Brownnosing within a Law Firm'?"

Nancy closed her eyes, trying to stay unemotional as far as Mark was concerned. He would be shocked if he ever discovered how she felt about him. *Secret love, secret sorrow.*

"Are you sure you're set financially, Nan?" Mark asked.

How easy it would be to accept his help, she thought. *Then I'd have an excuse to stay in touch with him.*

She forced herself to nod. "I received a grant and a loan and a Soroptimist scholarship for women returning to do graduate studies. The first two are renewable for three years as long as I keep my grades up. And thanks to you I've been saving like Scrooge,'' she assured him. ''I'll be fine. And someday I'll even be rich and not have to worry about where my next dollar is coming from.''

A flash of concern troubled Mark's features, then he nodded. ''Here comes the waiter,'' he said, retrieving the check before she could react. ''This is on me,'' he insisted. ''I can afford it, you can't. I'll miss you, Nan. I don't think I'll ever find another assistant as sharp as you. You could approach the bench and plead any of my cases right now.''

''Thank you, but the system says I can't,'' she murmured. ''So it's off to school again for this struggling assistant.'' She smiled at him, and his gaze seemed to caress her face. She longed to reach out and touch him, to follow the fine line just beginning to appear at the edge of his mouth.

The years would always be kind to Mark, she decided. Ten years from now he'd be more handsome than ever as maturity carved its mark on him. Maybe when she finished school he could become part of her life again. But only time and fate would tell.

''We've been through a lot of struggles together, haven't we?'' he asked.

She nodded.

His gaze lingered on her, making her uncomfortable. ''Stay in touch?''

Nancy brushed a strand of her rich brown hair away from her cheek and glanced away. ''That goes both ways. Now that the new expressway is finished the miles will be closer,'' she told him.

''But the traffic will be worse. Every time they open a new expressway in this valley fifty thousand new residents arrive to use it. Anyway, you'll be so busy with your studies, you'll forget me within a few months. Send me an announcement when you graduate, though, and we can celebrate.''

Nancy followed him from the restaurant. At her Volkswagen Beetle he hesitated as if undecided about what to do. ''You've always been one of my favorite women,'' he said, kissing her forehead.

Nancy blinked away her threatening tears. ''Like a sister.'' She reached up and brushed her lips against his but broke away instantly. ''But that's okay for now. Call me occasionally?'' she whispered, her voice shaking with emotion.

''Of course,'' Mark promised. ''We all have to start over sometime. I read somewhere that these days everyone has at least three careers.''

''You'll be a lawyer until the day you die,'' she replied. ''With your track record nothing can stop you. You've been my secret role model all these years.''

He looked surprised.

''You didn't know?''

He shrugged. ''I tried to . . . look out for you. You were always special.''

''You've been like a big brother, but now the family is breaking up. Do you think we'll ever see each other again, Mark?''

His gaze swung from her eyes to her mouth and caught the tiny flick of her tongue as she tried to moisten her dry lips. His mouth opened as if he wanted to say something. Then he shrugged again. ''Who knows what lies ahead for us?''

''I know what lies ahead for me,'' Nancy said, her composure regained. ''A law degree and a lucrative practice. You have it. Now it's my turn.''

Suddenly Mark pulled her close and kissed her directly on her startled mouth, his lips warm and sensual. She could feel the contours of his hard, muscular body, and for an instant she felt a sexual hardness against her abdomen. When his mouth lifted from hers, she could hardly breathe.

"Money isn't everything, honey," he said, gazing intently into her blue eyes. "Keep your head on straight and do what's right. The money will come, but never let it be at the cost of integrity." He kissed her again, this time brotherly and irritatingly light.

She touched her lips. "Why did you do that?"

Mark grew somber. "A woman shouldn't be distracted by a man if she wants to practice law."

"I don't understand you," Nancy murmured.

"If you really want something and you're willing to work hard, you'll succeed. It's one of life's guarantees."

Nancy sighed. "Mark, you're very confusing. But of all the men I've ever known, you're the very best."

He turned away and walked to his low-slung powder blue sports car, one of the material signs of his newfound prosperity. He turned once and waved, then unlocked it and climbed in. For a few seconds she saw his blond head in the lighted interior, then darkness enveloped him and he sped away.

"I love you, Mark Bradford," she murmured, wishing he could hear her words and accept the truth she spoke.

CHAPTER ONE

MARK BRADFORD GLANCED UP from his cluttered desk as his door slowly opened. He had warned his secretary to keep away any and all intruders. She'd obviously ignored him, but as much as he resented the intrusion, he resented even more the law books, legal briefs and case folders scattered around the room on two chairs, his credenza and the floor.

He'd worked into the early hours of the morning, trying to find the right approach to use in presenting the summation that he would be making within a few hours to a jury he suspected had already made up their minds about his client. To make matters worse, he didn't blame them.

Nathan Weller is guilty as sin, Mark thought, but as his defense counsel, Mark couldn't let that truth color what he'd say to the seven men and five women selected to hear the case. Over the years Mark had always managed to find some redeeming value in a client, but not in the notorious Mr. Weller.

A jury of his peers? Impossible. How could the court find twelve men and women as wealthy and unscrupulous as his client, a man who had made and lost three fortunes in real estate fraud, each fortune larger than the previous one? Lately he'd moved into the lucrative area of buying his way onto the boards of several savings and loan associations across the Sun Belt of the Southwest.

Nathan Weller had even managed to get himself elected president of one ineptly managed association, and he'd raided its assets by ramming construction loans through the loan committee and into his own companies. The prosecuting attorney's case had been incredibly easy to substantiate. At times Mark wished he'd been on the other side of the case.

He'd let himself be persuaded to take the case by pressure from a senior partner, Robert Summerset. "Your track record is sterling, Mark," the partner had said. "Nate needs that. Yes, I know he's got a reputation, but most of that is due to the biases of the press. You know how the local media has been out to get him. They even tried to pin that car bombing a few years ago on him. But no man could be as evil as they've tried to paint Nate Weller."

Mark had read about his client for years, and as he'd listened to the senior partner's persuasive argument, he had tried to keep an open mind.

"People change," the older man had continued. "You and I have changed. Why not Nate Weller? He's been a friend since the boom years of the fifties. I can't let him down after all these years. But I can hardly handle the case myself. It'll mean a lot to me, to the firm...to your own career. You understand, don't you, my boy?"

Regrettably Mark had agreed. One case wouldn't matter, he'd rationalized. He had a string of successes that could absorb the predictable outcome of this one isolated case.

Now Mark leaned back in his chair and stretched. His vision seemed blurred. For several seconds he couldn't even make out who had entered his office. Maybe he needed glasses, he thought, rubbing his eyelids. He leaned forward again and squinted.

His secretary, Maude Williams, leaned against the closed door. "Mark? Sorry to interrupt you, but this was special. Forgive me." She smiled encouragingly.

He rubbed his left arm, trying to restore its circulation. Hours of clutching a pen had taken its toll, and bumping against a stone wall while jogging on a predawn morning two nights earlier had been a stupid thing to let happen. He'd never lost his balance while running before. His arm had been prickly and aching ever since.

"Cramp?" Maude asked.

He nodded.

"I'll bet you worked all night," she scolded. "You don't look so good. You're as pale as a ghost. Are you sure you're feeling okay?"

"I'm fine," he insisted. "I went jogging this morning up at Squaw Peak." He smiled at her. "Ever seen the sun come up over the peaks?"

She shook her gray head.

"A breathtaking sight. Too bad so many people prefer to sleep in and miss it. No matter how late I work, I always get up early and run."

She smiled. "For an old man you look pretty good. I'll admit to that."

He chuckled and stood up, stretching. "I'm as fit as a fiddle and ready to sway that jury in spite of their prejudices against evil old Nate."

She laughed. "Since you and I both know there's nothing good about Nate Weller, why do we put ourselves through this agony?"

"We're obligated," he reminded her.

"I'm glad I just type the papers and don't have to live with my conscience. I don't envy you lawyers. You earn your fees, especially today."

He stroked his burgundy tie. "I even wore this to catch their attention. I've never lost a case with my lucky tie."

She laughed. "You've never lost a case, period... at least not since I hired on six years ago. But when this case is over, you should get out of here and take some time off. Take a month and go to the Caribbean or fishing in the mountains."

He chuckled. "I've never fished in my life, and why would I want to tour some islands that don't interest me?" He flexed his arms a few times, but the exercise brought back the burning aches and discomfort, and he stopped, pretending he was finished. Maybe he'd make an appointment with a physician. He hadn't had a complete physical examination since joining the firm. How long ago had that been? Straight out of law school almost twelve... or was it thirteen years ago?

His mind grew fuzzy, and he wasn't sure just how long it had been. When did he pass the bar exam? Never mind, he thought. It didn't matter. "Did you need something?" He glanced at his watch. "I'm due in court in two hours."

She grinned and waved a finger at him. "Yes, you! It's time to take a break." She swung the door open wide. In trooped a contingent from the office pool area, followed by several of the partners and their legal assistants and secretaries.

"Happy Birthday, Marcus Bradford," they all began to sing, their voices blending in spite of the disharmony.

He swallowed, but the lump in his chest wouldn't go away. "Birthday?" He glanced down at his desk calendar. "I'd forgotten."

Bob Summerset, the partner who had talked him into accepting the Nathan Weller case, pushed his way through the crowd. "You work too hard, Mark. After today you're on vacation, a mandatory one." He waved his arms at the crowd. "Witnesses, plenty of witnesses. Now, my boy, come into the library. We have a little something for you."

Two secretaries took Mark's arms.

"I really can't take the time," Mark insisted. "I have work to do." He took a deep gulp of air, but it didn't relieve his need for oxygen, and each time he tried to twist and stretch to relieve a nagging ache right between his shoulder blades, the pain worsened. He couldn't remember lifting a heavy object, but then he couldn't seem to remember a lot of details this morning.

"Come on, Mark," Maude teased. "Don't resist. That courtroom will still be waiting whether you're a good sport or not. A guy doesn't turn thirty-six every day, so cooperate. We have cake and ice cream and even a bottle or two of champagne. And..." She grinned conspiratorially at her co-workers.

Amber Kellogg, a pretty blond legal assistant who had been assigned to Mark on the Weller case, handed him an envelope. "We have a gift certificate for you for ten sessions in a tanning bed. In Phoenix, Arizona, a good-looking guy needs a tan, and you've lost yours with all your jogging in the middle of the night. The tanning beds are at the health spa in this very building on the mezzanine. They open at six in the morning."

"Thank you," he mumbled.

Amber peered closer. "Gracious, Mark, you look like a vampire this morning. Smile so we can see if you have fangs."

He tried but didn't quite manage even a grin. He wished they'd all go away and leave him alone. His two hours had shrunk to an hour and a half. "I have a headache."

"Then someone get him something," Amber called.

"I'll get them," Maude replied, and disappeared.

Two aspirins, a piece of cake, and a paper cup of spiked punch was all he could tolerate before he sought refuge in the men's room. Maybe he was coming down with a bug, he thought, but this was April. Who got the flu in April? He hadn't had so much as a cold since grade school.

He pulled a toothbrush case from his trouser pocket and brushed his teeth, then swished out his mouth with mouthwash before returning to his office.

"Maude, I've got an hour left. Guard this door with your life . . . and your job."

"Feeling better?" she asked, following him into his office and peering at him. "I don't know if you look green or gray. I can call the bailiff and explain to him that you're sick. I'm sure they'll give you a day or two to recover. Want me to try?"

"I'm just tired," he replied. The lump in his chest had eased and his temples had stopped pounding. He tried to remember if he'd eaten pineapple the previous night. He was allergic to pineapple. No. Last night he'd skipped dinner completely.

Forty-five minutes later he shoved his notes into the briefcase and zipped it shut, then pushed the intercom. "Maude, I'm out of here. Expect me when you see me."

When he opened his door, Maude was busily typing at her word processor. She glanced up and he paused. "This case has taken its toll on both of us," he admitted. "Thanks for all the good help. Hope your husband will forgive me for the long hours you've had to put in."

She frowned. "You still don't look so good."

"I feel better, but kick me if I ever accept another case like this one."

"My pleasure," she replied, tapping a few buttons on the keyboard. "Ready to knock 'em dead with your closing argument?"

"Not really. But short of curling up my toes and dropping dead on the spot, I can't think of any way to get out of it, so... wish me luck, Maude. I may need it on this one."

MARK BRADFORD couldn't move or speak. Darkness engulfed him as he tried to ignore the voices that came through a shroud of numbness. Gradually he became aware of his chest lifting and falling without any conscious effort on his part.

"Mark? Son, can you hear me?" a man's voice called.

Mark tried to open his eyes, but his eyelids felt as if they had been sewn shut.

"Mark, honey, we love you," a woman murmured. The voice sounded vaguely like his mother's.

He wanted to sit up, but his arms wouldn't cooperate and his legs were leaden weights. He abandoned the idea and began to sink back into oblivion again. Another voice, that of a total stranger, disturbed him, and he wanted to tell its owner to shut up. His irritation shifted to anger. He wanted to lash out but didn't have the strength.

If these voices would just leave him alone, he'd go back to the burrow of darkness and search once again for the shimmering light and the mysterious glowing figure that beckoned to him from the end of a long tunnel on the other side. He'd almost reached it twice. Once he'd come close enough to almost touch the outstretched hand, but some force had intruded, and the figure had stepped away to blend with the bright emptiness.

"Mark, don't you dare die on us again!" a young woman's voice insisted. "I'll never forgive you." A hand touched his cheek, caressing him for a moment before warm lips replaced it. He felt a drop of moisture and realized it was a tear, but he couldn't fathom the cause.

"Oh, Mark, please, you've got to fight this," she coaxed.

Fighting was the last thing he wanted to do. If only he could turn over and pretend they were gone.

The woman's voice intruded again. "Mark, the surgeon says you'll be fine now, but you've got to try on your own. We lost you twice and Dr. Merrick brought you back." Something about her tone brought a vague recognition. Maybe if he could open his eyes he could see who she was. He felt the warm hand on his cheek again. Then it withdrew.

"Son, it's me, your father. Can you hear me?"

"Please, darling, open your eyes," another woman's voice pleaded. "You're my only son. I love you. You must fight this. You can. Not only for us, but for yourself. You've only begun to live. Please fight this. Please."

An unfamiliar man's voice intruded. "Give him a few moments, folks. His pulse is stronger, steadier, too."

A weight lifted from Mark's brain as he forced his eyes to open. He blinked several times. A glaring overhead light blinded him until a man in green leaned over him.

"How do you feel, Mark?" the stranger asked.

"Like a bulldozer ran over me," Mark wanted to say, but when he tried to open his mouth, he became aware of a tube rammed down his throat. Another smaller tube tickled his nostril, and the shadow of a noisy machine with asthma stood like a sentinel near his shoulder.

"Don't try to talk, young man," the stranger said. "Rest. You've had a rough go these past two days." The man patted Mark's shoulder, and in spite of the stranger's unfamiliarity Mark felt reassured.

He slipped into sleep again until a gentle touch on his cheek brought him slowly awake. The voices grew louder.

"I think he's turned the corner," the man in green said. "Mark, your family needs to say goodbye. They'll be back in a few hours."

Mark could only manage a subtle nod but was able to open his eyes and focus on the slender blond woman leaning over his side. *Jill, why are you here?* He hadn't seen his sister for three years, not since she and her husband had moved to Atlanta.

"I love you, Mark," Jill said between sobs. "You scared us all half to death. We'll be back this evening."

Mark's mother leaned over him, her silver hair shining above him like an angel's wings. "Take care, my darling."

His father, usually a man of stoic demeanor, touched Mark's bare shoulder and gave it a gentle squeeze. "Hang in there, son," he said, his voice breaking. "I thought we had this little problem beat. I'll never forgive myself for passing it on to you." His father straightened, leaving Mark to wonder what he could be talking about.

So tired. The room grew quiet. His mind seemed to be quiet, too, as if it had been vacuumed of its contents. The rustling of fabric, soft silky sounds with accompanying light footsteps brought him awake again and he opened his eyes. A woman in a white uniform injected something from a syringe into the tube near his wrist, then replaced a bag containing red fluid hanging on a hook above his head.

"That should be the last one he'll need," the gray-haired man in green said. "Page me if his condition changes. I'll be back in a few hours either way."

The silence returned.

Mark lay awake, trying to think. What had happened? The last thing he remembered was approaching the jury box to begin presenting his closing argument for the defense of Nathan Weller.

The case had involved many witnesses who would have preferred to retain their anonymity, and Mark had received more than one threat on his life during the long and complex trial.

What about the trial? He couldn't be here, strapped to a bed with a tube rammed down his throat, tubes coming from both natural and unnatural openings in his body, and a thousand-pound weight pressing against his chest. Had one of those threats been carried out?

Devastating fatigue sapped every ounce of energy. *So tired*. The courtroom. Had something happened in the courtroom? *Too weary to think*. Had he lost the case? For a moment he couldn't remember why he'd become so distraught in the courtroom. He'd never been one to overdramatize when arguing the merits of a case.

Why the blackout? It had swallowed him up after he experienced the most excruciating pain he'd ever known, pain that had ripped his chest open and exploded it into a million spears of torture. Someone must have shot him right in front of the judge and jury, but how could that have happened with all the security measures the court had implemented? Had they caught the hit man?

He tried to turn onto his side, but the restraints at his wrists kept him flat on his back.

"Can I help you?" the nurse asked.

"I want to get up," Mark mumbled around the tube in his mouth.

The nurse leaned closer and smiled at him.

"I want to get up." The words were clear in his mind, but his ears registered muffled, incoherent syllables.

"Lie still, Mr. Bradford," she said, patting his shoulder gently. "You shouldn't move. I'll give you something to help you rest. Tomorrow Dr. Merrick will disconnect the respirator and take out the tube in your chest cavity. Then we'll have you sitting up and you'll be able to take some broth and Jell-O. Doesn't that sound wonderful?"

THE NEXT MORNING Mark awoke to find himself surrounded by strangers until his gaze fell on the familiar face of the man in green from the previous day.

"Good morning," the man said, smiling as he touched Mark's forearm. "I'm Dr. John Merrick." He breezed through the other introductions, but Mark fell asleep before they were completed.

Late in the afternoon he awoke again to the voices of two women near his heasd.

"He's cute, isn't he?" one asked.

"Yes, but too young," the other murmured. "He looks so healthy, but you can never tell just by looking. We certainly know about that."

"I still think it's a shame for this to happen to someone like this. It's tragic," the other voice said.

Before Mark could open his eyes the voice of Dr. Merrick filled the room and the two women stopped their work.

"If I ever again catch you talking about a patient as if he can't hear, I'll have you both on the carpet." Dr. Merrick walked to the side of the bed and Mark got his first focused view of the man. "Good afternoon, my boy. Feeling better?"

Mark tried to speak around the tube in his mouth.

"Don't try yet," Dr. Merrick said. "We'll have that out in no time. Lie still while we turn you back into a functioning human being again. I want you to sit up on the side of the bed. If you manage that, we'll let you have a snack."

Mark tried to nod, then gave up. Instead he closed his eyes and tried to ignore the activity around him.

An hour later he could barely recognize his own voice when he heard the scratchy cackle. "What happened? Why am I here?"

Dr. Merrick studied the monitor near the head of the bed. "You had open heart surgery."

Mark's mind went blank. "No."

"That's what I said when they brought you in, but...never mind now," Dr. Merrick said. "Let's try to sit up. Here's a pillow. Hold it against your chest, and we'll help you."

Two nurses took his arms, and with Dr. Merrick's assistance they got him upright on the edge of the bed. Despite the intense pain Mark managed to sit unaided. The medical staff stayed close by. He sat for several minutes on the side of the bed. "The floor's cold."

"Get his slippers on," Dr. Merrick said, and something soft and warm replaced the cold floor.

Mark took a deep breath. "I'm hungry, but I don't think I can eat."

"The nurse will help you," the physician said. In a few minutes Mark had swallowed a cup of broth and a small glass of fruit juice. "It's a start," Dr. Merrick said.

When he was in bed again, the activity in the room quieted and only Dr. Merrick remained. "Feeling better?"

"A little," Mark replied, "but you must be wrong about...why you opened me up."

Dr. Merrick settled himself on a straight-backed chair close to the bed. "When they brought you here, you were in the middle of a massive heart attack. With your blood pressure as high as it was, it's a miracle you didn't have a stroke instead. Once we got you stabilized and did a few tests, you were rushed to surgery. We did a quadruple on you. Your heart looked like it belonged in a man's body twice your age."

Mark closed his eyes. "I don't understand. Damn it, I'm only thirty-six years old."

"Think back these past few months. There must have been warning signs. Shortness of breath? Chest pains? Pounding in your ears? Dizziness? Burning or a prickling feeling in your left arm? Nausea?"

Mark glanced out the window at the leaves swaying in the spring breeze. "Everyone has those symptoms when they run."

"Not the nausea." The physician frowned. "You're a jogger?"

"It's the only way I could get my head cleared," Mark replied. "Sometimes after a long day and too many problems I'd drive to Squaw Peak Park and run the trails."

"At night?"

"It's usually dark by the time I get out of the office," Mark admitted. "Sometimes I run before dawn. It's quiet then."

"Suicidal! Pure damn suicidal under the circumstances," Dr. Merrick said, getting to his feet. "You need your rest, son. Your family has been here every hour on the hour, but you've been asleep most of the time. I suggested they take the afternoon off and do the same, so take a nap. They'll be here to see you after dinner tonight. Any more questions?"

Mark turned away and closed his eyes. The physician was wrong, dead wrong. Something else had brought him here. He was too young to have had a heart attack. If he ever got out, he'd get a second opinion.

THE NEXT FEW DAYS were a blur for Mark Bradford. Dr. Merrick paid him several brief visits each day, but

Mark didn't want to talk about his condition or his course of recovery.

His parents and sister visited for ten minutes each hour. They never woke him if they found him asleep. The nursing staff became his constant companions, but they would only talk about casual subjects or items they'd watched on the television news. That was fine with him.

On the fourth day after the surgery Mark was rushed back into the operating room to repair a ruptured vein in his left leg that had doubled in size. The leg problem took his attention off his chest.

Dr. Merrick continued to discuss his condition, but Mark forgot the details of the conversations once the physician left the room. The nursing staff began to insist he walk with them around the circular hallways. The first trip was made in a wheelchair. To his surprise they encountered a steady stream of walkers. He began to recognize some of the men and women. None of them were even remotely close to him in age.

He let the staff coax him into a video room where he watched a series of short films, but the subjects in the films were older men, and as he viewed the segments, he thought of his father.

A few members of his law firm sent cards. Flowers weren't allowed. Only family members were permitted to visit, and he was glad. He didn't want to see anyone from the firm. They'd never believe their eyes. He'd lost thirty pounds, his blond hair curled untidily and needed a trim, and the spark had left his eyes. He could see that each morning when they insisted he shave himself.

ON MARK'S TENTH DAY in the cardiac care unit Dr. Merrick entered Mark's room and pulled a chair up close to the bed. "Mrs. Mahoney says you made it through the day with no arrhythmia. That's good. I'm cutting some of your medication and we're going to move you out of here tomorrow."

"I get to go home?" Mark asked, doubting if he could manage alone.

Dr. Merrick chuckled. "Hardly, Mark. You'll be moved to the wing next to this one for a few weeks. You won't be out of here until we're sure all that new plumbing and that new valve in your chest is working fine and you aren't going to have any more complications. This was very high-risk surgery, Mark, and complications aren't unexpected, but so far you've handled them well. We'll keep you on medication, but if that doesn't do the trick, you may be a candidate for a pacemaker."

"Great." Mark turned to stare out the window.

Dr. Merrick got to his feet. "Mark, your father and I had a long talk. He said he never told you about his father and grandfather."

"Sure he did. I grew up hearing about them," Mark replied. "They were early-day pioneers in Phoenix. My great-grandfather was one of the first men elected to the U.S. Senate after Arizona gained its statehood. We were pretty proud of him."

"And what happened to him?" Dr. Merrick asked.

Mark recalled the stories he'd grown up hearing. "He . . . he died in Washington, D.C., during his second term in office."

"How old was he when he died?"

"I think . . . about forty-five."

Dr. Merrick stroked his chin. "And your grandfather?"

"He and my grandmother took a cruise and—" Mark gazed out the window again "—he had a heart attack somewhere between Pago Pago and... hell, I don't remember." He glanced back at the surgeon. "You don't need to ask. He was forty-six, but so what? My father is sixty-one, and he's as healthy as a horse."

"But you're not." Dr. Merrick came to the side of Mark's bed. "You have a congenital problem. It's called familial hypertrophic cardiomyopathy. Familial means it tends to run in families. Defective genes cause the heart muscles to thicken. That puts a strain on the entire organ, especially one of the valves in your case. It was weak to begin with."

"And now you've replaced it. So I'm going to be fine?"

Dr. Merrick shook his head. "Your body produces more cholesterol than it can use. Your mother has high blood pressure and high levels of cholesterol, and so do you. Damn it, Mark, you inherited the worst combination from each parent and aggravated the condition by becoming a superstar attorney who thinks he must win every case at any price."

"Not my current one," Mark murmured. "It leaves a bad taste in my mouth. I just wanted to get it over with."

"Well, you succeeded. Read the papers when you get out of here. The case resumed after a two-day recess. One of your associates took over, played on the jury's sympathy about your heart attack, reminded them of your brilliant summation in progress and your dedication, and convinced them to aid in your quick recovery by finding the bastard innocent. And they did.''

"He was guilty as hell," Mark said.

"Then why did you take his case?"

"The firm needed the revenue...and I thought just this once that I could ignore the obvious. I'd never before defended a client I was convinced was guilty from the start, but I compromised. I...did a disservice to my profession."

"No, young man, not to your profession, but to yourself. You've paid dearly for it, but at least the press treated you gently. Your name was always associated with honor...and it still is, thanks to your heart attack."

"But what happens when I go back to work?" Mark asked.

"You won't."

Mark frowned. "Of course I will."

"The only way you'll reach age forty is to change your life-style, your profession, your attitude."

Mark's complexion turned ashen. "You mean I could die anytime, anyplace?"

"If you choose to keep going the way you have been."

"But others I know—"

"They don't have your genetic background," Dr. Merrick warned. "Mark, you're intelligent and well educated, good-looking, healthy except for this small problem."

"Small? It sounds as if I could drop dead any minute." Mark eased himself from the bed and groped his way to the window, a pillow dangling from his right hand as he stared blindly. *This can't be happening,* he thought. *I had plans. Everything was on target. I had plans, damn it.*

The physician joined him at the window. "If you were smart enough to pass the bar exam, you're smart enough to change professions. What else can you do?"

Mark thought back over the years. "I earned my bachelor's degree in accounting and passed the CPA exam, then decided to go on to law school. I do tax returns on the side occasionally."

Dr. Merrick chuckled. "What a way to relax. What else interests you?"

Mark shrugged, finding no interest in the question.

"How about sports?"

"I played baseball when I was a kid. I played varsity ball in high school and two years at ASU until my classes demanded all my time."

Dr. Merrick's dark brow arched. "I manage a Little League team. My two youngest sons play in a league on the northeast side of Phoenix, and they talked me into it."

Mark looked skeptical. "How does a busy cardiologist find time to coach a kid's baseball team?"

"We all have the same amount of time, Mark," Dr. Merrick replied. "It's up to each of us to decide how to use it. I need the diversion to stay sharp. I've brought in two younger physicians to take over part of the practice."

"Then you gave up the money?"

"There's more to life than big money and a successful career."

"Not for me," Mark murmured half to himself.

Dr. Merrick shook his head. "You can change. You see, Mark, I open up the chests of many men, men who are too young to be suffering from heart problems. It's a trend that grows worse every year. My wife and I talked it over, and we made plans for the future.''

"I made plans, too, but they didn't pan out," Mark said. He grew silent as he mulled over the drift of the conversation. "Are you saying that either I change or I die?''

"It sounds harsh but, yes, that's what I'm saying. You could go back to school or use some of the other skills you've got. Will you be strapped financially?"

Mark grimaced. "I made some good investments through the years. I can cash them in.''

"A small concession in order to live. Own a house?''

"A big one in Deer Valley.''

"Sell it!''

"But it's half paid for.''

"Great," Dr. Merrick retorted. "Get out from under the mortgage and use the equity to buy a little place in the country.''

"Now you're the crazy one," Mark said. "I've never had any desire to live in the country. I'm city born and bred.''

"Change," Dr. Merrick argued. "Buy a fixer-upper and paint the damn place. Putter around in the yard.''

"Doesn't that take physical stamina?''

Dr. Merrick laid his hand on Mark's shoulder. "You'll have it in a few months. Take my advice. Slow your pace. I don't want to see you back here in a year or two. The next time I might not be able to pull you through.''

CHAPTER TWO

"DON'T BE PIGHEADED," Jill Mahoney said. "Let me help you."

After a moment's hesitation, Mark accepted his sister's shoulder, draping his arm around her as she assisted him through his front door.

His parents followed them inside. His father carried a suitcase and an armload of books. His mother had a potted plant in each arm. Several bouquets of cut flowers were still in the two vehicles parked in his circular driveway.

Mark eased into an overstuffed rocker seconds before what little energy he had drained away. "I didn't think I'd make it," he admitted. "Thanks, Jill."

"You've been coming to my rescue for years in one way or another, Mark. Now it's my turn," Jill said, kissing his cheek. "I'll fix something for lunch while you tell Mom and Dad where to put everything."

"Toss the flowers into the garbage," he said.

Jill looked pained.

"Sorry. Take your choice. Give one to the family next door. Drop two off at the senior citizens center where I did tax work last year." He rested his chin against his fist. "I'll keep the spider plant."

Over sliced turkey sandwiches they recounted the past month, but Mark had nothing to say. He picked at his half-eaten sandwich and took a sip of vegetable soup from a mug. "What happened to my mail?"

"We put a stop on the delivery," his father said. "I'll go to the post office as soon as I finish eating and bring it to you. Why don't you lie down and take a nap?"

Mark closed his eyes, trying to hide the resentment building inside at the way his family had begun to hover around him. "Maybe I'll feel stronger if I take a few minutes and rest, but wake me when you come back with the mail."

Two hours later Mark awoke to the sound of muffled voices. Cautiously he sat up, holding the front of his shirt to ease the discomfort when he moved. He wondered if he'd ever feel normal again. His body had betrayed him. All his life he'd taken it for granted, and now he was vividly aware of each change in his heartbeat, each minuscule tug of pain that sent a message to his brain to beware danger. Life-threatening danger!

Fear had become his constant companion.

Dr. Merrick had given him the name of a support group of heart surgery survivors in his area. Dubbed the Zipper Club, they met weekly. The surgeon had strongly suggested he join them.

Mark had agreed to hire a housekeeper to stay with him for a month. Jill had made the arrangements with the manager of the senior citizen center and had interviewed three women. At least the woman his sister had selected wasn't a stranger. He had worked with her on a tax matter with the Internal Revenue Service. Now the tables were turned, and she would be reporting for work in two days. Jill insisted on staying with him until the woman arrived.

He got up long enough to say goodbye to his parents, then returned to bed. After another nap and a light dinner, he waited while Jill cleared the table and filled the dishwasher, then joined him with two cups of herbal tea.

"Ready to tackle the mail?" Jill asked.

"Not really."

"I'll do it for you," Jill said, quickly sorting sacks into magazines, disposable junk mail, bills and personal letters. "Let's do the personal stuff first," she said. "I'll open them and you can read them. They're mostly get-well cards."

Mark glanced at each card before tossing it onto an ever-growing pile in the center of the table. Several minutes later he pulled an ivory inner envelope from a matching outer one, then carefully withdrew an engraved card. "I'll be damned."

"Who's it from?" Jill asked.

"It's a graduation announcement," Mark said. "Remember Nancy Prentice? She used to be my legal assistant."

Jill leaned over his shoulder and studied the enclosed photograph. "I remember her. She was the pretty one with brown hair and those gorgeous blue eyes."

"She returned to law school."

"You introduced us once at the office when I came to have lunch with you," Jill said. "Gee, that must have been at least five . . . six years ago."

He nodded, still staring down at the announcement. "But she was going to attend ASU. This is from the University of New Mexico. She must have transferred. I tried calling her once but got a disconnect message." He read the announcement. "I knew she'd make it. She was always one very determined lady."

Jill refilled their cups. "It's good to see you interested in something. When is it? Good gracious, it's next week. Are you going to try to go?"

"No." He tossed the announcement carelessly onto the stack of cards and letters.

"Why not? If I went with you . . . I could drive and we could get there in a day, two at the most."

"Your family needs you in Georgia."

Jill grew pensive. "Did you and her...I mean...were you involved? I remember some of your other affairs, but not one with Nancy Prentice."

His brows furrowed. "She was just a good friend."

"Did either of you ever want more?"

Mark retrieved the envelope and dropped the photograph inside. "She was so determined to make it into law school that I didn't want to distract her." He stared across the table and past his sister's curious gaze. Nancy Prentice had always been there when he needed a sympathetic ear, but she'd never played up to him.

A vision of her oval face surrounded by chestnut hair, her blue eyes twinkling, came to him, and for an instant he could hear her melodious voice. Going by the photo, she hadn't changed much. If anything, she'd grown prettier.

Jill grinned. "You were always the epitome of an upwardly mobile professional WASP. Maybe you were too caught up with your own self-importance to dally with a lowly legal assistant."

"You're wrong," he insisted, feeling his heart begin to pump harder. "Nancy Prentice understood our relationship." He glanced across the table at his grinning sister. "And we didn't have a relationship, not a sexual one. I'll admit I...maybe I was tempted a time or two. But Nancy is more like a sister. She needed me as a role model . . . a mentor," he murmured.

"How noble. My brother, the mentor of beautiful young career women," she teased. "I'd love to ask Nancy Prentice how she felt about the rules you'd laid down for her. Maybe she would have preferred . . . another type of relationship."

"Jill, cut it out. It's water under the bridge now." He changed the subject, and they chatted for several minutes about their mutual friends and where they had all settled.

"Nancy Prentice may be very disappointed if you don't show up," Jill said.

"I wouldn't want her to see me like this," he said, staring out the window for several minutes.

"Mark, what's really troubling you? You'll be all right with time. Soon you'll be almost the same man you used to be."

Mark shook his head. "That's the operative word, Jill. *Almost*. I'd make a poor financial risk. I'm a worse physical risk. No woman in her right mind would go into a relationship, knowing up front that she'd more than likely become a young widow, and even if I managed to stay alive for a few years—hell, I don't even know if I could. . . ." He stared past his sister. They'd always had open discussion about life, even sex, but this was more than he was willing to discuss with anyone, even Dr. Merrick.

Jill touched his hand. "Give yourself time to heal. That career protection policy of yours gives you an income."

"It doesn't even equal my mortgage payment on this damn house," he countered.

"But surely it'll carry you until you can return to practice."

"Dr. Merrick said I can't have a legal practice. He described the dire consequences if I didn't change. He seems to think I can't handle the pressure. So you see, Nancy Prentice would be very disappointed to see her old hero now."

"You're too harsh on yourself," Jill said.

"At first I refused to listen to Dr. Merrick, but I've decided to take his advice, at least for the present. No more stress in my life. It could end tomorrow, so I'll live each day to the fullest and take what comes my way. I'm putting this house up for sale. Maybe I'll buy myself an old hound dog and a pair of bib overalls and move to the country."

Jill laughed. "I'll believe that when I see it. Want me to buy you a pitchfork as a housewarming gift?"

He chose to ignore her remark.

"Why not a little place on the edge of the desert or in an older part of town," she suggested. "Phoenix is full of older neighborhoods. They're lovely and the people are older and more settled."

"Sounds great. It'll keep me sedate, and pretty soon I'll be shuffling right along with the rest of the neighbors."

"Mark! That's disgusting," Jill scolded. "Just don't jump into something without giving it careful thought."

"I jumped into this heart attack." He rapped the table with his fingers. "I don't remember giving it careful thought." He rose from his chair, holding his chest again. "Right now the only decision I'm going to make is to lie down in my own little bed. I'm not good company tonight."

"I'll be here if you need me," Jill murmured.

He stopped at the doorway and slowly turned to gaze across the room at his sister. "Sorry if anything I've said offended or upset you," he replied. "See you in the morning . . . and thanks. You and Nancy Prentice have a lot in common. You're a great listener, and so was Nancy."

"Perhaps she had a greater incentive than I do," Jill teased. "I grew up with you. I love you because you're my brother. Maybe her reasons weren't so sisterly."

His features remained solemn. "You do have a way of planting ideas, Jill."

But later that night while he lay awake he ran his hand lightly up and down his chest a few inches from the wide incision. He was only fooling himself, he thought. He would be making a major mistake seeking out Nancy Prentice or anyone like her. Female attorneys were in demand everywhere. She'd probably be choosing between lucrative offers from the best firms across the country.

She was about to start a new career, one she'd been working toward for more than a decade.

His best-laid plans had been yanked from him in an instant. He had no intentions of ever seeing her or any of his business acquaintances again. He would send her a congratulatory card, maybe not even that. Then he'd sell his house, move and start his life anew, but without a damn pitchfork.

CHAPTER THREE

NANCY PRENTICE LOCKED her car door and slammed it shut, only to unlock it again to retrieve her attaché case. Racing up the stairs to her small second-floor studio apartment, she fumbled with her keys, listening to the repeated ringing of the telephone as she pushed the door open.

She ran across the room and grabbed the handset. "Hello," she called, clutching the instrument against her shoulder.

"Aunt Nancy, you're late," a young girl's voice whined. "Mama said you'd be here by now. Coach Bible is here and so are Amanda and Chris. They said I could ride with them, but should I wait? The game starts in thirty minutes. We need to warm up and . . . you promised."

Nancy glanced at her watch. "I know, honey, but I got held up in the office with a client. I can be there in twenty minutes. Let me talk to your mom." She waited while muffled voices came over the line. "Linda, is that you? Sorry, I'm late, but it couldn't be helped. Should I meet you at the park? Where is it?"

"Nichole is disappointed, but she'll survive," her sister Linda said. "She can ride with the coach and his two kids. I'll wait for you here, but hurry, okay?"

"I'll change into something cool and hope the traffic keeps moving," Nancy promised. Replacing the handset, she went to her bedroom. She found a pair of blue cotton shorts and a red-and-white-striped knit tank top. She didn't relish the thought of sitting in the sun for two hours watching children fumble the ball and strike out with regularity, but she had promised Nichole.

Her white leather thongs felt delightfully comfortable on her bare feet. She wished she had time to polish her toenails, but Nichole would have difficulty understanding her reasons for being late as it was. At nine years of age Nancy's niece had focused all her interests and energy on her first year in Little League baseball, displaying an eager determination to practice this year so she could qualify for a major league team the next year.

Reaching for a straw Panama hat decorated with a red, white and blue festive band, Nancy perched it on her short curly brown hair. Maybe she'd let her hair grow out again. No, short hair helped her to look more mature. She had trouble enough convincing clients she was thirty-three years old. She took her driver's license and a twenty-dollar bill from her wallet, grabbed her keys and slammed the apartment door behind her.

She would have preferred to stay home, soak in a hot tub, then climb into bed early and read legal briefs until she fell asleep. But unfortunately time to herself wasn't on her schedule tonight. It seldom was, she acknowledged. Maybe next month. Or next year.

Her blond-haired sister, Linda, was waiting in a Taurus station wagon with its engine idling when Nancy rolled to the curb at her sister's home in Glendale, one of Phoenix's suburbs.

Nancy hopped out of her car, ran to the other vehicle and, opening the passenger door, slid inside. "Sorry."

Linda shrugged. "I know why your clients take precedence over relatives, but Nichole doesn't. Let's hurry."

Ten minutes later they found the last parking space in the dusty vacant field next to the ballpark.

"The game has started," Nancy murmured, surprised at the number of spectators crowded into the bleachers. "Who are all the people?"

Linda laughed. "Parents mostly, plus grandparents and friends. This is the early game. Wait until the major league teams get here for the 7:30 game. Then you'd swear you were at the national majors."

Nancy frowned. "Is that when the adults play?"

Linda laughed again and hugged her sister. "No, silly, they're boys and girls ten through twelve and the best players in the league. They take the game very seriously, just like grown-ups. Sophisticated plays, arguments over the rules. The umpires have their hands full sometimes between the players and managers and the parents."

Nancy scanned the crowd. "Do the parents misbehave?"

"Sometimes the tension of the game brings out the worst in a few of them," Linda confessed. "Some of them have their own copies of the rule books, and they argue with the umpires. Last year an umpire ejected two fathers from the games."

"I don't think I care to see that," Nancy said. "I never expected violence to be part of the program."

"If we weren't going out for ice cream after Nichole's game, we'd stay and watch the second game, too," Linda said. "Layne's two girls play in the majors."

Nancy thought of her two sisters and their growing families. Linda was expecting another baby in four months, Layne two months later. Sometimes she had trouble keeping her nieces and nephews straight. "Angie and Rachel?" she guessed.

Linda nodded with a proud grin. "And Zack and Chuck are playing in the Pony League for older kids, but Layne says the team is having trouble with the manager. Zack says they have two girls on the team this year, but the manager thinks girls should be banned from baseball."

Nancy followed her sister up the steps of the left-field bleachers and edged her way past knees to a vacant spot in the middle of the row. "That sounds like sex discrimination."

"That what I told Layne, but she says the manager has the final say. He plays musical chairs with the league offices each year and he always makes a generous cash donation to help buy the uniforms. This year he's the league vice president, and he's quick to remind everyone that the manager rules the team."

"But that shouldn't excuse him from the rules. What about fair play? Don't the other officials speak up?"

Linda grimaced. "If the other managers won't challenge him, he can make the girls sit on the bench the entire season. The other managers are busy with their own teams, and the parents are afraid that if they complain, the manager might make it rough on the kids, so it's a catch-22 all around. Maybe someday someone will come along to find a solution, but for now let's enjoy the game and be thankful it's not our problem.''

''Does the league have a president?'' Nancy asked. ''Doesn't he have the final say? Or there must be a board of directors.''

''The president is a wimp, and we don't have a separate board per se.'' Linda murmured to the person sitting on the other side of her, then turned to Nancy again. ''Our team is winning by one run in the bottom of the second. Let's watch the game.''

Nancy scanned the field, trying to find her niece, but the children all looked alike in their maroon T-shirts with Braves splashed across their chests in white. And they all wore matching maroon baseball caps. The other team wore green-and-yellow shirts and caps.

''Where's Nichole?'' Nancy asked.

''Playing second base,'' Linda said, pointing, then waving. A small child waved from her position several paces from the second-base bag.

''Strike two!''

Nancy's attention shifted to the umpire, who crouched behind the catcher. Dressed in navy blue shorts and a lighter blue short-sleeved shirt, the man was tall, probably six feet at least. Sandy blond curls brushed against his shirt collar, but his head was hidden behind a navy baseball cap turned backward and a catcher's bulky black face mask.

The umpire jumped out of the way when the catcher missed a wild pitch. ''Ball.''

The next pitch was a foul tip. Umpire and catcher repositioned themselves behind the plate and the game resumed. When the batter connected with a pitch directly over the plate, the umpire jerked off his face mask and stepped away from the action. The ball landed and bounced once near the shortstop. He caught it and threw it to Nichole, who tagged a base runner out at second. Then she threw it to the pitcher, who tossed it to the catcher . . . but too late.

"Safe," the umpire called as the runner at third slid into home. The man turned to speak with the score-keepers sitting at a table behind the backstop, glancing briefly at the crowd in the stands, then turned back to the playing field. "Play ball."

Nancy's heart jumped. The umpire put his face mask back on, leaned over the catcher and put one hand behind his back. "What's he holding?" she asked.

"A counter," Linda said, "so he can keep track of the count."

"What count?"

"The strikes and balls, silly. Don't you remember anything about baseball or softball?"

Nancy sighed. "I've never had any interest in athletics. You know that." She concentrated on the umpire again. For a moment she'd thought she'd recognized him, but the man she'd lost track of would never waste his time umpiring a baseball game, especially one involving children.

Yet, as she thought back over the years she'd worked at Burnside, Bailey, Summerset and Zorn, she remembered that whenever the firm had held its annual picnic Mark Bradford had always umpired the baseball games.

Play continued, but Nancy's interest had shifted from the game to the man behind the plate. "Who's the umpire?" she finally asked Linda.

Her sister craned her head over the spectators. "I met him once, but I don't remember his name. He's new this season. Cute, isn't he?"

Burying her hands between her knees, Nancy frowned. "He looks familiar, that's all. He looks like an old friend. I must be wrong. He'd never be around here." She raised herself a few inches off the bench, trying to get a better look at the man. "Mark lives in Deer Valley."

"I think this guy walks to the games."

Nancy sighed. "I must be wrong."

"Who's this Mark fellow?" Linda asked, glancing at her. "An old flame?"

Nancy shifted on the bench. "Don't I wish. He's just a good friend, or at least he was. I would have been willing to get involved, but he never acted interested in me that way. He treated me like his little sister."

She studied the profile of the umpire. The chain links of the backstop made it hard to see him, but the man's movements continued to remind her of Mark. "This guy must be Mark's look-alike. The last time I saw him he was climbing his way up to a lucrative partnership in one of Phoenix's most prestigious law firms."

"I thought that was what you were doing," Linda said.

Nancy's gaze stayed on the umpire. "It's a slow climb, I'm afraid. Twenty-six other attorneys newly admitted to the bar are hanging on to the same rung of the ladder that I thought was mine. You see, we were all hired at the same time. Law firms carry on a hiring frenzy at graduation time. New counselors work cheap without experience."

"Cheap, my foot!" Linda exclaimed.

"Well, modest, but when the senior partners bill at up to five hundred dollars per hour, our rates seem relatively inexpensive."

"It sounds like a terrible way to work," Linda replied. "So why don't you track this guy down if you care about him?"

Nancy's blue eyes were troubled as she turned to her sister. "Since I transferred out of state, we lost track of each other. I sent him a commencement announcement, but he didn't even take time to respond."

"Well, you can drool over the ump. I'm going to watch the game," Linda said.

Nancy's attention stayed on the blond umpire. Finally she tugged at her sister's shirt. "He was busy. That's why he couldn't come to my graduation."

"You're making excuses, Nancy. It isn't like you."

Nancy ignored the remark as she continued to study the umpire. "Then I went to London on that fellowship. When I got back, I called his firm and found out he was no longer with them. I asked around, but no one remembered him except one guy, and all he told me was that the bigger they are, the harder they fall. But he was a rat himself, so I didn't ask him to elaborate."

"Look him up in the phone book," Linda whispered, her attention torn between watching her daughter and paying attention to Nancy's rambling dialogue.

"I did, but the operator said there was no one by that name listed. I guess he moved away."

"Then watch the game."

The crowd screamed and applauded as the Braves scored two runs. Nancy brushed a stray curl from her forehead and readjusted her straw hat. "I'm probably wrong."

"What?" Linda turned to her.

"That guy couldn't be Mark," Nancy reminded her, pointing toward the umpire. "He'd never stoop to this."

"Stoop?" Linda turned sideways and stared at her sister. "Is there something less than honorable about umpiring a baseball game for kids?"

Before Nancy could clarify her remark screams came from the field, and the sisters turned their attention to the action.

"Strike three. You're out!"

The team on the field went into their dugout and the other team took the field. The umpire removed his cap and face mask, then pulled a red kerchief from his hip pocket and wiped his forehead. He spoke to the scorekeeper and her assistant, smiling at both women.

Nancy jumped to her feet. "It *is* him!" She began to work her way past the knees of the other spectators.

"Where are you going?" Linda called.

"To speak to the umpire." Before Linda could stop her Nancy skipped down the bleacher steps, only to find herself blocked by a crowd of customers who swept her toward the snack bar. Maybe the umpire *wasn't* Mark, she thought. Undecided and aware of her dry throat, she dug out some coins and joined the lineup at the counter. "A medium root beer," she said, trying to avoid being bumped by several rambunctious children purchasing strings of red licorice.

"Oh," the woman at the counter groaned. "That's the third out in a row. Our team isn't doing so well."

"The Braves?" Nancy asked, pleased with herself that she could remember Nichole's team name.

"No, the Giants," the woman said. "They were the league champs last season, but this year...they stink."

"But the season's just started, right? They could still improve," Nancy reminded the woman, wishing she'd return her change. She *would* speak to the umpire, Nancy decided, but she had no idea what she would say if the man did turn out to be Mark Bradford.

"Ma'am, you in a hurry?" the woman behind the snack bar counter asked, dropping Nancy's change into her hand.

"No. Can I help you?" Nancy asked.

"Could you take this drink to the ump?" The woman smiled and waved over Nancy's head to the home plate area. "The umps get free drinks, and this umpire is special. He's good. He's patient with the kids, and we want to keep him happy. Do you mind?"

"Not at all." Nancy took a drink in each hand, but by the time she made her way to the edge of the backstop, play had resumed for the fifth inning. She waited and sipped her own drink as three children in a row struck out, including her niece. The umpire removed his face mask again. A coach waved her onto the field, and she walked to home plate, her heart pounding against her ribs as Mark Bradford looked up at her.

MARK'S EYES OPENED wide in astonishment.

"Thirsty, Ump?"

"Nancy? Nancy Prentice?" He groped for words. This woman was the last person he'd ever expected to see again. "My God, what are you doing here?" He took the paper cup from her hand, his fingers brushing against hers. Her hand was shaking, and she jerked it away once he held the cup.

"I could ask the same of you, Mark."

"I'm umpiring a Little League game. Then I'm coaching." In spite of his better judgment he couldn't stop the smile spreading across his face. "And you?"

"My niece is on the Braves. She's . . ."

He held up his hand. "Don't tell me. I wouldn't want to be accused of partiality." His mind raced ahead. "Are you staying for the major league game?"

She looked puzzled.

He turned away and placed his drink carefully on the grassy spot against the backstop. "The second game," he explained turning again to her. She stood a few feet away from him, her empty cup dangling from her fingers. *Beautiful,* he thought. *More beautiful than I remembered.* The years since they had last seen each other had been kind to her, bringing her face a lean maturity that blended charm with youthful loveliness. Later he would wonder why he'd done such a fool thing, but he held out his arms. "Got a hug for an old friend?"

To his surprise her blue eyes filled with moisture, and she bit her lower lip. "Of course," she whispered, stepping into his embrace.

He didn't remember her being so slender, almost delicate. Her hands pressed against his sides before sliding to his back to hug him tightly.

"Mark," she murmured. "Oh, Mark."

Once before he'd felt time stop. Then he'd been in the hospital, hovering on the edge of death. Now, as his arms tightened around Nancy Prentice, time seemed to stop again. All his stiff resolve—to forget his past and forget all his hopes for the future—began to bend and buckle.

A tear slid down Nancy's cheek. "Oh, Mark," she whispered against his shirt. "I thought I'd never see you again." She eased back and gazed up at his face. "Where have you been? I thought you'd fallen off the face of the earth."

"Maybe I have." Before he could say more several maroon-and-white-shirted children surrounded them, and for Mark reality snapped back into focus.

"Aunt Nancy, you're holding up the game," Nichole complained. "Ump, we gotta finish the game. Can't we play ball?"

Mark looked down into the face of a pretty young girl with brown curls who struck him as a child version of Nancy Prentice.

Nancy pulled away from Mark and smiled fondly at the curious child. "This is my niece. Nichole Jackson, meet an old friend of mine, Mark Bradford."

"Is he your boyfriend?" Nichole asked.

Nancy cleared her throat. "No, just a dear friend." She looked up at Mark. "I guess we're holding up the game."

He nodded. "Can you meet me after the second game?"

"What time is that?"

"About 9:30. We can go for coffee."

"I'd love to."

Unable to suppress his pleasure, he called in an overly enthusiastic voice, "Play ball. Batter up!"

The spectators in the bleachers applauded, and for the first time Mark became aware of how public their reunion had been. Nancy's cheeks flushed and she turned away, her hips swinging attractively in a pair of blue shorts as she hurried from the field.

The game resumed and he tried to resist the impulse to search for her in the stands.

"What was it, Ump?" the catcher crouched in front of him called.

"Huh?" Mark asked, disoriented for a moment.

"The pitch," the boy whispered.

Mark had no idea. "Ball," he called, clicking his counter and hoping he was right. Most of the calls for the game had been balls.

The pitcher slumped on the mound, obviously displeased, but the catcher nodded in agreement. "Right on, Ump. I told Joey he's pitching outside all the time, but he won't listen. He's gotta get tighter, or we'll lose every game."

Mark pushed thoughts of Nancy Prentice from his mind. He hadn't seen her for years. Why get excited about running into her tonight? So what if she seemed genuinely pleased to see him? Besides, he'd put his past life behind him, and that included her.

The innings dragged on, a series of strikeouts, errors on the part of nervous batters and inexperienced young players, and so many balls he'd stopped keeping track of them beyond the current batter. Wasn't that what the scorekeeper was for? More than once he'd been forced to turn and ask for the count.

The Braves' manager called a time-out, and Mark pulled his face mask off. He caught a flash of red and white in the stands. Nancy Prentice waved to him, and he raised his hand in reply, feeling a surge of pleasure in spite of himself.

Perhaps Dr. Merrick was right about him taking his life too seriously. He'd followed most of his cardiologist's advice. The equity from his four-bedroom home in Deer Valley had enabled him to pay cash for an older two-bedroom home in Peoria, a small community now almost buried beneath the encroaching edge of Sun City development.

Although he'd forsaken the idea of wearing bib overalls, he had given in to getting himself a dog, a gorgeous Irish setter bitch, now expecting her first litter of pups.

Mark had learned basic carpentry and home repairs during the past year from his next-door neighbor, Horace Moore, who had retired after working forty years in construction. He'd been surprised to discover the satisfaction of doing most of the upgrading on his house and garage himself.

As he watched Nancy disappear into the mass of heads in the stands again, he wondered how she would react to the down-scaling of his life-style. No snazzy sports car, no haircuts from high-priced stylists, no expensive dinners in revolving restaurants, no reserved parking places in multistoried garages and no costly air-conditioning to keep his home cool.

He didn't mind giving up all that, but the loss of his large backyard swimming pool still irritated him. He'd always loved to swim, and the exercise would have helped his ongoing recovery. But he'd had to learn to watch his dollars and cents—something he'd never expected to be concerned about.

The game resumed with little excitement, giving him time to speculate on Nancy Prentice. She represented life in the fast lane, and as much as Mark needed his newly established slower paced existence, sometimes he hungered for the nonstop, always frantic mode of living he'd thrived on. He still woke up in the middle of the night, thinking about legal strategies, about besting opposing attornies.

In his old life, the thrill of anticipating a verdict had been exceeded only by the announcement itself. He'd seldom lost a case, but when he had, he'd always gather his staff the next morning to rehash their strategy and try to pinpoint where they'd gone wrong.

Control. That was the missing factor in his new life. He'd lost control over his career and financial affairs, his future and, worst of all, his own body. Fate haunted him constantly. He could drop dead at any moment.

The game ended with the Braves winning six to two. Mark signed the bottom of the page in the score book, making the game official. As he handed the book back to the scorekeeper, he glanced toward the emptying bleachers. Nancy Prentice had disappeared.

CHAPTER FOUR

HAD SHE CHANGED her mind about staying for the second game? Most likely. Well, that was for the best, he decided.

In the snack bar he retrieved his red athletic bag and headed to the rest rooms near the school that bordered the playing field. At times he wondered if he had taken on too much. But he knew the rules and regulations of baseball and had loved the game since childhood. And when he answered a call for volunteers and workers in the neighborhood newspaper, he'd been pleasantly surprised to learn that umpires were compensated.

As he sat down on the toilet seat to remove his umpiring shoes and pull on a pair of athletic shoes, he smiled. A year ago he'd commanded a fee of two hundred and fifty dollars per hour just to listen to a client. If the case proved complex, the fee went up. Now he collected two-figure checks for a week's worth of umpiring and deposited them in his modest bank account, glad for the bit of extra cash. He reminded himself repeatedly to count his blessings. He was alive, after all, and regaining his health. Only measured against his past dreams, those blessings seemed meager.

Once, six months after his surgery, he'd seriously considered resuming his legal practice. Dr. Merrick had exploded. "I forbid it! You'll be dead in three months if you do anything that foolish." He had grabbed Mark's shoulders and actually shaken him. "It's suicidal, Mark. Have you discussed this with your family? Your parents? Your sister?"

"My sister is back in Atlanta with her husband and three children where she belongs," Mark had replied. "My parents are out of the country."

"At least wait another year, then perhaps we can reevaluate your condition. Mark? Listen to me. You have a lot to give to this world, but it doesn't have to be in a courtroom."

Mark had struggled with that reality for over a year and still hadn't completely accepted the physician's warning. But he'd tried each and every day when he woke up, mouthing aloud the good things in his life, questionable as they would seem to his former friends and associates.

He lived a satisfying life, not full, but satisfying. He had yet to merge those two qualities.

Unbuttoning his blue shirt, he took it off, rolled it up and stuffed it into his bag. Then he paused, taking a tube of cortisone cream from his bag and lightly massaging it into the wide incision running down his chest. A glance at his watch reminded him of the time, and he pulled on a maroon cotton sport shirt with Braves emblazoned across the back and Coach above the left pocket.

He had allowed himself to be talked into helping the manager of the major league Braves team one afternoon when he stopped by to watch them practice. He had already committed himself to umpiring six games a week, which kept him busy a minimum of three nights. No team played more than twice a week, but by agreeing to help the Braves' manager, he had tied himself down more than he had planned.

When he talked to the league president about any conflict of interest, the man had assured him there would be no problem. The man seemed uncomfortable discussing the matter, leaving Mark to wonder what would happen if a major conflict came up during the season. Another coach had advised Mark that the league president went to extraordinary lengths to avoid conflict.

After that visit, Mark had decided that he'd work around the ineffective president and resolve his own problems, whether they involved umpiring or coaching. How the man had gotten elected was a puzzle to all the managers and coaches, but the parents had the final say, and their votes outnumbered the volunteer leadership.

The umpires, contracted for a fee, were prohibited from voting, and Mark was glad. He didn't want to get entangled in politics, even at this level. All he'd really wanted when he signed on was a diversion from his other problems. He'd forgotten how much he loved baseball, and he'd been surprised the boys and girls on the teams had brought that love back to life.

He'd also been surprised to discover the joys of working with children. Getting along with kids was no problem, and he suspected it was partly because he had no children himself and because he *showed* no favoritism.

But he did have his favorites. They were the youngest players, those eight years and under, children whose biggest problem was to get their oversize gloves around the bouncing ball. He'd umpired several of their games and had waived any payment, doing it purely for the pleasure.

They were the sweet innocents of the league, excited about standing at the plastic T to take a swing at the stationary ball, and so thrilled when they connected that they often stayed at the plate to accept the applause from their peers and parents. Only the gentle encouragement of the coaching staff could get them to begin to run to first base.

Each time one of these starry-eyed little boys or girls gave him a smile, often with a missing front tooth, and called him "Ump," Mark's ego got a stroke almost as satisfying as winning a court case.

Walking across the playing fields to where his team was warming up, he scanned the gathering crowd, hoping he'd been mistaken about Nancy Prentice. She wasn't very tall, perhaps five foot four. He spotted her standing alongside the left-field foul line, watching him approach.

She smiled and extended her hands. When he reached her, he took them and gave a squeeze. "I thought you'd left."

"I came with my sister," Nancy replied. "They went for ice cream to celebrate their victory, but I had Linda drop me at her house so I could pick up my car and hurry back."

"I thought you might have changed your mind," he admitted. "I'm glad you didn't."

Her gaze swept up and down his body. "You've changed your clothes. You don't umpire this game?"

He grinned. "No, ma'am, this round I play coach."

"You look . . . nice."

He squeezed her hands. "So do you." He felt her begin to withdraw her hands. "Do you still want to go for coffee after the game?"

Her eyes grew round, and for a moment they glistened again. Then she looked away. "That's why I came back. Meet you at the snack bar?"

"Fine."

She turned to go.

"Nancy?"

She whirled around. "Yes?"

He shoved his fists into the pockets of his shorts. "It's good to see you again." He gazed intently into her face. "Maybe it's been too long."

"We'll catch up on everything," she assured him.

"My life has changed." He gazed across the field. "All my plans..."

"The best-laid plans..." She smiled and her voice trailed away.

"Often go astray," he finished.

She chuckled. "I don't think that's quite the way Robert Burns put it. Or was it Hemingway? Maybe Steinbeck."

"It doesn't matter who said it. The author was right."

They stood a few feet apart, neither speaking as they looked at each other.

The teams began to gather in their respective dugouts. "I should go," he said.

"I wish you could sit in the stands with me."

He grinned. "Maybe on a night when I'm not busy."

"I'd like that."

He watched her mouth widen into a smile and he felt himself draw closer.

"Play ball!" the umpire shouted.

"Gotta go," Mark said, waving to his team's manager. "If you get tired and change your mind, I'll understand."

"I've never changed my mind about you, Mark." She touched his bare forearm lightly.

He frowned. "I left my... I walked to the game."

"Then we'll take my car."

NANCY WAITED IMPATIENTLY as the innings passed. She tried to pay attention to the game's progress, but her thoughts were on the man who spent most of his time coaching the second- and third-base runners. When his team played defense, he called plays from the dugout.

He was thinner than she remembered him. His features had hardened into masculine lines that enhanced his already handsome looks. Perhaps she was prejudiced, she admitted. When she spotted him coming across the playing field between games, she had been unable to stay in the bleachers. While she'd waited for him to reach her, she'd tried to evaluate the changes in him.

He had always been a bundle of energy when she worked on cases with him. When he was made a junior partner in the firm, he'd taken several of them to dinner at the Golden Eagle Restaurant. He'd reserved the seat beside his for her, and when he made the official announcement, he'd thrown his arm around her and kissed her. Before she could analyze the kiss he had bestowed similar kisses on the other two women at the table and shaken the hands of the men who had joined them.

So much for his ability to see her as anything more than a friend, she thought. Even now she sensed some distance between them. True, they had only exchanged a few words. But his pleasure had been revealed in his open embrace at home plate.

Over the years other men had drifted through her social life, but Mark Bradford had been the standard by which they had been measured. She had never gone to bed with any of them.

Maybe she just hadn't met the right man. She glanced toward Mark, wondering how she would respond if he showed an interest in her deeper than one of friendship.

Don't be silly, she thought. *Mark getting impassioned over me? If only he would.*

The game ended with Mark's team winning two to one, and Nancy applauded along with the parents and fans sitting around her. From the dugout Mark searched the crowd as if to confirm her presence. She waved to him, and he gave her a grin and a victory sign and motioned to the snack bar. She nodded.

Be still my heart, she thought, grinning at her own corniness. Yet her heart continued to pound against her ribs. All over a promised cup of coffee. Her sisters would be surprised to see her now, her pulse erratic and her cheeks flushed.

Mark came out of the snack bar door, adjusting the maroon baseball cap on his head. "Ready?"

She smiled and took his arm. "I'm parked on the street. Do you mind walking a block or so?"

He shook his head. "I've discovered the joy of walking."

When they reached her car, she paused. "Do you want to drive?" She held out her keys.

"No thanks."

In minutes they were at an all-night café a mile from the ballpark, its neon sign blinking to potential customers and other restless creatures of the night.

"'Evening, Mark," a gray-haired waitress said with an affectionate grin. "How did the umping go?"

Mark chuckled. "Fine."

The waitress arched a brow at him. "No one threatened to throw out the ump?"

"Not yet," he replied, opening the menu. "They're still being gentle with me. Probably because they have no one to take my place. No parent has yelled an expletive at me yet . . . that I've heard, anyway."

"And the team you're coaching? Did they win tonight?"

The waitress seemed insatiably curious about Mark, Nancy thought as she tried to ignore them and concentrate on the limited selection of the menu.

"This is an old friend, Nancy Prentice," Mark said, bringing Nancy's gaze up from the grease-stained menu. "Nancy, meet a new friend, Lucy Sanchez. She's been serving me and listening to my complaints for more than a year now."

Lucy grinned. "You? Complain? You never complain. Ma'am, this guy is the most noncomplaining customer I have."

"Want your tip early, Lucy?" he teased. He looked across the table at Nancy. "This beautiful waitress knows more about me than anyone I know. Hope she never decides to blackmail me. I'm a goner if she does."

The waitress guffawed and slapped Mark's shoulder. "He's pulling your leg, ma'am, but he's an easy guy to like, that's for sure. Now, folks, what'll you have? Roast beef with all the trimmings is our special tonight. The gravy's made right here from scratch. None of that powder stuff in this place. Coffee, Mark?''

"Decaf," he said, still scanning the menu. "And a chef salad without dressing. Hold the ham and cheese and give me extra turkey." He glanced across the booth at Nancy. "This is my treat. Order anything you want."

Nancy studied him, reading through his mask of polite etiquette. "I'll have the same but with a side of French dressing," she said, smiling up at the waitress. "And you're right. Mark is an easy person to like." She ducked her head when he glanced up.

They ate in silence for a few minutes. "Tell me about yourself," Mark said. "Practicing law at long last?"

"With a vengeance," she replied. "I'm one of the masses at Staley, Jennings and Kaufman."

He arched a brow. "You started at the top. Are they still downtown?"

"They're in a new high rise a few blocks from the federal building. I have my own office on the eleventh floor and my own reserved parking spot, name stenciled and all. It's great. We get a lot of—" She glanced at him. "I'm so comfortable being with you that I forget we're not working in the same firm. Our client base is confidential and I was about to spill the details. Stop me if I forget and go too far."

"Of course. What kind of cases do you enjoy the most?" he asked.

She filled him in on some of the more interesting cases without compromising the confidentiality of her clients. "But you know what I've learned recently? I like working with the client more than pleading their cases in a courtroom. I don't trust the other attorneys.''

He chuckled. ''Didn't I warn you about cynicism when you first decided to go back to school?'' She nodded, and they returned their attention to their meal.

He finished his salad and pushed the plate back a few inches. ''Sounds as if you're on your way.''

''Oh, I am, but it would be a lot easier without all the bloodthirsty competition. Some of the other newcomers are like sharks during a feeding frenzy. Fortunately our cases are assigned to us on a rotation basis, and occasionally I get lucky when a super plum falls into my lap.''

His eyes seemed shielded. ''I remember those days.''

She sighed. ''Most of my work is nuisance cases and make little difference in the grander scheme of things, but I love it.''

''I'm glad,'' he said. ''You wanted it and now you've got it.''

She took a sip of cool coffee. ''What about you, Mark? How is your practice? Busy? You always tended to overload yourself. Are you learning to pace yourself now that you're older? You must be...thirty-six?''

A chill ran up her spine when he stared back at her from across the table. His posture stiffened, and she could almost see the barrier that he erected across the table.

''Yes, I've learned to pace myself. I was thirty-seven last month...and I no longer practice law.'' Before she could recover from his shocking announcement he stood up. ''It's late, and you probably get to the office early." He smiled, but the effort seemed strained. "I'll take care of the bill. Meet you at your car." He retrieved the check and headed for the cashier's stand, forgetting about a tip.

She searched in her purse for loose change and dropped several coins onto the table, then ran to catch up with him as he exited into the darkness. "Mark, what do you mean? Have you gone into private practice... out of your home? Please, Mark, slow down and talk to me."

He paused and gave a nonchalant shrug. "I don't practice law." He repeated the statement as if he thought she were incapable of understanding its meaning. He didn't offer any elaboration as they left the parking lot of the café. Some sixth sense told her to refrain from asking any more questions. He'd confide in her when he felt comfortable.

"Drop me off at the ballpark," he said, rolling down the window and letting the warm spring breeze drift through the small car.

She turned off the air-conditioning and looked askance at him. "I'll be glad to drive you home."

He shook his head. "I left my athletic bag at the snack bar. The ballpark will be fine."

The playing field was engulfed in darkness as they bounced over a speed bump and rolled to a stop near the darkened snack bar. He gave her a mumbled goodnight and got out, then closed the door gently, as if he didn't want to wake up the neighborhood.

She waited, the car's engine still idling, while he unlocked the padlock on the snack bar door and disappeared inside. In seconds he reappeared with his red bag and replaced the padlock. He turned to wave, then headed across the dark playing field.

Bewildered by his sudden shift in mood, she remained in the parking lot. Something was wrong, but what? Why had he refused to talk about himself? The waitress knew more about him than she did. Maybe she should go back to the restaurant and confront the woman. No, she thought. The woman would defend Mark's right to privacy. And it *was* his right. But why had he shown such pleasure at first seeing her and then clammed up?

A gate creaked, then clanged. Curiosity got the best of her, and she left the car and ran onto the field, searching for him. A dog barked and she heard Mark's voice. The dog hushed as if he knew the night walker.

Before she could talk herself out of it she ran back to her car and started the engine. Shifting into reverse, she left the parking lot, turned onto the street, then toward the front of the school yard. Her instinct had been on target. A block ahead she spotted Mark. Staying well behind him, she followed in her car, but he never looked back.

His shoulders were hunched slightly, as if he carried secrets too heavy for a solitary mortal. A mile from the park he walked past the café, tapped on the window and waved to the waitress, then walked faster into the darkness.

Several minutes later Nancy glanced at her trip indicator. He'd walked two miles from the ballpark and still showed no sign of reaching his destination. *Walking is great for your health, Mark, but aren't you carrying it a bit far this late at night?* She recalled his habit of jogging in the predawn mornings. Perhaps he'd always been a night person.

She knew she might be risking everything if she misplayed her next move. He had always been special to her, and sometime during the years she'd worked with him, she'd fallen deeply in love with him. It had been a gradual process, one that had snuck up on her so slowly that by the time she realized what had happened she could do nothing but accept its realty.

Her sister had been right. One-sided love was painful, and unfulfilled desire worse. But it was neither love nor desire that motivated her tonight. It was concern. He needed her. He just didn't know it yet.

She pressed her foot on the accelerator and sped up alongside him as he reached the three-mile mark. She tapped her horn lightly and pushed the button to roll down the passenger window.

Mark stopped abruptly and turned, a grim expression hardening his features when he recognized her.

"Hi again," she called. "Would you reconsider a ride home?"

CHAPTER FIVE

MARK DROPPED his athletic bag onto the sidewalk. He should have known that Nancy Prentice would never let him get away without an explanation about his career change, but he had no intention of discussing the matter.

She had always been a tenacious researcher, and when they worked together, she had always come through for him. Now he found himself feeling the brunt of her tenacity.

Cutting through the darkened school ground had been a clever escape route...except the hunter had been his unrelenting former assistant.

She had tracked him down and called his bluff. The next play would be his. Should he reveal all his cards, or keep a few close to his chest? The thought of her reaction to his scarred chest was more than he cared to speculate about at the moment.

He was tired. The day had been long, too long. His appointment with Dr. Merrick was scheduled for ten the following morning, and he wanted to get a clean bill of health.

''Well?'' she called.

''Why not?'' he replied, not wanting to take the time to evaluate the wisdom of accepting her offer. Damn it, it was only a ride to his front door. How could that complicate his life?

He tossed his bag behind the seat and climbed in, scrutinizing the red leather interior. "Nice," he said. "Just the right touch of class for an up-and-coming career woman."

"You sound cynical... or envious," she said.

"Me? Of course not."

"Then hypocritical. Don't you still have that flashy baby-blue Mercedes?" she asked. "Of course you wouldn't have it. It would be four years old by now, and if my memory serves me correctly, you always drove the current year's model." She grinned. "What's parked in your driveway this season, Mark?"

He stared ahead into the quiet darkness. "A 1982 Ford truck with the tailgate removed."

She glanced sideways. "You? Driving a truck? I don't believe it. You were always a classy guy, Mark. Wouldn't a beat-up old truck clash with the other vehicles in the parking lot?" She chuckled. "Do they make you park in the alley?"

He fought down the urge to remind her that he didn't work in a prestigious legal firm anymore, but that would only fuel her already burning curiosity.

"As a matter of fact, I do park in the alley sometimes," he said. "I've outgrown the need to prove my self-worth by way of the car I drive. I've been down that road and I know where it can lead. If you need a car to reflect your success, so be it. I was merely observing." He slammed the door shut, plunging them into darkness.

She shifted gears but kept her foot on the break. "I don't *need* a car to express anything." She narrowed her eyes, then sighed. "I'm sorry, Mark. What you drive is your business. I just don't think of Phoenix as a truck town."

"That depends on a person's needs," Mark replied. "You have your reasons and I have mine. Can we move on now?"

She shrugged. "If I knew where you lived."

His mouth softened. "Two blocks west, then take a right. It's the last house on the left. If you go too far, you'll plunge into the irrigation canal."

Several minutes later she rolled to a stop in front of his small adobe stucco house and killed the engine.

He sighed. He yearned for a few hours of meaningful conversation with a trusted friend, without the platitudes that he'd begun to receive from his own relatives.

But now he had put himself in a new quandary. Although he needed a friend, he didn't want anything more significant. Would he be able to keep this woman at arm's length? Perhaps it would be wiser to say goodbye, slam the car door and never look back. After a year of adjustment, his life had become orderly. Dull but orderly, he thought. Wasn't that the way he wanted it ... needed it? Nancy would cause trouble.

"Do you have time for coffee or a glass of wine?" he asked, surprised at his own suggestion.

She jerked her key from the ignition and smiled. "Thank you. I thought you would never ask. You were angry at me back there, but you're wrong about me and my little red car. Cars can be status symbols, but this one isn't. I drive it because my brother-in-law works for the agency and he got me a super price."

"Sounds plausible," he admitted.

Silence divided them again.

"Mark?" She turned to him. "If you don't want me here, just say so. I'm a big girl now. I can handle rejection."

When he turned and saw the emotions playing across her features, he gave up his feeble attempt to keep his life orderly. "Nan, you're the last person I expected to see tonight. You, of all people, are the last one I'd want to hurt." He reached out and ran two fingers through her soft, short curls. "You have pretty hair."

"It's just plain brown," she replied.

"No, it's not, and I've studied it for years," he admitted. "It's chestnut and it's...lovely, soft and silky." He couldn't have pulled his fingers from her head if his life had depended upon it. "I hope you never decide to change its color." He pulled one of the curls out to its tip and let it coil back into place. "It's still bouncy, but you used to wear it longer."

"Judges and juries don't take bouncy-haired women seriously. I learned that on my first case."

"You lost it?"

"Yep, but now I'm glad. It hardened me," she said, leaving the car. "Softness has its place, but not in the courtroom." She followed him up the stone walk to the front door and inside.

When he flicked on the switch to the lamp in the corner of the living room, he was thankful he'd tidied the place earlier in the day. He turned to find her studying the interior. "Not very big," he said.

She smiled at him. "It's twice the size of my studio."

He frowned. "Nothing could be that small." In the kitchen he retrieved a coffee mug and a stemmed glass from the cupboard and held up one in each hand. She pointed to the wineglass.

He filled her glass with Chablis from a large green jug. "It has a twist of lemon. I think you'll like it." He took a bottle of sparkling water from the refrigerator and filled his own glass.

She gazed over the top of her glass as she took a sip, then lowered it. "Delicious. I drink alone?"

"I've given up wine, women, song...and all my other former vices," he replied.

"Do you still jog?"

"No."

She pointed a finger at him. "You always loved jogging at night. You don't do that anymore?"

"Night jogging can be hazardous to one's health."

"You mean from drunk drivers and reckless automobiles?"

"No...but I walk a lot."

"Day? Or night?"

"When I can't sleep," he admitted.

"You have trouble sleeping at night?"

"Occasionally. If I get pains..." He shrugged. "We all get aches and pains sometimes."

"So what do you do for fun and frolic?"

He glanced away. "Not much." He began to feel as if she'd cornered him and the corner was narrowing with each question. "Umpiring keeps me busy during the evenings. Later, if there's nothing good on the tube, I walk. All the dogs in the neighborhood know Belle and me."

Her cheeks blanched. "Who's Belle?"

"An Irish setter," he said. "She's asleep out back."

"You? You have a dog? You never wanted to be bothered with a pet. I remember you saying that once. Susie Watkins took a day off to help her German shepherd have puppies and you docked her. You said that didn't qualify as sick time."

He looked away. "And I'm going to be eating my words on that subject. Belle is expecting her first litter in two weeks."

"Oh," she teased. "Will that make you a papa or an uncle?" Before he could explain she broke into lighthearted laughter. "Mark, the midwife. I'd like to see that. Do you take her to Lamaze classes, too?" she teased.

He grinned. "Hardly. How do you know about Lamaze classes? Surely you haven't...?"

She glanced away. "No, I've never married, never had a baby, never even...came close. But I have dozens of nieces and nephews."

"Too bad," he replied. "The only reason I could think of that would cause you to drop out of law school would have been love and marriage and babies. No, that's wrong. Love and marriage shouldn't make a difference, but babies might."

"They might," she agreed. "What about you? It's been four years. Married and divorced already? That could explain your change in...I mean changing cars and everything. Did you give up law in order to avoid paying high alimony?" Suddenly the teasing drift of their conversaton stopped. "Oh, Mark, do you have children now? Is that why you're involved with the baseball program?"

"No children," he said, recalling his vow not to bring any into the world. Then he added, "No marriage, past or present."

"But...no woman? Women streamed through your life like salmon in a river."

He glanced away. "Not anymore."

She stepped closer, frowning as she studied him. "You're serious about no love life? Poor Mark."

"I'll survive, and as for Belle, we'll manage. My neighbor has offered to help."

"I've never seen a birth of any kind." She brushed her hair away from her forehead, displaying her uneasiness with the subject.

"You're welcome to come and be part of the party. This is Belle's first litter. Mine, too. I may need help."

She began to pace the kitchen, touching the fridge and reading a note held by a magnet, then putting her glass on the counter. "You used to say how silly people were who went overboard on their kids and pets. What made you change?"

He leaned against the sink and studied her. Would she understand all the changes he'd been forced to make? Most people didn't. "I was lonely, so I got a dog."

Her laughter filled the room again, and outside Belle gave a single, mournful bark. "You lonely? I still find that hard to believe. What happened to all the women who used to be so important to you? Good grief, Mark, the only times you ever paid any attention to me was when you invited me to dinner and cried on my shoulder because some aggressive lawyer you'd managed to seduce had revealed that all she wanted was Mark, the Mentor."

"I never cried on your shoulder, but I did appreciate bending your ear," Mark replied. "So I tended to be too trusting. I thought all those women were sincere."

She pursed her lips. "They were all beautiful, as well. Didn't I try to tell you that beauty and sincerity were mutually exclusive. You never learned, did you? So now you're a reclusive umpire who has given up a lucrative career? Why?"

"I have my reasons. They're personal."

Silence hung between them for several minutes.

"You amaze me, Mark," Nancy said. "What do you do now to earn a living?"

"I have a small accounting practice," he offered. "I do volunteer legal counseling at a senior citizens center... and I earn spending money umpiring Little League games."

"It sounds unbelievable," she replied, her gaze never leaving his face.

He emptied his glass and put it in the sink. "Come into the living room and we can talk."

He led her into the other room and motioned her to take a chair, but she shook her head and retrieved her keys from the coffee table.

"We haven't been communicating, just talking at each other," she said, avoiding his curious glance. "I'd better get on home. I have some reading to do."

"Legal briefs?"

"What else does a lawyer read for bedtime pleasure?"

"I've discovered American history," he replied. "I read discarded history textbooks for pleasure."

"Surely, you jest." She stepped closer. "You look very tired, Mark. Are you okay? Have you been ill?"

"It's been a long day," he admitted. The unexpected touch of her fingers sent tiny tongues of flame across his cheek.

"You have these sexy character lines running down your cheeks," she teased, caressing them slowly, until she reached the corners of his mouth. Her voice grew husky. "I don't remember them ... from before."

He felt his body begin to stir. "Nancy... don't...please. You'd be making a dangerous mistake."

"Why?"

One look into her glistening blue eyes made him ask the same question. Why? He never knew when or how his hands became buried in her soft, springy curls or when he eased her closer, but when he stared down at the most sensual pair of lips he could ever remember seeing, the wall of protective ice began to melt.

"May I?" he murmured.

"I'd be disappointed if you didn't."

No normal man could resist, and tonight for these few moments he felt as normal as any virile male with a woman in his arms.

His mouth covered hers, savoring the warm softness, the sweet, moist taste of the inside of her lip. His hands slid downward, lingering on her silky throat before gliding over her shoulders to her ribs. She pressed against his chest, and he stroked the rounded sides of her full breasts, playing with her passion as he worked erotic little circles with the heels of his palms.

Softly she moaned his name. The sound brought him to his senses. He was letting hormones rule his head, his physical needs overpower his firmly established boundaries.

"Nan, go easy," he hissed. "You don't want what you think you want."

She gazed up at him, her eyes dark with passion and need. "I've always wanted...this." Her hands slid around his sides to his chest.

Beneath the fabric of his shirt the ridge of scar tissue tightened, sending his aroused body an overpowering reminder of why this couldn't and shouldn't continue.

He grabbed her hands and forced them down to her sides. "It's almost midnight," he said, trying to ignore the confused expression in her eyes. "Didn't you know that this house turns into a giant pumpkin and I become a rat at midnight? You'd better hurry home, Cinderella."

"You could never be a rat," she murmured.

"Maybe you don't know me anymore."

She stared across the distance now looming between them. "Perhaps not," she admitted, stepping farther away.

Outside, the cool night air brought a soothing sense of composure to Mark as he followed Nancy to her car and tried to ignore the dissatisfaction in his thoughts and body.

"Will you be coming to more games?" he asked.

"Perhaps. Do I have a reason?"

He studied the tip of his shoe. "Don't you have dozens of relatives playing?"

He regretted his remark when he saw her chin lift. He'd seen that movement of her pretty chin many times during long, tedious research projects when others wanted to give up. She had never been a quitter once she'd set her heart and mind on a target. He'd never want to be her target, yet he sensed he'd become exactly that.

"Three nieces and three nephews," she replied. "I'm busy at work, but I promised them all I'd get to as many games as I could. I think one of them has a game tomorrow night."

"I umpire both games tomorrow."

"And Saturday?"

"The major Braves play an early game," he volunteered. "We finish about seven."

She unlocked her car door, and he waited for her to get in. Instead she slammed it shut. Belle began to bark, and the neighbor next door turned on the porch light and stepped outside.

"It's okay, Horace," Mark called, waving a greeting to the older man. The man acknowledged with a casual wave and went back inside.

When Mark's attention returned to the curly-headed woman glaring at him, he knew that once again she was about to call his bluff. He tried to distract her. "I didn't mean for us to wake up the neighborhood. It's a quiet place to live."

Nancy straightened her slim shoulders. "Damn it, Mark, if you won't ask, then I will," she said, keeping a death grip on her clutch purse. "Will you have dinner with me on Saturday after the game?"

"Sure." He couldn't tell who was more surprised. He'd had no intention of asking her out.

She opened the door again and got in. "Good. We'll go to some quiet place and it will be my treat." Her full lips tightened into a narrow line. "I suppose you think I'm being pushy."

He grinned. "Assertive. Isn't that the operative word for today's woman?"

"I knew those workshops would pay off someday. Good night, Mark." Without a backward glance she rolled up her window, gunned the engine and sped into the night.

NOT UNTIL NANCY REACHED the parking area of her apartment complex did a nagging thought materialize. The last time she'd seen Mark they'd had dinner at an expensive restaurant called Mummy Mountain Retreat and he'd told her about buying a large home in Deer Valley. That was miles north and east of where she'd taken him tonight.

Peoria, Arizona, was an almost forgotten town overshadowed by the huge Sun City retirement development and the growing suburb of Glendale. Many of Peoria's citizens lived below the poverty line. Some still tried to operate small farms, but most had sold out to developers in recent years. Her sister lived in one of those developer's look-alike tract homes.

That night at Mummy Mountain Mark had boasted about his newly acquired four-bedroom home and its swimming pool. She doubted that Mark's yard would have space for any kind of in-ground pool. He'd boasted that he'd be the first owner of the house and that it would be a great investment. The house she'd just left had to be at least forty years old, perhaps older.

Mark was quickly becoming one gigantic puzzle, but she'd solved puzzles before, including one that had consisted of a thousand solid red pieces. If she could master that monstrosity, she could solve the puzzle of Mark Bradford.

He hadn't replied when she asked him if he had been sick, but she could see for herself that he'd lost weight. She knew two men who had died of AIDS complications. They had become emaciated in their final months. Could Mark . . . ? She shoved that possibility aside, knowing that he wasn't homosexual or a drug user, and though she knew he'd bedded a lot of women, she'd bet that the conservative and strait-laced Mark Bradford had taken proper precautions.

But he had lost twenty pounds or more. Chronic fatigue syndrome? she wondered. Epstein Barr syndrome? An eating disorder? He had picked at his salad. Maybe he'd simply become a vegetarian. Didn't vegetarians tend to be lean?

She tried to think of other ailments that would take a toll on a healthy man. Some type of cancer? But wouldn't he have said so? Unless it had been prostate cancer. Men could get embarrassed about that. Perhaps he was too young for that problem. He was too young for a heart condition, too. Perhaps he'd undergone some type of routine surgery and experienced complications that had changed his life-style.

The important thing was that now he had recovered...well, almost. He was lean and tan and in good physical condition. The proof of his good health had become obvious when she felt his reaction to kissing her.

Maybe she'd misread Mark's disinterest in her over the years. Could he have just been displaying one more of his noble traits? He had always been her knight in shining armor.

Well, I'll find out, she vowed.

CHAPTER SIX

"YOU DID FINE on the stress test, Mark," Dr. Merrick said, settling himself in his upholstered executive chair behind a formidable walnut desk.

"And the cholesterol?" Mark asked.

"Still a little high, but a hell of a lot better than the 385 you had when we first met. Any new discomfort?"

"Only at night," Mark admitted. "It isn't really discomfort. Maybe it's just normal sensations. Sometimes I hear my heartbeat and I overreact. I start listening for every little irregularity. It skips, or it speeds up. I don't want to hear it, but it's as if I have a built-in stethoscope. The room is deathly quiet. I become aware of every breath I take, and sometimes it's as if I can't breathe without thinking about it. If I don't think about it, I'm afraid I'll stop and then die."

"But then you drop off to sleep?" Dr. Merrick asked.

Mark shook his head. "No. I get obsessed with listening. It gets worse and I hear every heartbeat. I think it's missed several beats and . . . I can't ignore it. I've thought about calling you, but that would be stupid. Why wake the rest of the world?"

Dr. Merrick waited patiently without commenting.

Mark ran his fingers through his blond hair, hating to admit his paranoia. "It scares the hell out of me.

That's when I get up and bring my Irish setter inside. She likes to sleep on the foot of my bed.'' He examined his hands. "She snores and I need her...the sounds she makes...someone else alive in the room.''

"You're attuned to what's happening, Mark,'' Dr. Merrick said. "That's good. Before you were ignoring everything. And if you think there's something really amiss, call me.'' The physician grinned. "You won't wake me, at least not at first. My answering service stays awake around the clock. I sleep like a log.''

They discussed the test results, then the physician modified Mark's medication and added more items to the growing list of approved activities. He leaned back in his chair and studied Mark. "You've never asked me about sex. I assume you're sexually active again. Any problems there?''

Mark shifted uncomfortably in his chair. "Is this the day of judgment?''

Dr. Merrick scowled. "I never judge my patients. I take them the way I find them and try to give them a new lease on life. I think that's what we've done for you, Mark. I've been seeing you every month or so, and if you continue to progress as you have been, and you don't have any relapses, we won't need to have another of these get-togethers for six months.''

Mark nodded. "That sounds great to me.''

Dr. Merrick's scowl deepened. "Frankly I'm concerned about your growing cynicism. You have your whole life ahead of you.'' He waved his hand in the air. "I'll bet you put on a front for your family and friends, but when you come here...well, let's talk about that.''

Mark slumped deeper into his chair. "What does that have to do with my sex life?"

Dr. Merrick grinned. "One can affect the other. Have you resumed sexual activity . . . or avoided it?"

Mark looked away. "I tried once . . . about three months after the surgery. I couldn't . . ."

"Get it up?" the physician asked, chuckling.

Mark didn't respond.

"I'm not surprised. I had you on some heavy doses of blood thinners and beta blockers. They can screw up a man's ability to perform. But you've been off those for months now. Are you still having trouble?"

Mark's thoughts shot back to the previous night with Nancy Prentice. "I quit looking for female companionship. Maybe I did avoid it . . . until last night." He smiled. "I met a woman I knew years ago. Frankly I was surprised at what happened during a simple little kiss."

"So she's someone special?" Dr. Merrick asked.

"No."

"Liar."

"She could have been, but not now," Mark retorted.

"Why not? If she's willing, why would you not be?"

"She deserves a better future than becoming an early widow."

Dr. Merrick leaned forward. "What the hell does that mean?"

"You said yourself that if I came in again in a year or so, you probably couldn't save me. I've become a realist, Dr. Merrick. I could drop dead anytime. Nancy deserves better than that. She's young. She'll want children. If I pass this genetic defect on to my children, I'd be giving them the same death sentence my father gave to me."

Dr. Merrick bolted from his chair and left the office, the door slamming behind him. Before Mark could decide whether he'd been dismissed or not the physician returned with an armload of books, followed by his secretary carrying a tray with steaming coffee cups and two videocassttes.

"Am I free to go now?" Mark asked, knowing he wasn't.

"Hell, no, Mark Bradford," Dr. Merrick said, dropping the load of books into Mark's lap none too gently. The videocassettes topped the stack. "Get him a box," Dr. Merrick said to his secretary. "I'm giving him homework, and tell Jane to schedule Mark another visit in thirty days for his exam. A written exam, not a physical." He waved her toward the door. "And don't disturb us until I say so."

Once the door closed behind her Dr. Merrick sat down and slowly drank half his cup of coffee. Mark followed suit. This morning he was too exhausted to argue. He'd lain awake for hours after Nancy left, and had finally gotten up and taken Belle for a long walk. Dawn had broken before they had returned to the house. Then he'd slept until 9:00 a.m.

He chanced a glance across the desk. "Let me have your sermon. I can feel it coming, so fire away." He ran his hand through his hair, then tried to relieve the knotted muscles in the back of his neck. "I feel as if I've been dragged through hell this past year."

"Maybe you're the one doing the dragging," Dr. Merrick said. "You're not the only man to have heart problems."

"No, just the youngest."

"Wrong. I had a patient a few years ago who had pernicious anemia," Dr. Merrick said. "He'd had it from boyhood. His family considered him 'the puny son,' and to get away from his own mother's protectiveness, he moved to Santa Fe. Good-looking young man, sensible and creative, too, but when he met this cowgirl who was the picture of health, he went into a period of denial. It almost cost him his life, but that woman loved him enough to hold his hand through his recovery. He's past forty now and living the good life and will continue to if he follows the doctor's orders."

"And the moral of this story is . . . ?"

"The moral is, there's always someone worse off than you are," Dr. Merrick said. "We got you in time. You could have made it through the trial and gone jogging that night, had the attack and died because no one knew where you were. You could have been found the next weekend by some little children on a picnic with their family."

The office grew quiet as they finished their coffee. The physician leaned closer. "You miss your law practice, don't you?"

"It was my life," Mark admitted.

Dr. Merrick rocked his chair. "So it was an extension of your masculinity. You were forced to give up the practice of law and now, as if to do penance, you've given up sex, not just for something like Lent, but for the rest of your life. A complete emasculation of your manhood. Is that it?"

Mark hesitated. "I didn't think so." He thought about the year of hell and the swings in emotion and attitude he'd gone through. "So what if I do decide to have an affair? I still won't subject the woman to anything permanent."

"If the woman loves you, why would it be a subjugation? Doesn't she deserve to have a say in the matter?"

"Nancy Prentice has a promising legal career ahead of her," Mark explained.

"So she has what you were denied but still want?"

"Don't put words into my mouth," Mark replied, angry at the other man's insinuation. "I meant that I would never ask her to give up—"

"Who said she has to?" Dr. Merrick began to pace the office. "She can be the wage earner and you can be the social volunteer."

Mark chuckled. "You're saying I can be a house husband? I suppose I can stay home and take care of the kids, too?"

"There weren't going to be any kids," Dr. Merrick reminded him. "Have you changed your mind? Mark, do you resent being born? Would you have preferred never to have lived?"

He gave that question careful thought. "No... maybe at times."

"Do you like the work you're doing?"

Mark nodded. "Yes, but it's not enough to support a family."

"That depends on what a family needs. Love, a safe place to live, good meals on a regular basis, parents to love them unconditionally, parents who love each other."

Mark joined Dr. Merrick in his pacing, selecting the other side of the office. "This is all premature. I just met her again last night."

"Are you going to see her again?"

Mark stopped behind his chair. "Saturday night after a baseball game."

"That's great," Dr. Merrick said, dropping back into his chair. "You let nature take its course. Does she know about your surgery."

"No."

"Tell her."

"That would end everything before it began," Mark said.

"Don't sell her short. And if a kiss leads to more and she's willing, make love to her. She may need it as much as you."

"That sounds irresponsible," Mark replied. "She'd probably get the wrong idea, read all kinds of intentions into it that I couldn't fulfill. It wouldn't be fair to play games with her."

Dr. Merrick sighed. "Mark, for an intelligent guy, you can be incredibly dense sometimes. Talk to her. Tell her how you feel and why. If she's an attorney, she must be sharp. What does she look like? Is she pretty?"

Mark gave a brief description of Nancy, and the doctor listened without comment until he finished.

"You must make a fine-looking couple," Dr. Merrick said, stroking his chin. "Take these books and read them. Mark them if you need to, and view the videos as many times as you need. Let her see them with you. And for hell's sake, get over this fatalistic attitude that you're going to drop dead any minute."

"But it's true."

"We're all going to do that and no one knows when. Live your life to its fullest. A good woman can make that life worthwhile and fuller than you ever imagined."

For a fleeting moment Mark could imagine Nancy involved with his day-to-day activities, but he couldn't shake the lingering doubts as to the wisdom of such a scenario. "Maybe I'll bring it up...maybe not."

Dr. Merrick extended his hand. "You give it a try, Mark. Take a risk. Without it you'll never know. Would you want to die never knowing about this Nancy woman?"

"I'll think about it," Mark replied, accepting the physician's extended hand.

Dr. Merrick grinned. "You have a day and a half. Well, I have other patients waiting, so take care of yourself, young man, and let that woman into your life."

Mark filled the box with the books and videos, then paused by the door. "What about my diet? When I go out to eat, there's not much on the menu that fits the list you gave me."

"Lean red meat is fine a few times a month," Dr. Merrick said. "Chicken is good, but the skin and fat is just as bad as the fat on red meat, so cut it off. Fish is great, but make it fresh if possible and broil or bake it. If it smells, put it back. Good fish doesn't smell. Skip the butter and whole milk products."

"Red meat! Wonderful. I've been living on vegetables, fruit and fish," Mark said.

"I don't see you turning green," Dr. Merrick remarked good-naturedly.

Mark rubbed the side of his neck. "But I've noticed these ridges starting to form. Do you think they might be gills?"

Dr. Merrick slapped Mark on the shoulder. "Not unless you start breathing through them. Keep up the good diet, but treat yourself to a forbidden meal occasionally. One or two a month won't kill you. And never skip your medication. With your body chemistry you could be a total vegetarian and you'd still have high cholesterol. Between the powder and pills, though, it's coming down a few points each month.''

They discussed diet changes for a few more minutes, then Dr. Merrick rushed off to his next patient.

Outside, Mark paused, scanning the activity in the parking lot. A mother ran after two young children as they scurried toward the entryway to the medical building. An older couple, their heads close as they talked, hurried toward a car parked near Mark's truck. A fire engine's shrill siren sounded in the distance, followed by the wail of an ambulance.

Yes, there were others with health concerns, many far worse than his own, but that didn't make accepting his own problems any easier. He unlocked his truck and climbed inside, pausing before sliding the key into the ignition.

Before he would let his optimism get a loose rein he'd think carefully about what his physician had said and bide his time. He'd gone through these emotional swings before. This one would run its course just like all the others. All he needed to chase it away was a tinge of discomfort in his chest.

He would eat a normal meal for a change when he went out to dinner with Nancy, but he had no intention of divulging his health problems to her.

BY THE TIME Nancy pulled into the parking lot of the ballpark, the aroma of fried chicken from the bucket she'd brought had whetted her appetite, and she yearned for a piece.

But she was determined to save all the pleasures of the evening to share with Mark. She had invited him to dinner but, after mulling over the invitation all morning, had changed her plans and decided on a picnic instead. He was a man bedeviled by many secrets. A restaurant would be formal. He didn't need that as an excuse to avoid her questions. He'd done enough of that already.

For the first time since joining Staley, Jennings and Kaufman, she had left her work at the office. This evening was for relaxation and pleasure. Perhaps if her wistful dreams came true, tomorrow, as well.

She slammed her car door, trapping the aroma of fried chicken and hot biscuits from the fast-food restaurant inside, and headed for the playing field. She spotted Mark leaning over with his hands on his knees as he and a boy of about eleven whispered to each other near the pitcher's mound. Anyone observing him could tell he was marvelous with children.

Finding a seat on the highest row of the bleachers, she leaned against the backrest and took advantage of his preoccupation to watch him unobserved. After working together for ten long years, they already knew each other's likes and dislikes, how the other person thought and felt about important issues. They could leap over the awkwardness of getting to know each other the way strangers had to... except at moments, she sensed he was very much a stranger.

She had never known him to be interested in children before, never heard him talk about his family. She knew he was the son of a successful politician, that his family went back to pioneer Arizona stock. She didn't even know if he had siblings. He'd always struck her as an only child, but as she studied him, she vaguely recalled being introduced years earlier to a tall, slender woman who might have been a sister.

As she admired him from her perch in the bleachers, she thought back to those years when her initial infatuation evolved into much more. Something gnawed at her thoughts. Had she only known a carefully constructed facade of this man? Had he shielded his inner self from even his closest co-workers?

Perhaps this weekend would answer all her questions. She smiled, knowing she was letting her imagination run wild. But why not? If she'd misread Mark's interest in her, she'd go back to her regular life and try to forget what might have been.

Two days, only two days since she'd met him again...and they had stretched an eternity. Friday had been hectic with two new clients assigned to her, but as she read through the folders to get a feel for each case, her thoughts were on Mark. If only she knew how he felt, and what was wrong with him, and why he'd given up a lucrative career.

Mark left the playing field and took up a position by the dugout, gripping the wire with his strong fingers and leaning his forearms against it for balance. His lean derriere would catch the eye of any alert woman. The tails of his shirt were neatly tucked beneath a western-style leather belt. Each time he moved she could imagine the ripple of muscles across his back.

His chest would be well developed, of that she was sure, but not hairy. Someday she wanted to lie beside him, running her finger from his throat slowly down to his... A blush swept up her cheek at the thought of being with him, naked, satiated. What kind of lover would he be? Tender? Masterful? Impatient? With her lack of experience she hoped he'd be understanding and tender.

Dangerous, she thought. Jumping to conclusions. They were simply friends, renewing an old acquaintance. Torn between wanting his undying love and fearing his rejection, she absorbed his every movement as he paced thoughtfully for a moment before sending a hand signal to the pitcher.

Yes, she admitted. Mark Bradford was the only man she could ever be involved with. She'd decided that years earlier.

Although he'd teased her that he had given up wine, women and other vices, she was positive he had exaggerated. Anyone as handsome and charming as Mark had to be fighting off the women.

She bit her lip to keep from laughing out loud. The crowd roared as the Braves' pitcher struck out two batters in a row and retired the side. The next inning started and she stirred restlessly. What if he didn't want a picnic? What if he'd changed his mind and announced his intention to go home?

The crowd cheered as the players came off the field. Sighing, she leaned back and closed her eyes, ignoring the game completely. She played with the key ring in her lap, waiting for the next inning to begin, but her mind kept weaving scenarios of her and Mark.

"Is this seat taken?" a man's voice said, and her eyes flew open.

"Mark?" Her gaze darted from his somber face to the playing field, surprised to find the field empty. "What happened to the game? Where are all the players?"

He grinned. "Those last two runs broke a tie, and we won five to three. Weren't you paying attention?"

Her gaze flew back to his face. "It's over? You mean, you're all done now? We can . . . ?"

"We can do whatever your heart desires," he replied. "I'm yours for the rest of the night."

CHAPTER SEVEN

NANCY CLOSED her eyes. *If only you meant that.* Knowing the remark was innocent of double meaning, she nodded. "Good. The food is in the car."

"I thought we were going out."

"I decided it would be fun to have a picnic instead...right here somewhere. Is there a tree where we could sit and eat?"

"Sounds okay." He removed his cap and ran his fingers through his dampened hair, then adjusted the cap back on his head. He seemed ill at ease.

"If you'd rather... I mean." She noticed the pallor around his mouth. "Are you okay?"

"A bit tired," he admitted.

She squeezed his hand. "Then you can rest and eat. I have tons of food. Can you help me carry it?"

"A pleasure," he replied, following her when she began to work her way down the half-filled bleachers. When they reached the ground, he draped one arm around her shoulder and guided her through the milling crowd. Several of the children called, "Hi, Ump," and Mark nodded back.

The Braves' manager called to him and he excused himself, returning to her a few minutes later. "Practice tomorrow afternoon," he explained. "We're in second place, but it's only ten days into the season. We don't want to get overconfident."

Perhaps it was only her imagination, but it seemed as if he pulled her closer as he chatted. He described the game, naming some of the players and their parents.

"You enjoy baseball, don't you?" she asked.

"Who doesn't?"

He stopped and she looked up to find him studying her. "What's wrong?" she asked, unsettled by his scrutiny.

"I missed you," he admitted as his hand brushed her cheek.

Her heart thudded against her ribs. "It's only been two days...but I missed you, too." Did he plan to kiss her right here in this parking lot? They were surrounded by latecomers for the second game.

A little boy raced up to them and skidded to a dusty stop. "Hi, Ump," the boy gasped, displaying two missing front teeth. "Remember me? I'm Butch! You umping our game tonight? I sure hope so. We win when you ump."

Mark ruffled the boy's spiky blond hair. "Sorry, Butch, I'm off duty tonight, but you play your best. Maybe you'll win without me."

"You betcha," Butch replied, and raced off.

Nancy sighed. "The children like you."

He slid his hand to the back of her neck and eased her forward. "And I like them. What about you, Nancy?"

"Like the children? Sure, but it's not the same as having your own playing. I can tell that by what my sisters say."

"I didn't mean the children," he said. "What do you think of the ump?"

"I think he's sort of...special. He's got a cute tush, and he's a fair and just umpire, and I've always liked him . . . a lot." Her last words were buried against his shoulder.

She didn't know who had taken the first move. It didn't matter, she thought, relishing the strength of his arms around her and the feel of his conditioned body beneath the fabric of his shirt as her hands slid around his waist.

The blast of a horn from a car less than three feet from them jolted them apart. "Find a secluded spot for that, folks. We've got a game to watch." The driver, a florid-faced bull of a man, made a lewd gesture and guffawed as Mark and Nancy stepped aside.

"This way," Nancy said, hurrying to her car to cover her embarrassment. When she opened the hatchback, the aroma of chicken turned her empty stomach into a knot.

"You take the box of food and I'll carry the pillows and a blanket to sit on." When they reached the large grassy field, he pointed toward a huge mulberry tree at the edge of the park.

"We can get a clear view of all three playing fields," he said. "The second games are about to begin."

Under the tree he took the blanket from her and shook it out. "Sorry about that redneck in the parking lot," he said. She handed him the pillows and he caught her hand. "So I have a cute tush? No one ever told me that before."

She grinned and avoided a reply, instead concentrating on unpacking the meal. "I thought about you all day," she confessed. "I've concluded you're a health food nut, so I bought the chicken from a place that cooks it in corn oil." She glanced up. "I hope you're not completely vegetarian. Maybe you don't eat meat at all?''

''Chicken's fine.''

''And I made the potato salad.''

''Does it have eggs in it?'' he asked.

She nodded. ''You don't eat eggs?'' Before he could reply she unscrewed the top of a wide-mouthed thermos. ''Here's some steamed rice. Surely you eat rice?''

He nodded. ''Rice is great. What else?''

''Fresh veggies,'' she replied, opening a tray of carrot, celery, bell pepper sticks and buds of cauliflower and broccoli. ''I know you're watching your figure, so the dip is low-fat yogurt.''

He reached for a carrot stick. ''If you noticed, I have a good-looking behind, then you'll be interested to know I've made a study of my own, Prentice. Your curves are in all the right proportions and in the right places.''

She ducked her head. She was too old to blush at a man's compliment. ''Shall we eat?'' she suggested. ''I have a thermos of orange juice. Surely you drink orange juice?''

She handed him a paper cup. He removed a small blue pill from his shirt pocket and discreetly slipped it into his mouth before he drank the juice. He didn't offer an explanation and she didn't ask.

He's truly sick, she thought, her mind racing over the ailments that could strike a man in his prime. *No, he's fine,* she decided when he reached for a chicken thigh and seemed to enjoy eating it. He avoided the potato salad, and she wondered if she'd screwed up on making it. But when she took a small second helping, it tasted fine. *He just doesn't like it.*

They watched the games as they ate. Mark provided a running commentary, pointing out the players' errors and successes. Little by little the game began to make more sense to her.

When she reached past him to get a celery stick from the tray and started to crawl back to her spot, he grabbed her by her waist and hauled her onto his lap, then dropped her to the blanket to settle between his legs.

"You can see better from here," he murmured against her ear as she settled against him. He encircled her loosely with his arms, pointing out players as he talked.

His open display of affection made her lightheaded. For years she had wanted him to show something, anything, to give her a hint that he felt the chemistry between them. When she took him home a few nights earlier, she had almost jumped into his arms. Had she given him the impression she was easy? *Oh, God, does he think I'm always available to... men?*

"Mark?" She hardly recognized her own voice. It sounded shy, unsure, disturbingly feminine and not at all the assertive and self-confident woman she liked to think she was.

"Hmm." His warm breath caressed her earlobe. Then his mouth touched the sensitive skin below the curve of her jaw.

"I... please don't do that." She giggled as he nibbled the side of her neck. "I can't think straight when you do that."

"You always think straight," he murmured, kissing her again. "I know you, Prentice. I worked with you for years."

"But, Mark...did you ever notice me...as a woman?"

"Occasionally," he confessed.

Startled, she jerked free and turned to confront him. "You did? You really did?" She leaned back on her haunches. "I never knew that."

He grew solemn. "You had a bright future and I wasn't going to complicate your life. But my behavior didn't keep me from having my share of lustful thoughts."

She reached out to touch his cheek. "Oh, Mark, that's wonderful. And it *was* noble. You've always been a man of principle. But I would have been satisfied with a simple dinner invitation."

"We went to dinner a lot," he pointed out. "And I used to bend your ear, filling you in on all my cases and strategies."

"I'm always available for a good talk, Mark. I'm your friend. Bend my ear anytime." Suddenly she sensed his mood was changing, as if he was distancing himself from her again. "Mark? Why did you really give up your practice?"

He concentrated on the game in the middle baseball diamond for several seconds. "The pressure got the best of me."

Had he suffered a nervous breakdown? She had never thought about a mental collapse when searching for reasons behind his career change. "Are you okay now?"

"I'm getting better day by day," he replied, meeting her gaze directly. "Live each day to the fullest is my motto. It's served me well during my recovery."

Recovery? Drug or alcohol? Some other chemical dependency? She sensed another attempt to shift the conversation away from his private life. She'd begun to recognize the signs. A tensing of a muscle in his cheek, a slight narrowing of his eyes. Usually they were warm and as green as the desert sagebrush, but when her questions crept too close, his eyes darkened and became cloaked in secrecy. She would have to be careful to respect the unstated yet almost visible ground rules he'd established.

"Mark? I knew about most of your women," she said, studying the two rings on her right hand. "You never asked much about the men in my life."

He tried to tuck a curl behind her ear, but it was too short. "I assumed there were many, but I knew you could handle them."

She looked up at him. "None of them were serious." What would he think of her now? That when she fooled around with men, she kept it casual? She couldn't elaborate without revealing an intimate secret of her own.

"Why not?" he asked, glancing toward the middle field when the crowd began to roar as a double play began. "Never met the right man?"

She knew he was only half listening. "Yes, I've met him, but he doesn't know how I feel," she replied, hoping her voice was soft enough so that he wouldn't hear her.

The crowd in the bleachers roared their approval as the catcher tagged the runner trying to slide into home plate. "That was a great play," he said. "Those Pony League players are super, don't you think?"

"Sure, Mark," she replied, and began to cover the food containers. The mood between them, warm and intimate a few minutes earlier, had become neutral. Perhaps she had been too open and honest with him.

Just when she began to feel he was interested in her, he'd shifted gears and left her isolated.

"Aunt Nancy, Aunt Nancy!" a young girl shouted.

Nancy glanced up to find several of her nieces and nephews running toward them.

"Company," Mark said, scanning the curious children's faces. "Relatives of yours? Wait." He pointed at a familiar face. "I know you. You're Nichole," he said, grinning at the youngest girl.

Nichole giggled. "And you're the ump who hugged my Aunt Nancy."

"Guilty," Mark replied.

The children's attention shifted to the leftover food.

"Help yourselves," Nancy said, not wanting to cart it all back to her apartment. "Mark, this is Larry," she said, pointing to an eight-year-old boy. "Larry and Nichole belong to my sister Linda."

Larry opened the thermos of rice and made a face. "Yuck. Who eats rice at a picnic?" He grabbed the last drumstick and began to strip it bare to the bone.

Nancy shook her head and shrugged toward Mark. "Next comes Angie, who's ten, and Rachel, who's eleven. They play on the major Yankees. They belong to my other sister, Layne, as do Zack and Chuck."

She motioned to two gangly young teenage boys, each concentrating on a chicken breast. "Zack is fourteen and Chuck is fifteen. They play for the Pony League Cubs. Zack is the second baseman who made that double play you were so impressed with."

"Great arm," Mark said. "Stay in shape and you'll make the pros . . . maybe."

"Gee, thanks." Zack reached for the last piece of chicken, a wing.

"Kids, this is Mark Bradford," Nancy continued. "He coaches for the major Braves and he umpires a lot of the games."

Zack nodded. "That's why we're here. Nichole told us you were an ump."

Mark nodded and extended his hand. "I umpire three nights a week, mostly minors. I've never done your league."

"We didn't think so and that's even better," the oldest boy, Chuck, said. "We need to ask an expert."

Nichole grinned at Mark. "Mr. Bradford is an expert. He did one of our games and we won."

Mark laughed.

Zack looked disdainfully at his younger sister. "That makes it sound like he cheats in your favor."

Nancy sidled closer to Mark, dropping her hand around his broad shoulder. "Mark would never cheat. He's a very honest person."

"Thank you for defending me, Counselor," Mark murmured. "Now, kids, tell me what's bothering you." He seemed to be enjoying the undivided attention from the six children who quickly consumed the leftover food.

"Got any more?" Rachel asked, scraping the last few kernels of rice from the thermos.

"You cleaned me out," Nancy said, packing up the containers and stashing them in the box. "Tell us what your problem is."

Zack pulled his baseball cap closer over his eyes. "It's sorta tricky... and we don't want to get into trouble for asking."

Mark looked from one anxious face to the next. "Does it involve the rules?" he asked, extracting a worn rule book from his hip pocket.

"How'd you guess?" Angie asked. "Go ahead, Zack, ask him. If Aunt Nancy trusts him, he's probably okay."

Mark and Nancy exchanged curious glances, and Mark winked at her, sending her heart into a flutter.

"Spill it, kids," Mark said. "What's the question?"

Zack scooted closer, as if he didn't want anyone else in the park to hear him. "I think our manager is breaking the rules. Chuck says he's just using good judgment. We have this girl. Her name is Sarah Burns, but we call her Sadie. She's been on my team ever since T-Ball, and I know how good she is. Ya see, Mr. Bradford, we have two girls on our team this year, and Mr. Fischer, our manager, won't let 'em play...ever!"

Chuck punched his younger brother. "That's because they're girls and can't throw as hard as us guys, stupid. He told us that."

"Stupid, yourself," Zack said, jerking away from his brother's intimidating fist. "Sadie is really a super player. She hit more home runs last year than anyone on the team, and she made the All-Star teams two years in a row. If she was that good before, how come she turned into a dork this year? Tonight is the first one we've won. If Mr. Fischer would have let Sadie play, we could have won all three. Does he have a right to bench her and Beth just because they're girls?"

Nancy turned to Mark. "He can't do that, can he?"

"I've never looked up the rules, but it sounds illegal to me, just on established sexual discrimination law in general."

"Has Sarah talked to the manager?" Nancy asked, giving Mark a chance to research the rule book.

"Sure," Zack replied. "She's pushy, and that makes the manager even madder. Her parents complained to the president of the league, but he's a number one nerd. I'll bet if you opened him up, you couldn't find a backbone, and if you did, it'd be yellow."

Mark glanced up from his rule book. "You mean Mr. Glenn? He's not so bad." He grinned. "Unless a problem comes up. I have noticed a certain lack of..."

Zack nodded. "Go ahead and say it, Ump. He's a wimp. Mr. Fischer runs him, so Sadie won't get any help there. We told her to see Aunt Nancy 'cause she's a lawyer."

"Yeah," Nichole chimed in. "Aunt Nancy can sue him, and Sadie will get a million dollars and buy the league and fire Mr. Fischer, so all the other girls will get a fair chance. Someday I might wanna play Pony League baseball."

Nancy shook her head. "It's not as simple as that, kids. First Sadie and her parents would have to come up with positive proof that the only reason she doesn't get to play is her sex. Being a girl isn't a valid reason to bench her."

"Right! So sue the manager!" Zack insisted. "I don't always like playing with girls, but when they're good, that's different, and Sadie's terrific."

Chuck squeezed his way into the circle. "Mr. Bradford, could you and Nancy come to our next game and spy on him? Sadie's sorta cute, and she deserves a fair chance."

Mark seemed hesitant to get involved in the dispute.

"Let me check around," Nancy said. "I'll see if there are some precedents for taking action. I'll let you know."

"Great," Nichole said, clapping her hands. "Aunt Nancy is gonna sue the manager and get him fired."

Nancy held up her hand. "Wait a minute. I never said I'd take the case. I'm up to here with cases already." She drew her hand across her neck. "Hiring an attorney costs megabucks."

"Unless they take it on a contingency basis," Mark added, explaining to the children what he meant.

"Gee, how come you know about suing people?" Zack asked.

Nancy patted Mark's shoulder. "He used to be an attorney," she said. "That's where we met." She could feel Mark's shoulder stiffen beneath her touch. "But he's retired now. Still, he might be willing to research the case...."

Mark got to his feet. "No, I couldn't." The children scrambled to their feet.

Zack helped him shake and fold the blanket. "But why couldn't you still check out the rules, Mr. Bradford?"

Mark stared across the field for several seconds, then looked down at the boy. "I'll check out the rules, but that's all. I can't...maybe your aunt can find someone who will at least talk to Sadie and her parents."

"What about coming to our next game?" Zack pressed. "Aunt Nancy promised to come to our games as well as the rug rats' games. She owes us that." Zack whipped out the league schedule from his pocket. "We play next Tuesday. You umping?"

Mark checked his own schedule. "I have an early game to work, but after that I'm free." He looked across the children's heads to where Nancy stood watching him. "Want to go see a big league game?"

"I'd love to," she murmured, afraid her voice would reflect her willingness to go anywhere in the universe with him.

"Now that that's settled, let's get out of here," Mark said, putting his schedule away. He glanced at his watch. "It's past ten and they'll be turning out the lights any minute now. Do you kids have rides home?"

Larry giggled. "Our moms are cleaning up in the snack bar. They said to be there when they close up."

"Then you'd better get a move on," Mark said. "The front window just got lowered."

"Do you know our moms?" Rachel asked. "Aunt Nancy and our moms are all sisters."

"That much I know," Mark replied. "Are they as pretty as Nancy?"

Surprised by his remark, Nancy grabbed the blanket and pillows. "Prettier."

"Maybe I should decide for myself," he said. "Can I meet them?" Several eager children yelled their agreement.

Mark picked up the box of empty food containers and beckoned to Nancy. "Come on, Prentice, let's see who's right . . . unless you're embarrassed about introducing me to them."

Her cheeks had returned to their normal color by the time they reached the closed snack bar.

"This is Linda," Nancy said. "You can tell her from Layne because she's blond." Everyone laughed, and Linda nodded her approval to Nancy.

Layne extended her hand. "I'm the redhead and the oldest. You're the best umpire we have this season. I'm so glad you're with us and I'm glad our little sister has found a reason to give up being a workaholic for a while."

Mark chuckled. "You three don't look anything alike." His gaze swung from one sister to the next.

"But who's the prettiest?" Rachel asked.

"Well," he replied, stroking his chin thoughtfully, "I'm partial to women with short curly brown hair, but blondes are beautiful and redheads are ravishing, so I believe it's a tie."

The sisters laughed and gathered their respective families. "Very diplomatic," Linda said. "Nancy's told me a little about you. I can see why you seldom lost a case. Now, kids, it's time to get home, so scat." She turned to Mark and Nancy as the children ran to a nearby station wagon. "Keep her distracted from those legal briefs she reads all the time, Mark."

"I'll do my best," he promised. He stood directly behind Nancy, and as they watched the two families drive away, Mark's hands settled on Nancy's shoulders. Across the field a man opened a metal box on a utility pole and turned off the floodlights around the three playing fields, plunging the area into darkness.

Nancy tensed, then relaxed as Mark's arms surrounded her. She leaned her head back against his chest. "It feels so good to stand here, just the two of us," she whispered.

He turned her in his arms. "Do you have plans for the rest of the evening?"

"No...do you?"

"If you're willing, I want to spend it with you." His lips brushed hers but left before she could respond.

Desire began to build inside her. "Where?" she whispered.

"At my place," he murmured, claiming her mouth again.

CHAPTER EIGHT

WHEN HIS MOUTH LIFTED from hers, Mark could barely make out her features in the darkness. "Will you come home with me, Nan?"

"Yes, oh, yes," she said, and he could feel her trembling in his arms.

His hands cupped her face. "I want to do more than talk or visit. I need you, Nan. God, how I need you. I want to make love to you."

"Yes... I want that also."

His thumbs grazed her cheekbones. "I can't promise you a future, but for now we can—"

"Don't try to justify this, Mark," she replied. "Being with you tonight is...well, it's something I've wanted for years. Don't you know that?"

He pulled her close again and held her, hoping and praying his decision would be a positive one for both of them. A sense of guilt flooded through him, and he tried to push it aside. Yes, he admitted, he had a selfish motive. If he made love to her successfully, he might be whole again. If in the process he bought her fulfillment, did that justify his actions? He wasn't sure, and his growing desire was making it hard to think logically.

Nancy's hand settled on his chest. "Your heart is pounding faster than mine," she said, laughing softly. She gazed up at him, and the adoration he saw reflected in her eyes brought a resurgence of guilt. *Maybe this is wrong,* he thought, seeing her vulnerability.

But they were consenting adults. Abstinence was a word foreign to their generation's life-style and vocabulary. They'd admitted to desiring each other for years. Tonight would be the culmination of those years.

"Let's get out of here," he said, easing his hold on her.

"I drove my car," she whispered. "I can't leave it here. It might be stripped by the time I came back for it."

"Then follow me home."

As he drove from the ballpark, Mark was careful to keep Nancy's car in his rearview mirror. When a traffic light separated them, he pulled to the curb and waited. This was a woman he didn't want to lose.

Soon the dark silhouette of his house loomed like a sentinel at the end of the street. He'd forgotten to leave the porch light on. He'd spent the day mulling over the consequences of asking her to spend the night. At least he'd been honest about his intentions. Playing games had no place in their lives, only up-front honesty and openness.

They would go inside and have a glass of wine. While they sipped the wine he'd describe his illness and explain how it had been the impetus for all the changes in his life. She'd understand.

He felt a moment of panic, wondering if he'd have difficulty making love. He didn't know how he'd handle that. *Let nature take its course. I'll be okay,* he told himself. *If I'm not, will she understand?*

He parked in the driveway and waited for her under the overhang of the dark porch. As she left her car and slowly approached him, he began to wonder how he'd ever thought of her in a sisterly fashion. She broke into a run and was in his arms.

She laughed with pure unbridled joy when he kissed her face, then the throbbing pulse at the base of her throat. He pushed the narrow strap down her arm in order to reach her slender shoulder, not wanting to miss an inch of her heated flesh.

His doubts about his ability to perform vanished when she pressed against him. He wanted to sweep her up and carry her to his bed. He needed her without delay. But that wouldn't be fair to her. Women needed prolonged foreplay, which usually paid off with shared ecstasy... if only he could maintain his patience.

"We should go inside," she whispered, slipping from his arms.

He fumbled with his keys, and she waited close beside him, shifting from one foot to the other.

"Hurry," she whispered.

The door opened and he pulled her inside, reaching for the light switch.

"No, keep it dark," she insisted, sliding her arms slowly up his chest and around his neck.

When her lips sought his, he forgot about drinking a glass of wine, about explaining his condition. His reservations about all the things he knew could go wrong vanished. Only the woman pressing against him mattered now. He ached with desire when her hips swayed back and forth across his loins. Did she know what she was doing to him, driving him crazy with need?

"Oh, God, Nancy, I want you in the worst way." He swung her up in his arms and carried her down the hallway and into his bedroom, stopping long enough to remove her tank top and bra before placing her on his bed. The room was dark, yet he could see the dim glow of her pale form. Her hips shifted restlessly, and he knelt to remove her shorts and panties.

She lay motionless, and he was glad she didn't try to hide her nakedness from him. Perhaps one of the benefits of sexual experience was a lack of pretense or false modesty.

"You're beautiful," he murmured. Her breasts were full and high. Her slender waist flared to rounded hips and down the shapely legs he'd admired each time he'd seen her.

She moaned softly as she turned her head to gaze at him, then closed her eyes. Dropping his clothing to the carpet, he lowered himself to the bed. She turned away, exposing her neck and throat to his eager kisses. He tasted her warm, delectable flesh and savored the throbbing pulse, then edged toward her breast. Each excited breath she took made her breast heave as his mouth approached.

When his lips touched its fullness, she moaned again, but the moan evolved into a soft groan when he took the aroused nipple in his mouth and rolled it with his tongue.

Her hands clutched his head, and he couldn't tell if she were urging him to continue or pleading for him to stop. Stopping was the last thing on his mind, and when her hand slid down his ribs to his hip, he shifted his attention from her lush breasts to her face.

He could barely make out her features in the darkness and wished he'd taken time to turn on a light. He wanted to see her eyes dilated with passion, her lips swollen after he kissed them again and again. He wanted to take time to explore every inch of her body. But each time she writhed beside him, his body screamed for progress.

"Mark, oh, my darling Mark, I love you so much," she murmured, seeking his mouth. "I love you, I love you. I've waited so long for you. Tonight . . . oh, to-night . . ."

His hand slid down her flat abdomen to the dark, inviting V of her legs, and she opened her thighs, encouraging him to explore her. Her moist heat burned his fingers and turned his own body into molten fire.

"Love me, Mark, love me," she cried, urging him onward.

He rose above her, wanting to be sure she was ready, but when he felt her hands on his hips, he lost his grip on his feeble control. He entered her slowly, striving to be gentle. She seemed small and tight, and he grew concerned that his hardness might hurt her. She lifted her hips slightly, drawing him inside.

When he encountered a barrier, he stopped. *No, this can't be,* he thought. "Nan?"

"Don't stop," she pleaded.

When he thrust deeper, he felt the quick tearing of her innocence. "Oh, God, Nan, you should have told me. I didn't want to hurt you."

"No, no," she whispered, but she stopped moving beneath him, and he knew she was biting her lip. "It's done," she said, pulling his head down. "It's too late to stop now."

"Sweetheart, if I'd known, I wouldn't have . . ."

She kissed him, her fingers flickering across his cheek when his mouth lifted from hers. "That's why

I couldn't tell you," she said between kisses. "I've waited...I knew why, only I thought...it would never happen. Please don't stop now."

Her fingers traced his lips, and he caught one between his teeth, running his tongue across its tip before releasing it. "You're magnificent," he whispered, kissing her again.

His natural urge to thrust was overpowering. This night was quickly becoming a night of uncontrollable urges. The thought made him smile. "Sweetheart, we were fools to let the years go to waste."

"But not tonight," she replied as her hips rose to meet his next thrust. "You didn't hurt me, not really. I feel...special, alive inside. Oh, Mark," she moaned, and her hips rose to meet him again. "Mark, don't stop. Mark, oh, Mark..."

Her thrusts became as frantic as his own until he felt her body tremble beneath him, her breaths coming in gasps as her arms tightened around his body.

He buried his face in her hair and gave in to the overwhelming need to claim his own climax. When it swept through him, its intensity sent the room whirling, as if an earthquake had struck his small house.

His heart pounded in his ears, and he expected it to explode right in his chest and stop beating forever. *Oh, Lord, will I die in her arms?* Fearing the worst, he rested his head on the pillow and tried to overcome his panic by taking deep breaths. Slowly his breathing returned to normal, and the throbbing in his ears lessened.

Giving in to utter exhaustion, he collapsed beside her, then rolled onto his back and pulled her close, holding her in his arms as peace and utter tranquillity replaced the prospect of dying. He'd taken a risk and now could claim sweet victory over his own body as he savored her declaration of love and her warm body beside him.

Her cheek rested on his shoulder, and her arm slid around his rib cage as she relaxed against him. She ran her foot up and down his calf, then slid it between his legs, and the intimacy of the gesture brought a familiar tightening in his chest, but this tightness held no danger.

"Sweetheart," he murmured. Then exhaustion surged through him, and he sought refuge in the arms of Morpheus and Nancy Prentice.

WHEN NANCY AWOKE, Mark's bedroom was bathed in the subtle glow of predawn light. She lay drifting between sleep and wakefulness, reliving the sweet memories of the previous night.

She'd been reluctant to tell him of her lack of experience, and when he made the discovery, she'd been terrified that he'd stop. Why did men hesitate to be a woman's first sexual partner? Did they feel an added responsibility, as if they would be expected to... to what?

He'd promised her nothing. She had told him all she wanted was a night, a single night with him. Now she knew she'd lied, but that lie had been necessary. Now she would have to reconcile his conditions with the deep love she felt for him. She pressed her hands over her eyes, trying to stop the threatening tears. One night would never be enough.

She raised herself on an elbow and looked at Mark. He lay on his stomach, his face toward the window, breathing slowly and deeply as if the night had truly exhausted him. She smiled. *Satisfaction,* she thought.

She had satisfied him. That should count for something. In spite of all the books and articles she'd read, all the talk shows that had focused on the subject of sex, nothing could take the place of firsthand experience.

This morning she understood the power of loving sex—the power to bond a man and woman forever. But reality quickly swept that fantasy aside. Most of the men she knew considered making love to a woman anything but a commitment. Many had made it plain that they thought they were entitled to sex as the natural conclusion even to a casual date.

Regardless of his reaction to their night together, she had no regrets. She resisted the urge to smooth his blond hair and awaken him. Last night, during their lovemaking, she'd become concerned about his ongoing bouts of fatigue. She recalled the moments when he hesitated, as if to catch his breath. Then she discounted them when she recalled how forcefully he had brought her to fulfillment before letting himself go.

No, fatigue hadn't been a problem, she decided. He was a thoughtful, passionate lover who had considered her own needs before his own. Tears threatened again. She took a deep breath to relieve the choking in her chest.

Slipping from the bed, she grabbed a terry-cloth robe lying over the back of a chair and left the room, anxious to freshen herself before he awoke. She found the bathroom two doors away.

Flecks of red on her inner thigh and a lingering tinge of soreness reminded her of the changes that had taken place in her body. A shower removed the blood, and the soreness wasn't great enough to stop her from wanting him to make love to her again. Memories of her own ecstatic response to his thrusts reawakened a burning desire in her to experience that thrill again.

A few minutes later she stepped from the shower and grabbed a towel, dried quickly and slipped back into the robe. Mark's after-shave clung to the robe, and she pulled the lapel over her face to inhale his essence.

Returning to the bedroom, she was disappointed to find him still asleep. The room had lightened considerably. She dropped the robe back onto the chair and slid beneath the sheet. In the distance she could hear the hum of an old-fashioned evaporative cooler.

She wondered why he didn't use air-conditioning. Economy, she decided. Throughout most of the summer the dry desert air of the area could be cooled adequately by the water-cooled unit.

Mark groaned in his sleep, and she moved closer. He rolled onto his back. She was torn between letting him sleep and enticing him to wake up and make love to her again. Playfully she slid her hand across his body.

Her fingers reached his breastbone and stopped. She leaned over him to see what she had encountered. A thick ridge of scar tissue ran down his breastbone the entire length of his chest, an ugly red ridge that looked as if he'd allowed a giant earthworm to be implanted under his skin.

She screamed.

Mark's hand shot out and grabbed her wrist. "Don't touch—" She knew he was glaring at her, but her gaze was glued to his chest. What on earth could have necessitated such drastic surgery?

"You've had your chest opened."

His fingers eased around her wrist. "It's...sensitive. Please don't touch it."

She tore her gaze from the incision and looked at his face, but it floated in a misty blur. "But why?"

"I had a heart attack," he explained. "I had by-pass surgery."

The terror of the scar's message tore away what little control she had. She blinked, sending hot tears splashing down her cheeks. "Why didn't you tell me what was wrong with you?" Her anger spilled into her words. "You should have told me."

"We both had our secrets last night," he murmured, closing his eyes as if to block her from his sight.

"Our secrets were hardly equal," she argued. "You could have died."

His eyes opened and he turned to her. "I nearly did...twice. But not last night."

"But...you're too young..." She wiped her cheek with the heel of her hand. "If you had died, I..." She put her forehead against his shoulder for a few minutes, then placed a gentle kiss on the upper part of the scar, ignoring the tension in his body when she touched him. "Oh, Mark, thank God you're alive."

When he relaxed again, she put her open palm lightly on his chest, being careful to avoid the incision. She shifted onto her stomach and gazed at him. "How could I have not noticed it last night?"

For the first time since he'd awakened, he grinned. "We were concentrating on other activities last night." His hand slid into her hair, and he tugged her closer until he could brush her mouth with a kiss.

"Mmmm, you smell gorgeous this morning," he murmured, his eyes still heavy with sleep.

"I've been up and had a shower."

He played with the curls at her temple. "I had no idea you were...a virgin. I didn't think there were any left in the Valley of the Sun over the age of sixteen."

"I can only vouch for myself," she admitted, struck by a moment of shyness.

"Why?"

She frowned. "Why no men before you?" She gazed across the room. "I couldn't...bring myself to..."

A troubled expression flashed across his face. "I didn't take precautions last night. It's a little late to be asking, but is there any danger?"

"I'm on the pill, so we didn't make a baby." She touched the tiny throbbing pulse at the base of his throat. "I couldn't be carrying anything. You're the one who...are you at risk?"

He lifted her fingers from his throat and kissed them. "I've had three blood transfusions. They were from certified blood banks, but just in case my cardiologist has tested me several times. I've had blood tests for diseases I've never heard of until I woke up in the cardiac care unit of the Arizona Heart Institute in Phoenix." He reached out and caressed her cheek. "Do you want to see my papers?"

His remark, a weak attempt at humor, struck her the wrong way. "Don't ever joke about this, Mark. Why didn't you let me know? I could have been with you."

"It struck out of the blue," he said, and his smile slid away. "I didn't have time to send out invitations."

"Tell me about it."

He eased her head down to his shoulder and began to talk. As his story unfolded, she began to understand the devastating experience he'd lived through. Her tears flowed, but she didn't cry out or move.

"You'll never know the quandary I was in when you walked up to me at the ballpark," he admitted. "I'd reconciled myself to living a celibate life and never telling a soul, except my family, about my condition. You see, I was put on some heavy blood thinners and beta blockers, all powerful medications."

"But those must have been necessary for your recovery," she said, tracing down his chest an inch away from the incision, circling around the bottom to come up the other side.

He stopped her hand before she reached his throat. "Does it hurt?"

"Not exactly," he said. "I'm trying to explain what happened, so stop distracting me. Your fingers...send little messages to other parts of me."

"What other parts, Mark?"

"Be serious," he chided her. "This is important. Some heart patients lose their ability to...they can't...I tried once and failed. I figured I'd better not risk that embarrassment again."

She began to giggle, and he rolled her off his shoulder, pressing her against the pillow. "What the hell is so funny?"

She slid her arms around his neck. "That wasn't the problem you had last night. I distinctly remember. And there were other times recently when I felt... anyway, you can forget that problem, Bradford. That's one excuse you can't use with me."

"And what was my problem last night?" he asked as his hands slide down her body, lingering to explore the curves and valleys along the way.

"Patience," she said. "You were very impatient." She felt him harden against her hip. She pulled his head down and kissed his mouth, sliding her tongue inside in search of his. He took control of the kiss, deepening its intensity until she had to pull away for air.

She nibbled at his lips a few times and smiled. "Now that I'm more experienced at this business of making love, could we try it again, this time a bit slower?"

"Nan, my precious Nan, you never cease to amaze me," he said as he rolled her over to straddle him. "Since you're trained to be the one in command now, you can do the work. Maybe that way it won't tire me so much."

She blushed. "What do I do?" When he showed her and she experimented with her own position, she smiled. Stretching herself along his body, she hesitated. "Will I hurt you?"

His hands ran up and down her back and hips, stopping to cup her buttocks and pressing her closer. "Somehow it doesn't seem to matter, sweeetheart."

Leaning closer, she kissed him, regaling in her new freedom to love him openly and bring him pleasure. As his arms tightened around her and he began to thrust upward, she knew they'd both made a commitment to each other regardless of what he might say in the light of day.

CHAPTER NINE

MARK ROLLED over with a groan, reaching for the woman who'd changed his life. His eyes flew open when he felt the empty pillow beside him. She'd been gone long enough for the fabric to cool. Angry at himself for his inability to stay awake after making love to her, he sat up and slid his legs to the floor.

Utter exhaustion had claimed him twice. Maybe he'd have a talk with Dr. Merrick about that. He'd wanted to hold her, whisper words of affection to her, tell her how important the night had been for him. Instead he'd rolled over and slept like a log. He hoped he'd had the decency not to snore in her ear.

Still groggy, he couldn't resist a peek out the front window to confirm that her little red car was still parked at the curb.

It was gone.

He frowned as he headed to the bathroom. Why had she left without a word? Their second time together had been more fantastic than the first, their mutual passions uninhibited and spontaneous. For a novice lover she had displayed amazing insight into what could pleasure him and had shown no embarrassment when he caressed her intimately. Why had she simply driven away?

He lingered in the shower, mulling over what his next move should be. Call her? No. She was the one who had left. She could call him.

Pride, male pride, he admitted. If protecting his wounded ego was more important to him than learning the reasons why she had left, he was a fool and didn't deserve her. No, he'd get dressed, give a thought to breakfast, then phone her.

Back in his bedroom he pulled on a pair of briefs and red walking shorts, then a short-sleeved white knit shirt. As he tucked in the tails of the shirt, he caught a glimpse of himself in the mirror. No, he decided, he'd hidden the scars long enough from the outside world.

The weather forecast for the day had been given as "sunny and warm," but in Phoenix that meant hot and dry. He'd wear a cool muscle top and to hell with the curious glances of strangers. Searching through his dresser, he found a comfortably worn blue-and-white top and left it hanging outside his shorts.

In the mirror he could see several inches of red incision. He'd already received an injection of cortisone to help dissolve the thickest part of the scar. Next week he'd get the second in the series. He wasn't sure they were helping, but the unsightly complication of the surgery had been difficult to accept. Other people he'd met had only a narrow pink line down their front. Maybe his scar would be like that in time.

The aroma of coffee wafted down the hall from the direction of the kitchen. He seldom brewed coffee by the pot anymore. By the time he'd drunk his one cup allowed per day and emptied the pot, the brew was a week old and tasted as if he'd boiled an old rag soaked in oil in the pot.

In the kitchen he spotted the coffeemaker filled with rich, fresh-brewed liquid, its orange light indicating its readiness. She had to be here. She hadn't run away. In the clear light of a new day he found it critically important that she had chosen to stay of her own free will. The house was quiet except for the soft strains of classical music coming from somewhere. Not inside the house.

He crossed the room to the back door and peered out. Belle, his Irish setter bitch, hadn't barked all morning. He glanced at his watch. After ten. She should have let him know hours ago that breakfast was late.

He opened the door and stepped outside. To his surprise he found Nancy Prentice sitting on the edge of the patio, her bare feet in the grass that had needed mowing a week earlier. She leaned forward, her arms around the dog's neck and Belle's face nestled against her front, as if the two were consoling each other.

The sound of a muffled sob came to him, and his heart lurched when he realized Nancy was crying softly into the dog's lush coat. "Good morning," he said.

Nancy flinched and scrambled to her feet, wiping frantically at her cheeks. She smiled, but it was tempered with turmoil.

Belle barked twice and came to Mark, her tail wagging.

"Good morning," Nancy murmured. Her cheeks were blotched with red welts. "I'm sorry. I must look a sight."

"You look wonderful," he said. He stepped closer and touched her shoulder. "Why the tears?"

She turned her back to him and wiped her eyes again. "I . . . I was fine until I started thinking about you...in the hospital and so close to death.'' She whirled around. ''Oh, Mark, what if you had died?''

His own smile was as sad as hers. ''Then I wouldn't be standing here consoling you.''

''But you could have. Mark, I felt so empty thinking about you...gone.''

''We all die sometime,'' he assured her. ''I simply had a brush with reality sooner than most people do.''

''But what about now?'' She stepped backward into the grass. ''What if something happens again? What if this time they can't...save you?''

''I live with that possibility each day,'' he admitted.

''Oh, Mark.'' Her face, stricken with terror, seemed to crumple before his eyes. He closed the distance between them, encircling her in his arms. ''Cry your heart out, Nan. God knows I have.''

He held her until her shoulders stopped shaking, then used the loose bottom of his muscle shirt to wipe her face dry. ''Let's take a walk,'' he suggested, guiding her to the four corners of the yard, describing his plans for a vegetable garden the next year, telling her how he planned to plant another shade tree and perhaps some fruit trees.

''So you see, I haven't sat down to die,'' he said. ''I take each day as it comes. Occasionally I plan ahead.'' He gave her shoulders a gentle squeeze. ''I was sullen and angry for months, but after I moved here and met Horace Moore, things started to improve. I'll introduce you to Horace sometime.''

He looked down at the top of her curly head, realizing the implication of his remark. How permanent would this newfound relationship prove to be? He didn't want to speculate on the pros and cons of that.

For today she was with him, and that would be enough.

When they reached the back wall of the masonry fence, he turned and leaned against it. "Yard needs mowing," he said aloud to himself. "I'd better get it done later today."

She kept her arm around his waist and looked up at him. "Can you do that? Operate a lawn mower and do manual labor?"

He studied her upturned face. Her complexion had returned to its lovely light tan and he couldn't resist dropping a quick kiss on her mouth. "I'm not an invalid. Didn't I prove that last night . . . and this morning? I just need to pace myself."

She blushed as the memory settled around them, bringing them close in its intimacy. He tightened his arms around her and enjoyed the quiet time. "When I got up, I thought you'd gone. I didn't see your car outside."

"I never went back to sleep," she replied. "You, on the other hand . . ." She chuckled. "Whatever happened to pillow talk?"

He grinned sheepishly. "I'll try to do better the next time." He watched her, pleased with the kiss she bestowed on his cheek. "Why did you move the car?"

"I peeked in your fridge and found it wanting," she said. "I made friends with Belle, and after I gave her breakfast, we took a short trip to the store for coffee, pancake mix and syrup—stuff like that. Your milk carton was almost empty, so I got another."

"Skim?"

"Of course. I figured you were on a special diet." She stepped free of his embrace and ran her hands through her hair at her temples, smiling nervously.

"Nan?" He touched her shoulder, and for a moment he expected her to pull away. "About last night . . . and this morning?"

"No strings, Mark," she said. "You made no promises and I asked for none. I'm protected and you're a safe partner for me."

"It's about more than safe sex, Nan."

She turned to him again. "Maybe."

A door banged next door, and Mark looked toward his neighbor's yard. Horace Moore's white head bobbed as he approached the fence.

"Morning, folks," Horace said, his voice low and rumbly. He ducked below the six-foot fence top, then reappeared to stand a foot taller than the fence. "Had to get me a stump to get a better view," he confessed.

"Good morning, Horace," Mark said, taking Nancy's hand and leading her to the wall that divided their properties.

"Well, Mark, aren't you going to introduce me to this pretty young lady?" Horace asked. His snow-white hair had been carefully combed, and Mark began to suspect his neighbor had been watching them from inside his kitchen. Horace folded his long arms along the edge of the fence and waited, a definite spark of curiosity in his brown eyes.

Nancy extended her hand. "If Mark won't, I will," she said, charming Horace with her smile. "I'm Nancy Prentice. I used to work with Mark years ago." She laughed. "I was a legal assistant and he used to boss me around."

Mark draped his arm around her shoulders. "She's right about that, Horace, but the tables have turned. Now she's a full-fledged attorney herself, and if I'm not careful, she may be bossing me. You know how overbearing female attorneys can get."

Horace chuckled. "Keep a firm rein on her, sonny."

Nancy chuckled. "You two sound like a pair of rednecked chauvinists. I'd like to think neither of you mean a word of it."

"Not me," Mark replied, pecking her lightly on her cheek.

"Me, neither," Horace said. "But I reckon you get two men together with a pretty woman and you bring out the male in them. Seeing what a pretty little thing you are, I reckon Mark forgets your profession when he's with you, right, sonny?"

Mark laughed. "Right, Horace."

They visited for several minutes, then Horace arched a white brow. "I see by the looks of your shirt, Mark, that she knows about everything?"

"Almost." Mark shifted uncomfortably. "Can't tell her all my secrets too soon."

Nancy glanced from one man to the other. "What secrets?"

The men exchanged knowing glances, but neither elaborated. Nancy let it drop, but some sixth sense told Mark it was only for the present.

"Forget I brought it up," Horace said. "Well, folks, it's Sunday, and if I don't get a move on, the preacher will be all finished before I get to church. You see, ma'am—" he grinned at Nancy "—I'm the chief inspiration for his sermons." With a polite nod he stepped down from his stump, gave a wave and disappeared into his house again.

Mark took Nancy's hand, and they walked toward the patio.

"What did he mean about more secrets?" she asked.

"We all have secrets," he said, circling the omissions he'd deliberately made when he told her about the cause and consequences of his surgery. "Can't tell you everything about me. There'd be no mystery left. Don't you have secrets?"

She grew solemn. "Not anymore." Under the shade of the patio she confronted him. "I spilled all my feelings, Mark, and that puts me at your mercy. Don't abuse it. Knowledge can be very powerful." She looked away, then rubbed her palms together. "How about breakfast? I already fed Belle, but she told me she loves pancakes and said that you seldom make them and when you do, you don't share with her."

He tried to look mortified. "Belle told you that? What a fickle animal. Give her a pat and she forgets her master. I'll have you know she gets at least a bite of everything I eat."

When he smiled at her again, he sensed that she had ignored his attempt at humor.

She frowned and edged toward the door. "I don't fully understand everything that's happened to you and why you gave up so much...but that's okay," she said. "Perhaps I should simply accept the miracle that you're alive. The rest is your business and I won't pry. I enjoy your company, so I do hope we can continue seeing each other." She hugged herself.

He laughed and pulled her into his arms. "Prentice, I misread you all these years. You never once came on to me."

"That didn't mean I didn't want to."

"We could have had ten good years. We'll have to make up for lost time." He gazed down at her adoring blue eyes. "Now give me a proper good-morning kiss and hug."

INSIDE, NANCY MIXED the pancake batter while Mark set the table. Belle lay on the tile floor, watching Nancy's every move.

"Patience, girl, I've made extra just for you."

The dog's tail thumped harder.

"But you'll have to wait your turn," Nancy cautioned.

The dog's tail slowed and she laid her nose on her paws, but her liquid brown eyes followed Nancy's every move.

"You've made a friend for life," Mark observed from the table near a window that overlooked the yard.

Nancy's gaze flickered from dog to master, then back to the griddle. She turned each small cake and mentally counted the time they needed to cook. "Pancakes are ready," she called, and Belle got to her feet, wagging her tail excitedly.

Mark got an old chipped plate from the back of the cupboard and held it out. "This is Belle's special Sunday plate," he said, nodding toward the animated animal. "She says she wants three, please."

"Done," Nancy replied, flopping three light cakes onto the plate. "Does she spread her own margarine and syrup?"

"Usually, but I'll do the honors today," Mark said. When the plate was properly fixed, he whistled a command and Belle trotted after him onto the patio.

He glanced up to catch her peeking out the window at him. By the time he returned to the kitchen, the plate was licked clean. Mark shook his head. "No manners at all. Scarfed those cakes like a dog, didn't she?"

"If we don't sit down ourselves, ours will be cold and Belle can have seconds," Nancy said, pouring steaming coffee into their cups. Halfway through the meal, she put down her fork and gazed across the table. "Does it seem strange to be sitting here with company? I mean, do you have other people..." The more she tried to explain, the worse it sounded.

"Do you mean women?"

"No, of course not," she replied. "I meant just...people."

He reached across the table and covered her fidgeting hand with his. "My sister was here once. My parents, twice, but we ate out. You're the first woman Belle and I have allowed to use this kitchen."

She couldn't control her smile of pleasure.

He squeezed her hand. "Do I detect a tinge of jealousy?"

"I'm never jealous," she insisted, then shrugged. "I was just curious." She got to her feet and gathered the plates and carried them to the sink. When she turned, she found herself trapped between his arms and the sink.

"Please try to understand," he said, his voice husky. "I went from superstar attorney to invalid in a matter of minutes. It was a difficult adjustment. Most of the women I knew were interested only in the superstar attorney. My appeal to the opposite sex was cut out just as literally as Dr. Merrick cut out the vein in my leg to do the bypasses. I lost my sex appeal."

"Not to me."

"You're the exception."

She shook her head. "A woman who would drop you because of what happened isn't worth your time." She tried to duck under his arm, but his reflexes were lightning-quick.

"I got your graduation announcement the day I came home from the hospital," he said. "You were the only woman I wanted to see, but I couldn't bring myself to get in touch. It doesn't matter now. I wasn't good company back then."

She touched the front of his loose shirt, being careful to avoid the sensitive scar. "I had hoped you'd come to the ceremonies, but I assumed you were busy on an important case. Still, I was disappointed. Then I decided it was the distance. Driving to Albuquerque was too much to expect even for a healthy person."

"I could barely make it from my bed to the table," he admitted. "I didn't want anyone to see me like that, especially not you."

"But if I'd known, I could have—"

"I would have rejected your pity."

"It wouldn't have been pity," she whispered. "It would have been . . . love and concern."

"I wonder if that would have made a difference." He tilted her chin, bringing her mouth up to his.

When he released her lips, she could feel the hardness of his need. "But now that doesn't matter," she whispered, kissing his throat.

"No, not anymore," he replied, stroking her nipples into hard buttons. "Maybe you're part of my recovery, Nan. Maybe more. Hell, I don't know. All I know is that I want you."

"Yes." She took his hand, and they returned to his bedroom where he took her to paradise again.

AS THEY LANGUISHED in the bed, she held him in her arms and stroked his shoulder muscles, relishing the closeness they'd shared, trying not to lose control of her emotions.

During the lovemaking, his strength had never faltered, and for the few brief moments when passion had carried them to new heights, she had almost forgotten the real world.

But when he rolled away from her and she'd seen the vivid reminder on his chest, tears of anger had lodged in her throat and she'd been thankful when he left the room for a few moments. By the time he'd returned, her eyes were clear and she could smile.

"Are you okay?" she asked, stroking his shoulder again.

He ran his finger around her areola and got an instant reaction. "I never thought I'd have this much virility ever again," he admitted. "You do something special to me."

She kissed his hair. "And you to me."

They lay quietly for several minutes.

"Tell me about your work," she asked, "but only what you want me to know. If I'm prying, tell me."

"I have a small office at the Peoria Senior Center a few blocks from here," he explained.

She tried to ignore the erotic movement of his cheek on her breast as he talked.

"I get it rent free in exchange for doing volunteer legal counsel for the center's clients."

So you haven't given up legal work completely, she thought. "What kind of cases?"

"Most of them involved problems with pension benefits and Medicare. Not exciting but satisfying. I enjoy taking on the bureaucrats." He grinned. "I strike terror into their little regulatory hearts when they discover I have a legal background.''

She laughed, squeezing him and savoring the intimacy they shared. ''I could lie here forever with you,'' she admitted, holding him against her naked breast. Yet, even as she enjoyed the suspension of time, she knew it couldn't last.

''I have to go to the Braves' practice at two,'' he said, as if reading her thoughts. ''Want to go with me?''

She mulled over his offer. ''I'd be in the way. Do you mind if I stay here?'' Her hand stopped its stroking. ''Maybe I should go home.''

He propped himself on an elbow, dipping to kiss her throat before gazing into her uncertain eyes. ''I'd rather come home to find you here.'' He glanced out the window. ''We still have several hours of daylight. Stay, please.'' His finger traced the line of her jaw to her ear. ''We'll do something special tonight.''

''We've been doing special things ever since I stepped through your door.'' She played with the blond curls near his ear. ''You wear your hair much longer now.''

He arched a brow. ''Haircuts and three-piece suits don't seem important anymore...and they cost money.''

She frowned. ''Are you...making it? Financially, I mean? Oh, good grief, that's none of my business. Forget I asked it. But that old truck, this house...''

He seemed to withdraw emotionally. ''They're not up to your standards, are they?''

She tried to pull him close again, but he sat up and dropped his feet to the floor. She scooted to his back and slid her arms around his rib cage, laying her cheek against his shoulder blade.

"Houses and fancy cars aren't important," she insisted, hoping he'd believe her.

"Then why the curiosity?"

She couldn't explain her need to understand all that had happened to him while they'd been apart. "What happened to your home in Deer Valley? You bragged about your swimming pool and all. And that glamorous blue Mercedes?"

"I sold them."

She knew she was treading in stormy waters, but she couldn't stop herself. "Why?"

He got up, grabbed his robe and headed toward the door. "I sold them because I needed the money to live on." He hurled the words back at her, then slammed the door behind him as he stomped out of the room.

WHEN MARK RETURNED to the closed bedroom door, he listened for sounds but heard nothing. "Nan?" No reply came. He turned the knob and eased the door ajar.

Near the window he spotted Nancy. She was dressed in the familiar tank top, shorts and sandals. She stood erect, her head held proud and her chin high. He half expected her to bolt from the room, but when she continued to stay at the window, he grabbed his clothing and dressed in record time.

"Are you leaving now?" she asked, keeping her back to him.

His heart ached as he approached her, not wanting the emotional fall that would surely come if they both let their pride rule their emotions now. "Not for a few minutes." He put his hand on her shoulders and eased her against him. "I'm sorry, Nan. I have no right to snap at you each time you ask a personal question."

The tension in her shoulders slipped away, and she turned, her eyes sad. "I didn't mean to pry. You're different and it's much more than the... heart attack. I wanted to know about what happened to change you so much. I care about you, not your cars or your houses or your bank account. Just you, Mark."

She laid her head gently against his chest, being overly careful to avoid the middle. As he embraced her, he resented her overt efforts to compensate for his condition.

"Mark, I'm not asking for you to love me, not yet," she said. "But that doesn't stop me from loving you. You have no say in that. You told me you'd given up wine, women and song, but have you given up the right to give and receive love, too?"

Unable to find the words he suspected she wanted to hear, he tightened his arms and held her, not wanting to lose her yet.

She gazed up at him. "Is it time to go?"

He looked across the room at the small clock on his nightstand. "Ten minutes." He hand moved slowly up and down her back. "Maybe we've done too much too soon."

She slipped from the circle of his arms. "Perhaps you're right, but unlike you, I have no regrets." She left the room, and he found her in the living room retrieving her purse from the sofa.

He knew he should say something, but the right words failed to come. He grabbed the long, lumpy athletic bag containing baseball bats and spare balls. "I'll follow you out."

She went to her automobile. He looked away when she fumbled and dropped the keys, then knelt to retrieve them. "Goodbye, Mark," she said, her shoulders stiff and proud. "It was wonderful while it lasted, wasn't it? I never expected this to be a one-night stand." She unlocked the door and slid into the seat. The door slammed and he turned away, not wanting to see her drive away, but when he heard the revving of the little engine, he turned around again.

As she backed out of the driveway, she glanced at him once. Then the car shot ahead down the street.

His heart thudded in his chest, but he tried to ignore it. They'd spent less than twenty hours together, found paradise in each other's arms, and shared an intimacy like none he'd ever known. And they'd talked, or at least had tried to talk.

Therein lay their problems. On a physical level they meshed perfectly, but when it came to the normal give and take of being together, he had overreacted to each and every attempt she had made. He glanced up to see her apply the brakes three blocks away and make a sharp left onto the thoroughfare.

You're a fool, Bradford, he thought, knowing he'd kept her at arm's length rather than let her get close enough to experience his daily life.

Dull. His life would be considered dull by anyone who had known him before.

Dull. Had he been afraid of letting her stay because he didn't want to be seen as dull in her eyes?

Ah, those expressive blue eyes that had bewitched him for years. He wanted them to behold him with pride and love, to see the loyalty and admiration they'd always reflected, not disappointment and pity.

Tomorrow she would be back at her office, researching important legal cases, attending meetings with the senior partners where future partnership decisions were formulated and cemented. He could imagine her racing down a hallway in the massive stone courthouse to participate in hearings and jury trials.

He, on the other hand, would walk the several blocks to his office and settle into a half day of listening to impoverished older adults describe their lonely lives and their meager financial status. He'd listen attentively to their stories, then reassure them that he would try to help.

Often he suspected his clients wanted to talk as much as get their problem solved. And more often than not, he could resolve their difficulties with a minimum of research and a quick phone call to the right bureaucrat in the appropriate agency.

They'd settle on a small token fee. The men would shake his hand, their posture a little straighter than when they first came to him. The women would wipe their tears and kiss his cheek and invariably bring him a plate of cookies the next day. He'd thank them and wait for them to leave the office, then put a few of the cookies in a plastic bag to take home to Horace and Belle.

From two hundred dollars an hour to a plate of oatmeal cookies. Yes, his fee had changed. He had changed. Nancy Prentice had changed.

He tossed his athletic bag into the back of the truck and started down the street. When he got to the stop sign where he turned left, he braked, signaled, then made his turn. A few blocks ahead he spotted Nancy's red car pulled over to the curb. He eased up on the accelerator, and when the truck rolled past her car, he saw her head resting against the window glass. Her face was covered with a white tissue.

He drove on, but the image of her sitting in the car, weeping and suffering alone, gnawed at him. *You're a fool if you go back,* he thought. *She's strong. She'll recover.* A car in front of him slammed on its brakes and he did the same. In his rearview mirror he could still see Nancy's car, now only a dot of red in the dusty landscape.

Alone. He knew firsthand how being alone could cripple a person's anticipated recovery during an emotional or physical crisis. Hadn't he lived through enough of them himself? *Alone.*

Don't be a fool, Mark.

Crying? Over me?

Don't be a fool. Stay out of it.

A cloud of confusion lifted from his thoughts, and he made an abrupt right turn and began to drive along the dirt street running parallel to the road he'd come down.

You'd be a bigger fool if you didn't go back, he thought, estimating how many blocks he'd driven. Two more right turns and he was back on the main street. A block ahead he spotted her car, the only one for several blocks parked along the busy street.

Now what should he do? He'd already said he was sorry. Or had he? Had he told her that he loved her? He wasn't sure. A man said a lot of things during lovemaking, but had he said the important words at the right time?

Maybe she'll give you a second chance. He doubted he deserved it, and he wasn't ready to speculate on the consequences, but he knew he couldn't leave her alone.

Oh, pretty Nancy Prentice, you're in love with a fool, he thought as pulled up behind her parked car and killed the engine. *Thank God, you are.*

CHAPTER TEN

IDIOT, BLOCKHEAD, DOLT! Nancy searched her mind for other names to call herself. She'd jumped into Mark's arms again and landed in his bed, not once but three times. How could she have been so stupid as to imagine she could bare her heart and not get hurt?

Nincompoop. Dunce. Stupid, stupid fool!

All she'd wanted was to understand what had brought Mark to this cynical point in his life. How could he have reacted so insensitively? "Fool, fool, fool!" she shouted, not knowing this time who she was berating—herself or Mark. The words rang in her ears, and she felt thankful she was alone.

A tapping on her window brought her out of her self-indulgent tirade and she turned to find Mark standing beside the car, his hand on the door handle.

Her fingers sought and found the locking mechanism, then inched to the window button and rolled it down two inches. A blast of hot, dry desert air aggravated her discontent. "What do you want?"

"Can I talk to you?" he asked. She glanced up, but his head was somewhere above the top of the window.

"You're late for practice. You wouldn't want to disappoint the little kiddies."

"But I've disappointed you," he said, sliding his fingers into the opening.

Another gust of hot air swept across her face. "Go away." She pushed the button, and the window silently moved upward. She just wanted him to leave her alone. He'd done enough, made his position perfectly clear. Now what did he hope to accomplish other than embarrass her further?

"Ouch!"

Her gaze shot from the window control button to the window. Three of his long fingers were wriggling frantically, already turning purple, pinched between the top of the pane and the door.

Frantically she pushed at the buttons. The doors all unlocked at once and three of the windows rolled silently downward.

"Nan, damn it, unroll it before you amputate my fingers!"

Finally she found the right button and his hand withdrew. Scrambling from the car, she raced back to his truck, where he'd retreated, massaging the bruised fingers on his left hand.

"I'm sorry, Mark, I didn't mean to hurt you. Oh, my God, are they bleeding? Are they broken?" She looked up to find him scowling at her.

"I was worried about you," he said, his voice low and sad. "I saw you parked here and..." His hand settled on her shoulder.

She took his hand tenderly in hers and examined it. The skin on the underside of his middle two fingers was oozing blood. "You're hurt. Do you want to go home? Or to a hospital?"

He grinned. "I think I'll live without medical attention. Can we talk?"

"You'll be late for practice."

"We could both go to practice and talk afterward."

She took a deep breath and smiled. "I'd like that."

DURING A BREAK, Mark came to sit beside Nancy in the bleachers. "How about dinner at my favorite café?" he asked.

She looked down at her shorts and rumpled top. "I'd like that, but I need to change clothes at my place." She wiped perspiration from her brow.

"You must be roasting. Someone said it was over a hundred." He'd already removed his jeans and now wore a pair of jogging shorts that rode high on his thighs.

While he returned to home plate and began hitting pop flies to the team members in the infield, an idea came to her. She mulled it over, turning it around, searching for reasons why he'd oppose it, then decided to pursue it.

An hour later the manager and coaches called an end to the practice, and Mark bid the team goodbye and joined her. "It's a good thing we're going in separate cars. I need a shower," he confessed.

She smiled but didn't reply. A mile from her apartment building, she pulled into the parking lot of a supermarket with a deli department. She beckoned to him to follow.

Inside the refrigerated store she went directly to the deli counter and waved her hand. "My building has two swimming pools. Would you like to swim and eat inside? I have a balcony, but it's too hot to sit outside."

She expected an argument, but when he pointed out three different salads and an assortment of wafer-thin

meats and cheeses, she felt as if they'd reached a truce.
A bag of English muffins and a variety of fresh fruit
completed the menu.

Once in her apartment, he leaned against the door
and chuckled. "It *is* smaller than my place...but nice.
Couldn't you find a larger place?"

"I didn't want to spend the money." She dropped
her purse on the kitchen counter. "I made it through
law school by hocking my future salary. You know
how it is. So I want to repay the loans as soon as possible. I hate working so hard and having it all go to
interest. Sometimes half my salary goes to those
loans." She gave him a tight-lipped smile. "I'm
pleased to report that I'm past the halfway mark on
the principal."

His gaze flickered over the apartment and back to
her. "I haven't been swimming since . . . my surgery."

"Will it be safe for you? The exercise, I mean." She
looked away, not wanting to get drawn in to asking
more questions. The important thing was that he was
with her now. The day was winding toward its end,
and time was running out. Tomorrow life would return to the normal, hectic pace to which she'd grown
accustomed.

"I'll change into a suit," she said, trying to ignore
the unmade bed that filled a third of the studio apartment. In a bureau that she'd stored in a closet she
found a two-piece suit and a matching knee-length
cover-up, then sought refuge in the bathroom.

When she returned to the combination living and
sleeping room, he had moved to the table and was
flipping pages in a reference book she had checked out
of the law library at work.

"Your case involves guardianship?" he asked.

"Yes, two children are concerned about their father."

"And they want control of his assets?" he guessed.

"They feel they can manage his affairs better than he can. He's made some unwise investments."

"Don't we all?" He read a paragraph in the book and turned another page. "It's a matter of perspective."

She gazed across the room. "Are we about to have another argument?"

His expression grew solemn. "I listen to the conversations at the center. To the potential victims of guardianship cases, losing means losing control of their lives. To the children who want to protect their future inheritances, it's just prudent management." He closed the thick book and got to his feet. "I need a quick shower. Do you have a spare towel?"

She looked longingly at him. "The towels are on the racks in the bathroom."

He paused at the bathroom door. "Want to join me?"

Her heart thudded. "We'd never get to the pool."

"Maybe the pool isn't so important."

Erotic images danced in her mind as she gazed across the room. "I've never showered with a man."

He held out his hand. "Then come with me. This is your weekend for new experiences."

His offer was irresistible, and she stripped out of her clothing and let him lead her into the steamy enclosure. The slick bar of soap passed between them as they washed. When he offered to do her back, she turned around, but his hands wandered far from her spine.

When she turned again, he was fully aroused. The water sprayed over them as she took him in her hands, stroking him against her abdomen until he groaned and gritted his teeth to keep control. He leaned against the shower wall and lifted her in his arms. "Put your legs around me and hold on tight."

Amazed by his strength and agility, she felt him touch her, then slide inside. When she'd settled against him, she wrapped her arms around his wet back and whispered his name in his ear.

He began to move, and she matched his rhythm until the world seemed to spin and explode around them.

When at last she slid to her feet, the rapture that had swept her away left her spent. Dreamily she gazed up at him. "I could have never imagined anything like that ever happening to me." She leaned her wet forehead against his shoulder.

He lifted her chin and kissed her gently, then held her for a few more minutes before helping her from the shower. He tossed her a towel. As he dried himself, he pretended to be serious. "And no more distractions," he scolded.

"You're the distraction! I told you I'd never done that before." She grinned. "It was sort of fun, wasn't it?"

He smiled back at her. "Sort of."

In the main room again she handed him a tube of sunscreen, retrieved a pair of sunglasses and her keys and motioned him out the door.

When they stepped outside, noise from several boom boxes tuned to different radio stations assailed them. "Why did I assume a quiet swim?" he asked.

"I thought they'd all be up at the river or the lakes," she said. "Most of them go tubing every weekend."

"Do you go with them?" he asked.

"I have a few times, but they drink too much. One time a guy... well, he got out of hand, so I stopped going."

Mark looked around. "Is he here?"

She took his arm. "He moved out the next month."

His head bobbed, and she suspected he was counting the thundering radios. "How many?" she asked, hiding her grin.

"Sixteen. Do you think we could orchestrate a power failure?"

Smiling, she took his hand and led him to the smaller pool away from the parties. Only two other couples were in the pool.

She dropped her cover on a nearby bench, kicked off her thongs and dived into the water, expecting Mark to follow her. When she came up in the middle of the pool, she turned to find him still on the edge of the pool. He'd sat down on the edge but hadn't removed his shirt. The other couples were engrossed in their respective private conversations.

When it dawned on her why he hadn't joined her, she swam back to him, coming up between his knees. "Mark, no one will notice you, and if they do... flip 'em off."

His eyes narrowed.

She grinned. "That's what my nephew, Chuck, told me once. That's his solution to anything and everything that bugs him." She ran her wet hand up his thigh. "Come on, handsome. Join me for a swim."

He glanced at the others around the two pools.

"Then come on in with the shirt on," she said. "We'll pretend you're supersensitive to the sun."

As if her words had hit a raw spot, he stripped the shirt off and slid into the water. For the next half hour they swam and played, seldom touching but both aware of the sensual overtones between them.

The other couples left the small pool when the shadows of the building grew longer. "We've waited too long to sunbathe," she said, shooting him an appreciative look. "Anyway, you're tan enough."

"I work outside. Horace and I redid my roof last fall."

Her eyes widened. "So soon after...everything?"

"I pace myself."

She swam away underwater, turned and shot back toward him, coming up directly in front of him. "How do you feel?" she asked.

"Tight."

A blush swept up her cheeks.

He laughed. "Not that kind. I mean, my chest feels tight."

Her cheeks went from pink to pale. "You're feeling pain?"

He brushed the wet strands of hair from her cheek, pulled her into his arms and kissed her. "No, silly, the incision feels tight. Maybe when we're inside you'll let me use some lotion."

"Of course. I'll even put it on for you. I'll massage it ever so gently." She ran her finger lightly across his chest, circling one nipple, and smiled when it hardened.

"Cut that out," he warned.

"And what do you intend to do about it?" she teased, kissing him once before swimming away again.

On the other side of the pool she turned, enjoying the sight of him lounging against the opposite wall of the pool, his arms spread along the edge. He seemed contented, relaxed, almost happy.

They stayed in the water for a few more minutes. Then Nancy climbed out and dried off. "I'm starved. Let's go inside and have dinner."

"No wonder you're starved," he replied. "We never had lunch."

Thoughts of what they'd done instead brought a sparkle to her eyes and a blush to her cheeks.

He turned away and swam several laps of the pool, each one faster and more powerful than the previous one. When he boosted himself from the water, he was breathing hard but smiling.

She slid her arm around his bare waist and was pleased when his arm settled on her shoulder. As they passed the larger pool, Mark ignored the curious stares from some of the guests.

When they reached her small balcony, Mark glanced over his shoulder. "I feel as if I've run a gauntlet."

She patted his ribs. "But you made it, didn't you? You're too sensitive, Mark. But I understand." Inside, while he showered, she removed the deli food from the refrigerator.

When he joined her, she wiped her hands. "My turn," she said. "Fix it however you want." He began to empty containers into serving dishes. "See you in a few minutes," she said. When she closed the bathroom door, she hesitated for a moment, then left it unlocked, hoping he'd join her again, but he seemed content working in the kitchen.

Sighing, she showered and dressed in record time, selecting a sundress in shimmering blues and greens.

Tonight they could get to know each other better, but when they talked, she'd have to be extra careful to avoid any of the subjects that seemed to upset him.

Joining him again, she poured two glasses of sparkling water and added a slice of lime to each glass. "Do you have a match?" she asked, and when he shrugged, she removed the two candlesticks from the table. "Just as well. They get in the way of seeing each other."

He put the tray of cold cuts on the table and surrounded it with small dishes of the assorted salads and a platter of breads and condiments.

The food was half-gone when he leaned back in his chair and patted his stomach. "More than enough," he said. "I usually eat light in the evenings."

She smiled across the table but didn't speak.

"Why did you transfer from ASU to New Mexico?" he asked.

Taken aback by his question, she studied him carefully. "Is this one of the subjects that will cause an argument?"

He chewed his lower lip for a moment, then smiled. "No, because this is about you, not me."

"Fine, but sooner or later the scales must be balanced," she warned. "It's only fair."

"Later. Now why did you change schools?"

"Halfway through my second year one of the scholarship sponsors declared bankruptcy. It was one of those savings and loan companies that went under a few years back."

"Not HoHoKam Savings and Trust?"

"How did you know?" she asked.

"What other S and L closure affected so many people?" he asked. "Even me." He told her about his client, Nathan Weller, and his reservations on defending the man. "So you see, I paid a price, too, and Weller is free to do business again. You must have been devastated when no funds came through."

"I panicked," she admitted. "I drew my savings down to almost nothing in order to pay the semester's tuition, then learned about some generous scholarships in New Mexico, several reserved for women." She grinned. "Thank goodness some sexual discrimination still exists. My grade average was an honorable 4.0 and I transferred to New Mexico the next fall."

"Why didn't you get in touch with me when you were strapped for funds?" he asked. "I could have helped."

"Pride, Bradford, the same pride that kept you from getting in touch with me when you were sick."

"Touché," he replied, taking another piece of fruit. He reached into the pocket of the green-and-gray-striped shirt he'd brought in from the truck. When his hand came out empty, he looked troubled.

"What's wrong?" she asked.

"My... medication. I left it at the house."

"What kind? What for? How important is it?"

He scowled. "It could be life or death. I should always carry a vial of nitro, and I thought I had a little blue pill. I take a powder." He stood up. "I've got to get home."

"Mark?" She dropped her napkin onto the table and hurried to him. "I...I thought we'd...won't you spend the night?"

"I can't. If I start to get careless about—Dr. Merrick harps on the importance of taking it regularly."

Desperate to keep him with her, she took his hand. "Can't you at least stay for a cup of coffee? You've been without the medication all afternoon. Would another hour matter?"

He hesitated, obviously undecided. "One cup. I'm sorry, Nan, but maybe it's for the best. We can't fight if we stay apart." He sat back down at the table.

As they sipped their drinks, she studied his actions. She still knew so little about him, how serious his problem really was, how he managed to survive financially, what really motivated him. "Mark, I need to ask you one question. Just one, so don't get mad, and you don't have to answer me if you don't want to."

He leaned back in the chair. "Shoot."

"If you could have one thing, just one thing that would be more important than anything else in the world, what would it be?"

She waited expectantly for his reply. Would it be her? Did he love her enough to put her in first place? Or perhaps it would be his health regained. A family? No, that would come with the first, unless he considered them separate items.

When he remained silent, she couldn't resist prompting him. "Maybe you're contented with what you're doing, where you are. But most people are dissatisfied about something. What would you wish for more than anything else in the world at this very minute?" *To be with me?*

He studied the bruised fingers on his left hand, touching them lightly.

"I'm sorry about your hand. Does it still hurt?"

"It's tender," he admitted. "It'll be rough to hold a pen. I know you didn't mean anything, love. It was an accident." He looked across the table, his gaze drilling into her soul.

She waited, confident now that he did love her, that she would be his first priority. He'd called her *love*. Once before he'd called her sweetheart. He hadn't actually said the three important words, but he had certainly circled around them. Since he'd warned her about commitment, she'd not pressed him. She'd never considered herself a clinging woman. She wasn't going to become one now.

"If I could have anything in the world..." His gaze drifted past her and out into the fuchsia-and-pink sunset. "More than anything I want to...practice law again."

"Law?"

He frowned. "You're surprised?"

"Well...yes." She stammered to cover her disappointment. "I thought you gave it up."

"Not willingly."

"Then why?"

"Dr. Merrick said it could kill me."

"Kill you? How could it?" Torn between fear for his life and anger at the physician who had pressured him, she reached out and took his hand. "How could a profession possibly kill its practitioner?" She waited impatiently for him to explain.

"He attributed a lot of it to pressure. The stress seems to aggravate my condition."

"But, Mark, it's what you love. How could a job you love be detrimental to your life? If you're miserable now, isn't that stressful? Wouldn't doing what you love be healthier?"

He took her other hand and squeezed it. "Nan, I wonder if I could."

"Maybe if you got back into it slowly," she replied, resting her cheek against his heart and listening to its steady pumping. How could it be so unreliable when he looked the picture of vigorous good health?

He kissed the top of her head. "Maybe."

She leaned back to see his face. "What about the girl in the Pony League who's complaining? What if you used that as a test case? It's not precedent-setting, but it could give you a chance to test the waters."

He cupped her cheeks with his hand as he brushed his mouth against hers. "Nancy Prentice, being around you makes me feel like a winner again. I love you."

"I love you, too, Mark. You make me feel like a woman, a perpetually aroused yet fulfilled woman."

"Sounds like a contradiction," he said, kissing her harder. "If I took Sadie's case and won, I could start to build my career again. Then I could make some decent money and we could... If I returned to full-time legal work, we could have a future." He hugged her tightly, taking her breath away.

"Don't get too excited," she warned. "You haven't even looked at the case yet. Maybe the manager is in the right, not Sadie."

"Isn't any attorney worth his salt trained to represent either side of a case? I've been the devil's advocate before."

She frowned. "When you represented Nathan Weller?"

He gave her a halfhearted grin.

"And you paid a price."

"But that was different," he retorted. "After I win this Pony League case and build up a client base, I could get a larger place, someplace in a better part of town. I love that little house, but it's not exactly in the best neighborhood."

"It's quaint . . . but nice." His enthusiasm became infectious. "Do you have the reference books you'll need? I can get you some from my firm's libary."

He shook his head. "I never sold mine. They're packed in boxes in the spare bedroom."

She grinned. "So you never completely gave up on the possibility of returning to practice?"

"I'll get them out and build some bookshelves. I've had the materials for months." He glanced at his watch. "I do need to get home. The swimming was good for me, but I'm beginning to feel the effect."

"Can you drive home safely?" she asked. "Maybe you should . . . rest here first."

He tossed his head back and laughed. "First I'd pretend to rest. Then you'd lie down beside me and we'd start to fool around again. We'd make love and you know what happens to me after that. I conk out for hours, and we'd be right back in trouble, with me skipping the medication, because I'd wake up and want to make love again . . . and again . . . and you'd be late for work, and how would you ever explain your tardiness to those stuffy partners?"

She touched his lips to silence him. "I get the point. Go if you insist, but drive carefully."

He swung her around in a circle, lifting her feet from the carpet. When she touched the floor again, his mouth settled on hers. The kiss deepened, and he forced her lips apart as his tongue caressed hers. She began to move her hips across his groin, eager to make him change his mind about leaving.

Suddenly he jerked away. "Damn it, I can't concentrate when you do that."

"That was the idea," she teased.

"You've been seducing me ever since we met again."

She smiled. "Someone had to make the first move. You weren't going to."

"Reckon you're right, but I planned to. Busy tomorrow?"

"Very. We have depositions scheduled all day and most of the rest of the week."

He grimaced. "Then I'll meet you at the Pony League game on Tuesday evening. I have some tax extensions I have to clear up and some other obligations at the center." He kissed her again, this time lighter but filled with promise. "Goodbye, sweetheart, take care of yourself."

"You, too." She touched the slight dimple on his left cheek. "You're very special to me."

He studied her for several seconds, and for a moment she thought she saw his green eyes glisten.

"Prentice, you're the medication Dr. Merrick suggested I find," he said, shaking his blond head in amazement. He kissed the tip of her nose, and she grinned. "I don't know where I'd be today if we hadn't met again."

She laughed. "Keeping company with your dog Belle."

"And what about you?" he asked.

"Wondering where you were, how you were doing, if you were happy." She stepped out of his embrace. "Knowing that you're happy has always been important to me."

"Tonight, for the first time in a year, I'm truly happy," he said.

She held the door for him, staying on the balcony and watching until he was out of sight. When she returned to the apartment and closed her door, she glanced around. He'd only been there once, but now her apartment seemed incredibly empty without him.

CHAPTER ELEVEN

MARK SWISHED OUT the glass in which he'd drunk the prescription powder and set it in the sink. As he turned, he heard the soft whining of Belle.

He unlatched the kitchen door, and a flash of copper fur sailed past his legs. He followed Belle down the hallway and into his bedroom. The dog's tail beat the carpet in appreciation, and Mark knelt to greet her, scratching her behind her ears and grabbing the ruff at her neck and shaking her affectionately. She whined again and tried to lick his cheek. He pulled back just in time to avoid the wet caress.

"Belle, pretty girl, you're definitely my second choice for female companionship tonight, but you'll have to do."

Her tail thrummed in agreement.

"But not under the covers," he cautioned. "It's the foot of the bed. Understand?"

Her tongue lolled out one side of her mouth and she seemed to nod her understanding. Her belly hung low and her nipples had begun to enlarge. Mark knew she could have the litter within the week.

"I reckon expectant mothers are entitled to a little special treatment around this place," he murmured, stroking her fur. He changed into the jogging shorts he used at night, then checked that the front and back doors were locked. There had been a rash of break-ins during the spring. Belle trotted at his heels as he moved through the house. At least twice he'd had her to thank for thwarting possible break-ins at his house and that of his neighbor, Horace.

In the hallway he turned the evaporative cooler down to low. Belle stopped and waited. "Got to save electricity," he said. "Got to watch the pennies." He thought of Nancy Prentice's air-conditioned apartment and the pool available whenever she decided to take a dip. He'd had a pool at his Deer Valley home, and it had cost him a bundle to maintain, especially when he became too busy to do the work himself. The pool service company seemed to think anyone who used their service had money to burn.

Man and dog returned to the bedroom, and Mark opened the window a few inches. A gentle, warm breeze drifted into the bedroom. Belle cocked her head at him.

"Could be cooler," he admitted, "but it won't last much longer." He glanced toward the calendar thumbtacked to the wall next to his dresser. *July, August, September and half of October, then it'll turn cool.* Oh, God, for enough money to reclaim a few of the luxuries he'd once taken for granted.

He thought he'd made the transition to a simpler life-style, but since finding Nancy Prentice again, doubts had erupted at every turn. Maybe he'd been deluding himself all along. Horace had spent half a year convincing him of the advantages of living in a less affluent neighborhood, and he'd begun to agree . . . until yesterday. Was it only yesterday?

He jerked the spread and sheet down to the foot of the bed and dropped to the pillows, trying to block out the unrest that had besieged him since he'd driven away from Nancy's apartment.

She stirred his dreams, his nightmares and fantasies, and tonight all three had merged into one gigantic dilemma.

Could she have hit on something he'd never considered? Had Dr. Merrick overreacted in his insistence that Mark follow such a restrictive regime of recovery? If he watched his diet, took the medications and paced himself, why couldn't he get back into the legal profession and pick up where he'd left off?

For a decade he'd had it all, including a fine apartment along the north-central corridor in Phoenix, then the house in Deer Valley. His sharp-looking little blue sports car had been preceded by two BMWs and a classic Porsche convertible. And every time Mark had arrived at work in a new car, Nancy had been impressed.

Belle put her paws on the side of the bed, waiting for permission to climb on. He patted the mattress, and she leaped onto the foot, circled twice and lay down. The animal had been crucial during his recovery. Before his sister Jill had left for her home in Georgia, she had insisted he get himself a pet. She had dragged him to three different kennels before he'd found the year-old pedigreed bitch who had taken the choice from him with a swipe of her wet tongue on his outstretched hand.

He'd brought the dog home, still filled with doubts about having an animal to care for, and when Jill drove away in her rental car for the airport, he'd almost called her back. Rising panic had tightened his chest and weakened his already teetering confidence that he could manage alone.

The springs creaked as Belle began her predictable creeping away from the foot of the bed. She rolled onto her side, pressing her back into his calf, then his thigh and finally his hip as she crawled along on her side. He pushed an extra pillow behind his head and turned onto his back again before patting the bed. The dog dashed into his arms, sighing as if she were almost human when he hugged her.

"Belle, tonight you're truly my best friend . . . and you never talk back, do you?"

She barked, and the sharp sound reverberated in the quiet room. Chuckling, he put his arm around her neck. She settled against him again, her head resting on the corner of his pillow. In a few minutes he could tell that she was asleep.

She whined in her sleep, and when he put the open palm of his free hand on her side, he thought he could feel the pups moving. When he was first approached about breeding her, he'd declined the offer twice. The man had persisted, and Mark had finally agreed after a month of serious consideration. Now he was glad. Having the litter to care for and later place would give him something special on which to concentrate.

Puppies . . . babies . . . Nancy. He stroked the sleeping animal's coat and allowed his thoughts to drift. *Babies . . . Nancy Prentice.* His hand moved up and down the dog's shoulder and foreleg. *Nancy, love, do you want babies?*

When Dr. Merrick explained the gene that had caused his heart condition, he'd made an easy decision never to marry or, if he did, to avoid fathering children. Why subject innocent offspring to what he'd gone through? For months he'd held his own parents guilty of his condition. Several meetings with the Zipper Club in the neighboring city of Glendale had made him accept the situation and forgive his parents, but he had avoided discussing the matter with them.

But his decisions about marriage and a family had been made before Nancy Prentice had come sailing into his life again. How long? He stared up at the dark ceiling. Less than a week . . . four days? How could it possibly be only a matter of days?

He recalled the time they'd spent together. He grimaced in the darkness. Had their actions been premature? They'd certainly made up for the lost years. The thought of never having loved her or made love to her, of never again waking up with her by his side was inconceivable.

She's young, he thought. *Her sisters have families. They're both pregnant. She probably plans on a family of her own someday. Thirty-three years old?* Still young enough, but not so many years left. If she got involved with him, she might be sacrificing her God-given right to bear children.

Fifty-fifty chance. Dr. Merrick had said any child of his would have a fifty-fifty chance of being healthy or of being more like him than he'd ever imagined. The idea of having a child with Nancy Prentice held a special poignancy. He'd been as surprised as anyone to find himself getting along with the children when he started to umpire the baseball games. He seemed to have an innate ability to understand them, even though he'd had little contact with children other than an occasional visit with his nieces and nephews.

Fifty-fifty chance. But didn't that also mean that a child might be healthy and spared the defective gene? An image of a toddler with Nancy's brown curls surfaced in his mind, and he allowed it to play through his thoughts for several minutes.

Stupid, be realistic, he thought, sliding his arm from beneath Belle's head and rolling onto his side to stare out the window. How the hell could he afford a family? He could barely manage a budget for one.

The accounting service and legal work he performed at the Peoria Senior Center was funded by a grant from the state of Arizona and could be cut anytime the government changed its priorities.

He'd already applied for a renewal of the base grant and put in a second request to hire an associate, but what attorney in his right mind would accept a position with no job security, a meager salary that depended on the generosity of the state rather than the ability of the clients to pay, and no health or pension benefits? Yet there was more than enough work for a partner if that partner had the right attitude.

Although the grant agreement allowed him to charge up to fifty dollars per hour for his services, he'd voluntarily reduced it to thirty dollars, and that didn't allow for the research time required on the more complex cases. By reducing the hourly charge, he could take on more clients.

He rolled onto his stomach. Sometimes he felt like an old-time circuit-riding preacher who was forced to take his pay in trade and produce. At least he'd convinced his clients to make him cholesterol-free cookies. He'd even convinced a home economist from the university of Tempe to come and do a series of lessons on nutrition.

Belle scooted closer.

"Hey, girl, you're crowding," he whispered. Belle whined her guilt but didn't move away.

Who the hell said life was fair? Mine is a regular brier patch. Yet he *had* discovered a rose in his patch of thorns. Nancy Prentice's peach-colored cheeks were as fair as petals on a champion rose, and when he held her in his arms and made love to her, he knew somehow he had to find room for her in his troubled and uncertain life.

He needed her. Perhaps a little pruning and grooming in his own garden would make room for her, and together they could find happiness. His fist tightened.

Belle whined and pulled away, then jumped to the carpet and turned to look his way. "Sorry, girl." He followed her from the room and let her outside. When she was ready to go inside again, he secured the door and they returned to the bedroom. This time she lay down at his side, avoiding the foot of his bed completely.

"Go to sleep, girl," he said, stroking her lush fur. "Tomorrow we've got some serious thinking to do about our futures."

ON TUESDAY Nancy pulled into the parking lot of the ballpark and glanced around for Mark's truck. *Of course not,* she thought. *He walks.*

She hadn't seen him since Sunday, but he'd telephoned her on Monday evening for an hour after he returned from umpiring two games. He told her he'd finished unpacking his legal library and had taken some of the books to the center where he'd already moved the basic library.

"I'm glad to know you never really gave it up," she had said, and he'd reluctantly admitted he hadn't.

When she asked him how he felt, he had simply replied, "Fine."

"Miss me?"

"A little bit," he'd replied. "But Belle keeps me company."

"But she doesn't sleep with you," she'd teased, and he'd broken up with laughter.

She locked the car and walked to the snack bar. "Where is the Pony League game?"

A volunteer behind the counter pointed to the farthest field and grinned. "It's a hike and a half."

"But worth the effort," Nancy replied.

When she spotted Mark in the bleachers talking to another man, she knew she'd walk a thousand miles to be with him. He was dressed in his pale blue umpiring shirt and navy blue shorts.

His tan legs were muscular, and as she approached him, she recalled how they felt beneath her caressing hands. His skin was incredibly sexy and warm to touch, not overly hairy as some blond men could be. Everything about him was perfect in her opinion.

He glanced up, saw her and stood immediately, motioning the man to follow him. They met several yards from the noisy crowd.

"Good evening," he said, taking her hand and giving it a squeeze.

"I thought you were off this evening," she said, wanting him to pull her close, but he didn't and she swallowed her disappointment. *After all, this is business,* she decided. *Better conduct ourselves like professionals.*

"I'm subbing for a guy with a sick kid," he explained. "Nancy Prentice, I'd like you to meet Sam Burns," Mark said. "He's Sarah's father. I apologized for acting like an ambulance chaser when I approached him, but when I explained our reason for coming—"

"I say it's about time." Sam Burns removed his baseball cap and wiped his brow, then put the cap back on his partially balding head. "This has been going on for years," he said. "Sadie is my second girl to play in the Pony League. Debbie was on another team and got to play regularly, but this son of a bitch Fischer won't let Sadie or the other girl on the team play. He flatly refuses to let them do anything but warm the bench. My little Sadie's a damn good player."

Nancy shook his hand and was impressed with his confident grasp. "I can tell you feel very strongly about this. Why?"

Sam Burns beamed. "Remember back in the forties when the A-1 Queens and the Ramblers were championship teams in that old baseball league for women?"

Nancy grinned sheepishly. "I'm afraid that was before my time."

To her surprise Mark nodded. "My dad used to talk about the women's baseball league. It was a very popular sport during World War II. The games were often sellouts, and both the Queens and the Ramblers went on to national championships. But now people think girls shouldn't play because they might get hurt and permanently harmed."

"So can the guys," Sam countered. "Did you ever get hit with a ball in your crotch?" He glanced at Nancy. "Sorry, ma'am."

"That's why the boys wear jock straps and cups," Mark said. He glanced at Nancy, then added, "Sorry,

Nan." He returned his attention to Sam Burns. "Do the girls wear protection for their breasts?"

Nancy shifted uncomfortably at this turn of the conversation. "I didn't realize it was such a physical problem."

Sam frowned. "My girls do, and so do some of their friends. My wife and I talk to my girls about that sort of thing. She designed them each a protective vest. They can wear them under their shirts or over them. It doesn't matter. Fischer isn't smart enough to bench them for a valid reason like that. He's a chauvinst bastard who knows he's breaking the law, and I want to see that he doesn't get away with it."

"And that's it?" Nancy asked, sensing he might have other reasons for feeling so strongly about his daughters playing ball.

"Well, the girls' grandmother, my mother, pitched on the Ramblers the second year they went to the nationals. There was nothing *soft* about the way those gals could slide a fastball over the plate. They packed a wallop. I know, because I learned to catch working with my mother. She can still burn a pitch over the plate."

Mark chuckled. "Not many guys can claim that."

Sam nodded. "I reckon there's nothing that would please her more than to see her granddaughters play on a championship team. She comes to most of the games, and she knows that this is as far as girls can go around here, but damn it, Sadie's being cheated because of some overbearing, egotistical, self-centered bigot who can't see beyond his own balls—sorry, ma'am—and let my girl play."

Mark winked at Nancy, sending her heart skittering into double time. "How's the team doing?"

"Hell, they've lost every game but one," Sam said. "If he'd let Sadie play, they'd be in first place."

"We can't say that for sure, can we?" Nancy asked, looking from one man to the other.

Mark draped his arm around her shoulders. "Why don't we climb into the stands and watch the game?" He brushed his lips against her cheek when Sam Burns turned his attention to the game. "Bring a notepad?" he asked her.

"Always." She slid her arm around his waist but resisted leaning into him. "You?"

"I still know how to do research," he boasted. "I already have several pages. Maybe later we can compare notes."

"Your place or mine?" she asked softly.

He brushed a kiss across her mouth. "We'll decide the details later."

She followed him up the bleachers to a spot that gave them an unobstructed view of the entire playing field, yet directly behind the dugout of the Cubs.

The manager named Fischer paced back and forth in front of the dugout continually, stopping only to shout instructions to his players. Two girls who looked about fourteen sat huddled together on the bench. A skinny boy the same age held down the other end of the bench.

Fischer turned to the girls and growled an order to them.

"What'd he say?" Nancy asked.

"To pick up the equipment and the trash," Mark murmured.

"Damn that man," Sam Burns snapped. "I didn't pay her registration fee to make her his maid."

Nancy leaned past Mark. "Mr. Burns, does he make them do that often?"

"All the damn time. I told my Sadie to refuse, but she says it would only cause more trouble."

The manager crooked a finger at Sadie and she stood up. He beckoned again, and she went to him, glancing once over her shoulder toward the crowd. The manager pulled some coins from his pocket and dropped them into her hand. When one dropped to the dusty ground, he waited until she knelt to pick it up.

He called Sadie's name and she glanced up. While he spoke she slowly got to her feet again, holding the front of her blouse against her young chest.

"Did you see that?" Nancy started to get to her feet.

"Where are you going?" Mark asked, grabbing her hand and pulling her back down.

Nancy's head whipped around, her eyes narrowing with anger. "He's . . . he's . . . why he's nothing but a dirty-minded old man who gets his jollies from looking down the front of teenage girls' blouses. Mark, either you stop him or I will. I'll call the police and tell them—"

"Sit down, Nan," Mark insisted, tugging her back to the bench.

The runner on third tried to steal home and the catcher tagged him out, retiring the side and filling the Cubs dugout with noisy young teenage boys.

Mark, Nancy and Sam watched as Sadie left the dugout and ran across the field to the snack bar, returning several minutes later with a soft drink. She handed it to Fischer and returned to the dugout.

"The creep didn't even have the decency to buy her one," Nancy said. "Mark, if you don't take this case, I'll get my firm to handle it. That's a promise."

They watched a few more innings as the score against the Cubs grew. During the last inning, the crowd in the bleachers thinned considerably. Only a miracle could salvage a Cubs win.

The game ended with a score of ten to one against the Cubs. Sam Burns beckoned to his daughter. She grabbed her glove and started to leave the dugout.

Fischer, the slightly rotund team manager, jerked around. "Hey, Burns, you ain't done. Get your cute little ass back over here."

Sarah skidded to a halt.

"Burns, you're on cleanup," Fischer called loud enough for the lingering crowd to hear. "Get your ass in gear and help those two guys there."

Her mouth opened and closed.

"I don't care if you have a hot date or not, get hustling. Your boyfriend will still be panting when you're done here."

Sam Burns walked around the backstop and onto the infield. "Sadie, let's go," he insisted.

Fischer dug his heels into the dirt and whirled around. "Hey, mister, no one gets on the field but the teams, and this one doesn't leave until I say so."

Sam clinched his fists but kept them at his sides. "Sadie is my daughter and I say she's through for the night, Fischer. She's done enough picking up after you, you son of a—"

Mark laid a restraining hand on the man's arm. "Let's go, Sam. You and Sadie, could you join us for a hamburger and Coke? We'll visit." He turned to the young girl. "I'm Mark Bradford."

The girl smiled, turning her face into a lovely promise of emerging maturity. "You're the umpire for the majors."

Mark nodded. "And this is my friend, Nancy Prentice. Can you get away now?"

Sadie turned to her manager. For a fleeting moment Nancy sensed the fear that flashed across the young girl's features.

Before they could discuss her dismissal, Mark stepped closer. "Nice to meet you, Mr. Fischer. I'm one of the official umpires for the other divisions. Sadie's leaving now. She has an appointment with us." He turned away, dismissing the man. Retrieving Sadie's glove from the dust, he slapped it against his thigh and handed it to her, then offered her his arm. She glanced toward her father, back at the flushed manager and back at her father again. He nodded and she accepted Mark's arm.

Mark steered her from the field. "We know about Mr. Fischer's reputation," he whispered. "Let me tell you about our plans."

Nancy turned to Sam Burns. "While they get acquainted, will you escort me to the parking lot? You can trust Mark. He's the most ethical, moral, upstanding, noble, competent man I've ever known."

Sam chuckled. "With a recommendation like that he must be God incarnate himself."

"Could be," she replied.

They followed Mark and Sadie to the parking lot, keeping the pace leisurely to allow the man and girl to chat.

Halfway to the lot, Sadie stopped abruptly and clapped her hands. "Really?"

Mark nodded.

Sadie threw her arms around Mark's neck and hugged him. "Oh, Mr. Bradford, you've totally saved my life, absolutely, positively, totally saved my life. You're radical, totally cool...and you're gorgeous, too, for a mature guy."

CHAPTER TWELVE

"THIS ISN'T MCDONALD'S, but the hamburgers are great," Mark said as they studied the menus.

Nancy glanced at Mark, who sat beside her in the booth at his favorite café. "You eat the hamburgers here?"

He shrugged. "No, but they look good."

Sadie looked startled. "You don't believe in hamburgers?"

Mark grinned back at her. "I watch my diet." The waitress arrived and he folded the menu. "A vegetable omelet with egg beaters."

The others ordered hamburgers with French fries, and when the food arrived, they all ate quietly. After their plates were cleared and Sadie savored a chocolate sundae, Mark retrieved a notebook and pen from his shirt pocket.

"Now," he said, with a deep sigh, "tell me about yourself, the other girls and this Fischer."

Sadie swallowed a bite of ice cream and made a face. "Well, there's just one other girl. Her name is Amber Todd. As for Fischer, he's worse than a creep. He's weird and . . . it's hard to describe, but he makes me feel dirty."

Mark arched a blond brow at her. "I can understand that, but proving it in court may be difficult. We must prove that he singles you girls out for special treatment."

"Special abuse is more like it," Sadie insisted.

"Abuse," he conceded. "I could prove it, but you have to give me the ammunition."

For the next hour Sadie described the times when she made suggestions, offered to play, insisted that she be put in the game, did his bidding and cleaned the dugout. She related some of the remarks he'd made to the two girls on the team.

Mark held up his hand. "He actually called you 'a little bitch'?"

"When he wasn't calling us bimbos or cute asses or broads," she replied. "I called him a liar and he got furious." She pounded the table with her small fist. "Mr. Bradford, I make straight A's. How dare that creep call me a bimbo. Then he called me a 'dyke.' I didn't even know what that meant until Daddy told me. Can't I be a normal girl and just like playing baseball? I love playing it and I'm good at it, too. Ask my dad. Ask my grandma. She used to play semipro hardball. She's sixty-five years old, and no one is more of a lady than my Grandma Burns."

Sam Burns chuckled. "You get your baseball-playing ability from her, that's for sure, honey."

Mark frowned. "Doesn't anyone challenge him?"

"Chuck and Zack Andrews tried once, but he called them wimps and fags and threatened to bench them for three games if they sided with me," Sadie said. "Fischer said they had no balls." She ducked her head. "I knew what he meant, but...he shouldn't talk that way. And he's wrong, at least about Chuck. Chuck is..." She sighed dramatically. "He's radical."

"When the manager calls you insulting names, are they always sexually oriented?" Nancy asked.

Sadie looked puzzled.

"Pertaining to being female," Nancy clarified.

"Sort of," Sadie said, beginning to fidget in her seat.

"Can you tell us some of them?" Mark asked.

"Some of what he says makes the guys snicker and leer at us," Sadie said. She glanced at her father. "My dad will get mad if I tell you too much."

Mark shook his head. "There's no such thing as telling me too much, Sadie. Your father suspects what's been happening but hasn't been able to go to every game, so it's up to you to tell us everything."

She studied the empty sundae glass. "I really don't want to say them."

Mark slid his notepad across the table. "Then write them down." He waited while the girl agonized over the list of words and phrases that might help substantiate the accusation of sexual harassment and discrimination.

When the notepad returned to his side of the table, he studied the list, giving a soft whistle. "A gentleman, he isn't." He leaned back against the cushion and gazed at the other two adults as they read the list.

"Are managers allowed to talk that way?" Nancy asked, leaning against his shoulder to scrutinize the list.

"When an umpire hears that kind of language on the playing field, he or she has the right to eject the offender from the game," Mark replied. "Parents, too, if they get out of line. Doesn't anyone, especially the umpire, ever challenge this guy?"

"They're afraid of him," Sadie said. "He gives a lot of money each year to the league, and they need the money to pay the bills. I guess stuff like uniforms costs megabucks, so they let him get away with it."

Mark mulled over the girl's remark, then straightened. "Then perhaps we should include the league officials in the suit. They condoned his actions by their silence." He started to reach for the check, but Sam Burns grabbed it.

"This is on me," Sam said, retrieving his wallet and removing several bills.

"What's this going to cost?" Sadie asked. "Daddy, can you afford to do this? I can get through the rest of the season." She looked at Mark. "We don't have lots of money."

Mark patted her hand. "I'll take the case on a contingency basis. If we win, I get...twenty-five percent. The going rate is above that, but twenty-five is fine. If we lose, I get nothing."

"Twenty-five percent of what?" Nancy asked.

Mark inhaled sharply. "That's the challenge. Let me check into some things, like the league's liability and malpractice policies. I wouldn't want to cripple or kill the league, but I want to get this guy. I'll have to notify the head of the umpiring program. This puts me in a conflict of interest. There's no doubt about that." He smiled sheepishly. "I've grown accustomed to those weekly checks."

"I could—" Nancy began, but he interrupted her offer.

"No charity."

Nancy frowned at the snapping tone of his voice. "You don't know what I was going to say." She grabbed her purse and slid from the bench, trying to hide her irritation.

Outside, she stood in the parking lot, waiting for the others. Once again some invisible force had come between them. She turned at the sound of footsteps approaching. Her heart lurched at the sight of Mark Bradford walking toward her, his hands hooked in his shorts' pockets, his blond head bowed in order to hear Sadie's remark.

"Is that okay with you, Nan?" Mark asked.

Sam Burns and his daughter seemed to be waiting, too, as if her decision mattered.

"I'm sorry," she said. "I was...daydreaming. Is what okay with me?"

Sam draped his arm around his daughter's shoulder. "I work nights out at the Palo Verde power plant. I let the time get away from me. It's an hour's drive. Could you give Sadie a ride home? We live on the same block as Chuck and Zack Andrews."

Nancy smiled. "Of course."

"And could you drop me back at the ballpark?" Mark asked. "I'll walk home from there."

"We've already been that route," she reminded him. "I'd be happy to take Sadie home, and you, too, Mark."

Sadie kissed her father's cheek and said goodbye, then squeezed into the crowded space between the two bucket seats, balancing herself with a hand on each seat back. They chatted about school, baseball and boys and in twenty minutes they were in front of her house.

"Good night, Ms. Prentice. You, too, Mr. Bradford, and thanks for helping me. We'll teach that old creep Fischer a lesson, won't we?"

Mark climbed out and held the seat for Sadie's exit, then waited until she ran up the walkway and waved from the front door. Once she was safely inside, Nancy shifted gears and they raced into the night.

In the darkness of the car's interior she smiled and glanced toward him. "I feel as if it's time for me to ask, 'Your place or mine?'"

"Mine."

She glanced at him again, but he was staring straight ahead.

"I should start driving my truck," he said, startling her with his remark.

"So you won't have to be stuck with me?" She tried to hide her wounded pride. "Mark, what's wrong? I thought we'd...found something, something wonderful."

"We did, but—"

"You're not obligated. I told you I was a big girl now, but please don't jerk me around emotionally. You put your arm around me and pull me close, even in public, and I think you really like being with me. Then you dig a chasm and fill it with invisible monsters and I don't recognize most of them. You snap at me when I get too close. Why?"

She braked for a red light. In the glow of the traffic signal she tensed when his hand reached out and his fingers brushed her cheek.

"It's not what you think," he said.

"Then what is it?"

He stared ahead into the darkness. "How long has it been since we met again?"

Frowning, she pressed on the accelerator and turned onto his street. "Only a week. It seems like much longer."

"Come inside," he said as the car rolled into the driveway of his house. "We need to talk."

She parked behind his truck and silently followed him into the house. The last time she'd come home with him they'd forgotten all about talking and had tumbled into bed without a moment's hesitation, as if fulfilling their passions was the most important thing in the universe. This time she resolved to retain her self-control. Mark had some explaining to do before she allowed herself to be swept off her feet again.

He turned on the light switch and headed toward the kitchen. "I'll check on Belle," he called before disappearing into the dark backyard.

She glanced around the living room. He'd made several changes, she noted. One wall was now covered with bookshelves, and he'd moved in a large office-size desk, which was now cluttered with books. She smiled, remembering that he'd always pretended to be neat, but chaos had always reigned when Mark threw himself into a case. In spite of his doubts and his physician's warning he'd obviously thrown himself into this one.

Perhaps the challenge would help him recapture some of his old confidence and drive.

"Nan, come out here!" Mark shouted from the yard. "And turn on the light."

She ran to the exit. "What is it? What's wrong?"

"It's Belle," he called from the far corner of the yard. "She's started having her puppies. There's a blanket on that lawn chair." He waved toward the patio. "Put it down on the concrete, then come help me move her."

Nancy spread the blanket out against the wall of the house, then ran to him. The Irish setter lay on her side, straining to give birth to a third fat, red pup. Two older pups lay squirming in the grass, their coats almost dry.

"Oh, Mark, what do we do now?" she asked, feeling helpless.

"Let her lick this next one for a few minutes," he directed. "Then you take the puppies and I'll carry her to her new bed."

They waited until Belle seemed satisfied that all her babies were safe. Mark motioned to Nancy. "Take the puppies to the blanket. I'll bring Belle."

She gathered up the warm, squirming newborn pups and hurried to the patio to kneel on the edge of the blanket, only to find herself almost knocked over by a concerned mother who shoved her aside and lay down next to the pups. Immediately the dog began to strain again.

"Damn, I didn't even get a chance to grab her," Mark said. "She raced after you and the pups. Did she hurt you?"

Nancy reached out and touched the head of one of the pups, caressing the wavy copper coat. "I'm fine. I've never seen puppies being born before."

Mark grinned. "Then welcome to the Bradford Birthing Clinic."

He sat down crosslegged beside her, and together they watched as seven more pups were delivered over the next hour.

"Is it always so easy?" Nancy asked, embarrassed at her ignorance of such a natural process.

"Having babies?" He shrugged. "For dogs and cats, I think so. As for human beings...my sister says it's worth the effort." He glanced sideways at her.

"What do your sisters say? Don't women do a lot of talking about babies and deliveries?"

She picked up a puppy and brought it to her cheek. "He's..." She turned the pup onto its back and checked. "She's incredibly soft and warm."

Mark grinned like a proud papa. "You didn't answer the question."

She put the pup close to one of Belle's many nipples and watched it root around for several seconds before settling down to nurse. "I never had much interest in having babies until recently." She felt his gaze on her but couldn't bring herself to look at him.

"And now?" he asked softly.

"You'll misconstrue my answer."

"Try me."

She reached out and stroked Belle's head, scratching one ear. Belle's tail thumped the old quilt. "Having babies isn't so unthinkable...now that I've met you again."

Nancy looked away. When she turned back, her heart twisted sharply as she saw the unexpected brilliance of tears in his green eyes.

"Mark, what's wrong?" She scooted over on her knees, stopping between his legs, and placed her hands on his shoulders. "Oh, my darling Mark, what have I said?"

His hand cupped her chin, bringing it up where he could meet her troubled gaze again. "Let me tell you about my babies."

"Your babies? Mark, what are you talking about? You have children? You told me before that you didn't. When? How many? Who's their mother? Oh, my God. I can't remember if I asked you about previous marriages or not. I assumed—"

"I have no children." He reached out and drew her against him, cradling her in his arms. "Listen, Nan, listen very carefully, because what I'm about to say will probably change everything. You won't want my babies when I tell you... what really caused my heart attack. I was a walking time bomb and didn't know it."

"It doesn't matter," she said, her voice muffled against his shirt.

"But it does," he insisted. "Any child of mine stands a fifty-fifty chance of dying young or having a heart attack at an early age, just like I did. I have a genetic problem." He gave her a brief but concise medical explanation for his condition. "So now you can understand why I've decided to have no children. I can't take a chance on doing that to an innocent baby."

"But—"

Tenderly he stroked her arm. "So, you see, my darling Nan, if you want babies, you'll have to find another man."

Mark waited for her to pull away. No woman in her right mind would hang around now. "You deserve better than what I can give you. You're young, too young and healthy to saddle yourself with me if you want a normal family." Her head shifted on his chest, and he glanced down to find her staring at Belle and the pups.

"I had hoped you might... truly love me," she whispered.

The pain in his chest was almost worse than when he first became ill. He tightened his hold on her, knowing he should roll her off his lap, but afraid that if she left, he couldn't survive without her. "I love you very much, sweetheart, maybe too much, but if you have any sense at all, you'd hightail it for home.''

She slid her hand up his shirt and around his neck. "If I had to choose between having babies or having you, I have no choice. I love you, for better or for worse, with or without children. One week, one year, or one decade... it doesn't matter, because without you, I'd be dead inside. But I don't want to stay unless you really want me."

"More than life itself," he murmured, claiming her mouth with his. He wasn't sure if the groan he heard was hers or his.

The contentment he'd worked so hard to achieve in the past year had been brought into question by this woman in his arms. He wanted more than just her willing body in his arms at night. He wanted her beside him while he researched his cases, to help when he encountered roadblocks. They'd always been a terrific team. Now, with both of them practicing law, they would be unbeatable.

He needed her nearby when the house grew too quiet, when the doubts about reentering the legal profession gnawed at him, to hold his hand during his next examination at Dr. Merrick's office, to celebrate when the kindly physician assured them he was healthy and strong and that they'd made the right decision together.

They would be Bradford and Bradford, Attorneys-at-Law. There had been a time, years ago, when he speculated about having a son to join him in practice. That was no longer possible, but a wife—Nancy—would be even better.

"Let's go inside," he suggested, helping her to her feet. He clutched her face in his hands and kissed her mouth. "I'd hate to think you'd leave me tonight."

"Never, Mark," she replied, returning his kiss with one of her own. "We'll work this all out. You'll see. If we love each other, nothing will keep us apart."

He laughed. "It's us against the world. We'll be invincible."

CHAPTER THIRTEEN

"THANK YOU FOR SEEING ME," Mark said, settling as best he could in the cold metal chair. The three men staring back at him were the elected officials of the league. Only one was absent.

"What can we do for you, Mark?" Al Glenn asked. "Trouble with the parents? Are they giving you a hard time with your umpiring?" He laughed nervously. "Ya gotta watch them Little League parents. They have a notorious reputation. Why I remember once several years ago when two fathers actually came to blows right on the field. It seems the one—"

Mark held up his hand. "The parents have been fine. The few who have gotten out of line...well, I reasoned with them."

"Then a kid," Al Glenn guessed. "Some of those kids run wild at home, ya know. Regular little terrors, only you can't tell their parents that. They're perfect little angels in their eyes, so if you have a brat who won't listen, give me his name and I'll speak to the parents. But remember, we don't want to alienate anyone. We need these parents and their kids, or the league would curl up its toes and die." He chuckled, as if pleased with his handling of the difficulty.

"It's Fischer in the Pony League," Mark said, cutting to the core of the problem at hand.

The three men exchanged darting glances before returning their attention to Mark. "Stanley Fischer? He's pretty important to this league, Mark. He's kept us afloat more than once, and he's willing to be an officer. He's been president three times in the last decade, in fact, and he's managed the Cubs for fifteen years now. If you're having trouble with Stan, take him aside and level with him. He's a reasonable guy, really a good joe."

Mark started to speak, but Al Glenn interrupted. "Go easy on him, Mark, for all our sakes. He's got a temper, but we need him, and the kids like and respect him."

"Are you sure?" Mark asked, surprised that anyone who had watched the man in action could hold such an incredible opinion.

"There may be a few troublemakers who rebel at his style of management," Glenn admitted. "He's from the old school that says a kid should respect and obey his elders. Besides, Stan is a vice president. He's slated to be president again next year." He laughed nervously. "Each time he gets elected president he ups his donation to the pot."

"He buys the presidency?" Mark asked, trying to hide his dislike for Stan Fischer. "Isn't that a form of bribery?"

"Nah," Dale Redmond interjected. "It's just good sense on our part. We get his money and he gets his ego stroked and a big charitable deduction on his tax return."

"At the expense of the children?" Mark asked.

"Hell, what are you implying?" Al Glenn asked. "Is that why you asked for him to be excluded from this meeting? I figured maybe you wanted more money for umping, or wanted a guarantee about next season. There are no guarantees in this business, Mark. You'll find that out. As for next year, see Stan Fischer. He'll be the president."

Mark glanced at his watch. He was due at Nancy Prentice's apartment in an hour for a swim and dinner and hopefully a night of bliss. He grinned, letting his thoughts drift.

Al Glenn misinterpreted his action. "Glad to see you've changed your mind about Fischer. He can be abrasive, maybe a little too hard on his players, but he's a fine coach and we're grateful to have him as a volunteer in the league." As if his remarks had concluded the meeting, he retrieved his keys from his pant pocket and jiggled them.

Mark held up his hand. "Listen to me, fellows. Stan Fischer is an insensitive, chauvinistic male who verbally abuses all his players, sexually harasses his female ones and violates their civil rights by discriminating against them based solely on their sex. That's a federal offense if we choose to pursue it. He sets an incredibly bad example for his male players and he doesn't know the meaning of sportsmanship."

Al Glenn pressed against the back of his chair. "The hell you say."

The third man, who hadn't said a word, leaned and extended his hand to Mark. "I'm Murray Harper. Glad to meet you at last. Two of my kids play on the majors and one in the minors and they all say you're the best umpire we have." He turned to the league president. "Al, we've all seen this coming. Mark is right. Fischer is a one hundred percent son of a bitch."

Al blanched. "But we need him."

"And his money," Redmond added.

"Do we?" Harper asked. "What's the complaint exactly and what do you want us to do about it...and how do you fit into the complaint?"

"I've been asked to represent Sadie Burns and her father Sam Burns," Mark said, choosing his words carefully. "She's one of two girls on the Pony League Cubs. Fischer has made their lives miserable all season and neither of them has played since the season started."

Redmond shrugged. "We pretty much stay out of the operations of the individual teams. That's why they have managers and coaches. Fischer used to field championship teams consistently."

"Used to?" Mark asked.

"I'll admit he's been complaining about the caliber of kids playing ball these days," Glenn added. "He's right there. Today's kids are lazy. They don't try as hard as we did when we played ball."

"Any kid who cares enough to sign up and pay the registration is obviously interested in playing baseball," Mark challenged. "The manager sets the tone of the team. The Cubs have problems. They've won only one game this season."

"So sue the manager!" Glenn said. "Is that what today's parents do when their kids aren't on winning teams?"

"No," Mark said, leaning back as he scrutinized his opponents. "But a manager who harasses and ridicules the team members should be held accountable."

"That's malarkey," Redmond said. "A manager has to be hard on his players. That's how he gets the best out of them."

Mark scowled at Redmond and Glenn. "By calling the girls bitches and chippies and tarts—is that how he gets the best out of them? By making them police the dugouts and staying with them to ogle down the fronts of their shirts when they lean over? By never letting them have so much as a turn at bat just because they're girls, or assuming they can't catch a ball and banning them from playing a single inning? The two girls don't even get a chance to play during practice except to chase loose balls in the outfield."

"Maybe that's all they're good for," Glenn countered.

Mark stared the man down. "There's more. Fischer describes in anatomical detail all the reasons for his belief that girls shouldn't play ball. He does this during practice when the parents and spectators aren't present—but the boys on the team are. The only saving grace is that the boys are on to Fischer's style and they dislike him as much as the girls do."

"So why do they stay on the team?" Glenn challenged.

"They love playing baseball," Murray Harper said in support of Mark. "Baseball is the major community sport around this valley. I played. You guys played. Now our kids are playing. They deserve better than Fischer, regardless of how much financial help he gives the league." He looked at Mark. "What do you want from us?"

"Rein in Fischer. Lay down the law with him. Tell him that if he doesn't change his ways, especially toward his female players, he's going to find himself in deep trouble."

Al Glenn laughed. "And who's going to make trouble?"

"Me."

"You? What are you going to do? Hire an attorney and sue the bastard?"

Mark's gaze drilled into the other man's eyes. "I don't need to hire an attorney. I am one. My license to practice law in the state of Arizona is hanging on my office wall. And, yes, if Stan Fischer doesn't change in the weeks left in the season and treat the girls with respect and allow them to play, I plan to file suit against him for sexual harassment and discrimination on behalf of Sarah Burns."

"Go ahead," Al Glenn said. "We have liability coverage."

"Good, you may need it," Mark replied, feeling his blood pounding through his veins. The rush of adrenaline gave him a sense of euphoria as the meeting drew to a close. "We may include the other girl, as well, and if the league officials fail to take responsibility for solving this problem, I won't hesitate to include the league and its officials as defendants."

Murry Harper got to his feet. "Sue for what? An apology? Financial damages?"

"Both," Mark said, standing up.

"How much?" Dale Redmond asked.

"Sam Burns wanted to ask for a million dollars," Mark said casually as he put his notepad and pen in the leather briefcase he'd brought to the meeting.

Al Glenn's face turned gray beneath his ruddy complexion.

"But I suggested a more modest settlement," Mark said. "We haven't settled on an amount." He withdrew two papers from his briefcase. "Here's my resignation from coaching with the Major League Braves and from my umpiring duties. I'm sorry about giving up the umpiring, but I don't want a conflict of interest, and there would be one even though I have no involvement in the Pony League."

He shook the men's hands. When he got to Murray Harper, he said, "Sorry about all this, but Fischer has no business working with children. Someone has to take a stand." He handed each of them his business card. "Call me anytime you want to discuss the matter."

"So you're through with us?" Murray Harper asked. "Hate to see you go, Mark."

"Maybe next year I'll umpire again," he hinted.

"Doubtful," Al Glenn murmured.

"Will we see you at the games?" Murray Harper asked.

Mark ignored the tightening in his chest, took a minute to clear his thoughts and forced himself to smile. "I'll be observing and taking notes at every Cubs game remaining in the season."

"How DID IT GO?" Nancy asked, beaming at Mark as he sailed through her door.

"Great! Like old times. God, I loved it." He kicked the door shut and grabbed her, swinging her around before letting her settle against him. "I love you, sweetheart," he murmured, then claimed her mouth with an intensity that sucked her breath away.

If her heart raced any faster, she feared she'd faint in his arms. "And I love you." Her facial muscles actually ached from smiling so broadly. "I missed you today."

"Why didn't you call?" he asked. "I was inside all day until my little visit with the Three Stooges. I considered giving you a call and kidnapping you from that old high rise."

She grinned. "Where would you have taken me?"

"Up to the highest point of Squaw Peak to just sit with you and watch the world go by. Would you have come with me?"

"Tempting, but I was terribly busy with a new client," she admitted.

He kissed her lightly. "Me, too. I had a steady stream of worried seniors with small complaints. Most of the problems I resolved over the phone. It's amazing how intimidating a lawyer can be when he sets his mind to it."

"A nice guy like you?" she teased, stroking his cheek and touching his sensual mouth.

"How anyone could take advantage of an older man is beyond me." He kissed the tip of her nose and she giggled.

"That's what I mean," she tried to explain, but the pulse at the base of his throat distracted her. "Only a nice-guy lawyer would think that way. I know too many lawyers who only see a buck to be made, a case to be won, a deal to be struck. You see the person to be helped."

He shrugged. "I like to win a case or strike a deal. That's what I've been doing today." He looked beyond her head. "I gave the league until the end of the season to reform Stan Fischer before we file the suit. I'd been thinking in the range of a quarter mil, only I didn't tell them that. They think we're aiming for a full million. We'll keep them guessing."

She stroked the escalating pulse at the base of his throat. "You play fair. That's another reason why I've always loved you, even in the old days when I wasn't supposed to."

His hands slid into the hair behind her ears. "I think I loved you back then, too."

"You loved me enough to let me go," she murmured. Her arms slid up around his neck, and she leaned against him, enjoying the closeness. "Oh, Mark." She took a step backward, and he followed her, his lips clinging to hers. When they bumped against her bed, they lost their balance and fell across it, still in each other's arms.

"What about dinner?" he asked, rolling onto his back and keeping her pressed against him.

"Dinner can wait."

"NOW TELL ME about the meeting," she demanded.

"What meeting?" His fingers traced circles on her naked shoulder. "You have the most delectable skin," he added, kissing her lightly.

"The meeting with the officials." She grabbed his hands and held them against the pillow, but his caresses had already led her thoughts astray. "You don't fall asleep anymore after we make love," she observed.

"It's a case of conditioning and survival," he explained. "I'm getting used to making love, and afterward, you won't let me sleep. You want to talk . . . like now."

"Poor baby," she teased. "Now tell me about the meeting." She propped herself on an elbow and waited, admiring his features. Sexy eyes, she thought. Nice brows, intelligent forehead, gorgeous hair. She'd always thought he had beautiful hair, but then she'd never been impartial regarding Mark. She drew a heart on his chest, avoiding the sensitive scar. "You have a very sexy body," she said. "It's long and lean and hard, but soft to the touch in all the right places. You bring me great pleasure and satisfaction, Mark. Just in case I forgot to tell you.''

He grew solemn but didn't reply.

''I could spend the rest of my life like this, simply looking at you,'' she continued.

He drew her closer until he could touch her lips. His kisses were usually filled with passion and desire, but this caress became so tender that it brought tears to her eyes.

They lay quietly for several minutes. ''Now tell me what happened at the meeting,'' she insisted. ''And no more distractions.'' She proved her determination by slipping from the bed and pulling on a pair of red shorts and a matching knit tank top. ''Let's eat. You can tell me over dinner.''

She jerked the covers back, exposing his naked body, grinned suggestively, then hurried to the small kitchen area of the studio apartment and began to shove dishes into the microwave, ignoring the rustling of clothing behind her.

He joined her. ''What's for dinner?''

She cocked her head. ''I made spaghetti with meat-less sauce, garlic toast and tossed salad. I'll warm the sauce.''

He lifted the lid on the sauce. ''From scratch?''

''I cook from scratch occasionally.''

''It saves tons of money when a person is on a tight budget,'' he said, as if speaking to himself.

''You need a microwave oven.''

''I can't afford one,'' he replied, leaning against the counter. ''My special diet is a drag for you, isn't it?''

She wanted to respond but hesitated to disturb their easygoing mood. Several minutes later they sat down at the small table.

"Now tell me what happened at your meeting," she ordered.

He described the men and their attitudes. "Murray Harper is supportive of our complaint. I'm going to work on him as a potential witness. Dale Redmond is a fence sitter, and Al Glenn is about as spineless a man as I've ever met. I gave my written resignation from the Braves and from umpiring." He stared at his spaghetti as he twirled it on his fork.

"You need the umpiring money, don't you?" she asked.

"No, everything's fine," he insisted. "I have some investments I've never cashed in. I'll manage."

"I can—"

"No!" He carried his plate to the sink.

She sat silently in her chair, hating the sudden tension between them. "I'm sorry, Mark. I never mean to offend you, but I always manage to, don't I?"

His hand dropped to her shoulder and she flinched.

"I guess we have a long way to go," he said, pulling her from the chair and into his arms.

"If we love each other, why do we disagree so quickly?" she asked, burying her face against his chest.

He led her to the sofa and pulled her down beside him. "Pride. For me it's old-fashioned male pride. Since meeting you, I get angry all over again about not being able to make the income I once did."

"But you said once that you were debt-free. That must make it easier to manage."

"But there's no future for me," he explained. "Damn it, I used to bill from two hundred to four hundred dollars per hour. Now I get from twenty to forty dollars, and most of that comes from government grants."

"You have the satisfaction of knowing you're helping people in need."

"Platitudes, mere platitudes, Nan. Satisfaction doesn't pay the utilities or buy the groceries. Remember that fancy little blue sports car I had?"

She nodded. "It was my favorite."

"Mine, too, but it was the first item I sold," he said. "Next I sold half my furniture, followed by the house itself. I have nothing to offer you."

"I'm not asking for anything."

"But a man needs potential, a financial future in order to offer a woman something permanent."

"I have my own career, Mark. I don't need financial security from a man. I love you, and for now that's enough."

"I can barely afford a simple gold ring, and I certainly can't afford a fancy diamond," he said.

She pulled away to stare at him.

He gazed at her. "If I had something to offer you, I'd ask you to marry me, but we have no money to fall back on, we couldn't have children, and I could drop dead anyday."

"Oh? And what if I'd accept, anyway?"

"You'd be a fool."

"Try me." She rested her head against the sofa and studied him. "I'm committed to you, Mark. The legalities don't matter."

"Maybe not now, but they will someday," he countered.

"Then why don't we take them up when that day arrives."

Silence filled the room for several minutes. "We could exchange keys," he suggested.

She shook her head. "Not yet. You still need your privacy and I do, too. And if it doesn't work out, it would be awkward to ask for them back."

"So you have doubts?" he asked.

"Not for me, but until you're reconciled about your career we don't need to complicate matters. Maybe you're still healing. We can enjoy each other and work together on Sadie's case...and you can court me." She smiled softly and reached out to caress his cheek. "Will you stay with me tonight?"

"I'd be disappointed if you didn't want me to stay," he confessed. "But I'd always ask. Maybe we'll take turns. One night at my place, one night at yours."

"Wonderful," she said, sighing. "But I fly to Chicago the day after tomorrow. I'll be gone a week. Will you miss me?"

"You know I will. But we'll take advantage of tonight, and we'll have tomorrow at my place. Wait until you see the puppies. Their eyes are about to open and they've started to crawl around. They're making an old dog out of Belle. Keeping track of ten puppies at a time drives her crazy."

She snuggled against him again. "Let's cook dinner for your neighbor Horace—what was his name?"

"Moore," he replied. "You really want to invite Horace to dinner? He'd love that. He won't admit it, but he's lonely."

"Then please invite him," she said, excited about getting to know his neighbor better. "You decide on the menu and I'll come from work to your place and

we'll have fun. Then after Horace leaves, we can—''
she kissed his throat ''—make out. How does that
sound?''

"Making love to you is much more than simply
making out," he replied, nudging her face upward.
"Sometimes I feel as if I've given my soul to you, Nan.
You make me feel complete in a way so special that
words fail me."

CHAPTER FOURTEEN

NANCY LISTENED to the ringing of the phone at Mark's end. A month had passed since their dinner with Horace Moore. In the meantime Nancy's cases—including one that had taken her out of the state—had kept her too busy to do anything but work. She'd been able to find time to spend only two nights with Mark.

Now she found herself alone on a Saturday night, stuck in a hotel room in Boston, where she'd tracked down a reluctant witness on an important case. She could fly back to Phoenix, but she and Mark would have had only a few hours together, and part of that time would be spent driving back and forth between the airport and her or his place.

She considered inviting him to fly to Boston but knew he couldn't afford the airfare and wouldn't accept a complimentary ticket from her. They would have to be satisfied with a frustrating phone call.

"Yes? Hello," Mark said from thousands of miles away.

"Hi, it's only me," she replied, unable to keep the choking sound from her voice. "I miss you so much."

"I miss you, too. How's the case going?"

"As usual," she replied. "And yours? Did Fischer reform? Is the season over?"

"Ended this evening," he said. "The Cubs lost and ended their season with a one-and-ten record. Fischer threw a tantrum right on the field and made a perfect ass of himself. Then he lit into the girls, accusing them of jinxing the team. Can you imagine anyone doing that?''

"Did you keep notes?"

"I got all his insults but one," he replied. "They were all sexually oriented. He stormed off the field and didn't even bother to help pick up the equipment. The coaches and the kids all pitched in and helped. It's a shame Fischer doesn't realize what a good group of players he has. With a little encouragement they could have taken the championship."

"Now what?"

"He'll get served tomorrow morning," he explained. "I could tell by the end of the first week that he had no intention of changing, so I went ahead and prepared the complaint."

"When do you get a date on the court calendar?"

"That may be the hang-up," he admitted. "You know how crowded the docket is. This case may receive a low priority."

"What if the press picks up on it?" she asked. "Do you expect media coverage?"

"I don't know, but I've cautioned the Burns family about that possibility," he said. "We'll cope with that when and if it comes."

"How about you? Are you feeling fine?"

"Great. I've never felt better. If this case is any indication of how I'll do when I get back into the rat race, maybe I can reconsider my financial future. How about that?"

"We'll see, but don't overdo it, Mark. You tend to be a workaholic. Are you taking your medication?"

"Pretty much." There were a few moments of silence. "I've forgotten a few times, but Dr. Merrick said that wouldn't make a difference. When will you come home? Can I pick you up at the airport?"

"No, don't do that," she replied. "My plane gets in at four in the morning, so I'm going to bed and hibernate for a day. I always suffer from jet lag."

"Want me to come over and keep you company?"

"You'd be making love to a zombie."

"Who says we'd have to make love?"

She giggled. "We always seem to. Give me a few days to recover." She glanced at the tiny calendar in her checkbook. "Why don't you come over on Thursday evening? That gives me a day to sleep, two days to get reoriented at work and a day to straighten up the apartment. See you at six?"

"Wild horses couldn't keep me away, sweetheart," he replied.

MARK'S TELEPHONE RANG midmorning on Thursday.

His secretary called to him. "It's for you. She says it's important but wouldn't give me her name."

Mark nodded. "I'll take it. I'm sure it's Nancy Prentice. Would you close the door, please?" He waited, then picked up the receiver. "Nan?"

"Yes." Her voice sounded breathless and sensual.

They'd been apart for the better part of a month. He ached for her at night and longed for her during the days, wanting to share so many things with her. "I've missed you, honey."

"I know, and I hate to make this call because I've got bad news, Mark."

"Dinner is canceled." A wave of anger surged through him.

"The partners have called a staff meeting for this evening," she explained. "It includes dinner followed by a meeting that may last past midnight. They always run longer than scheduled. There's talk of another firm being brought in. I hope not. There are too many legal experts running around here already. They're like rats in a maze. I'm so sorry, Mark."

He swallowed his disappointment. "Tomorrow?"

"I'm afraid not. I have to go back to Boston. They booked me on a flight tomorrow afternoon. Then it's on to Chicago for a week. I'm going with two other attorneys. One is a partner. This is a very big case, Mark, and some of us will get promotions out of it. You know how important that is to a junior-grade counselor like me."

"Sure, a chance to live in the fast lane." He flicked his pencil against the desk to vent some of his irritation. "Call me when you get back . . . if you can find time."

"You're mad, aren't you?"

"Why would I be mad?" he replied. He took a few deep breaths and exhaled. "Of course, I'm mad, but I'll get over it. You have your career. I have mine. You know where you're headed. I know where I've been."

"You make it sound as if we're incompatible. Mark, what are you trying to say? I love you. My career has nothing to do with that. I never expected you to—you resent my job, don't you? That's not fair, especially now that you have a chance to move back into a full practice. Why are you acting like this?"

"Forget I said anything," he said, redirecting his anger inward. "Partners can make or break you, Nan, but don't forget your own personal ethics. Promise me that?"

"Why, of course," she replied, but her voice had grown cool. "I've got to go. My secretary is holding a call. I'll phone you from Boston."

"Sure, that's fine. Have a good trip. We'll find some other time to be together." He hung up and stared across the room at the closed door. He'd been insensitive to her predicament. He remembered how important each and every case was to a beginner's career. She couldn't simply walk away from it all.

But he had. No, that wasn't entirely true. He'd been struck down and dragged away and been given an ultimatum to change or die.

The room became a suffocating box, and he had to get outside for a breath of fresh air. To his disappointment his secretary followed him onto the large patio where an enterprising volunteer had painted a shuffleboard court. Several teams were involved in a tournament.

"Have some juice and a snack," his secretary, Joyce Adams, said. "It'll rejuvenate you."

He took the glass and two cookies that appeared to be filled with twigs and flakes. At times he hated the healthy diet he found himself bound to, but the cookies turned out to be tastier than they looked and his anger dissipated.

"Who's Nancy Prentice?" Joyce asked. "You've doodled her name on your calendar several times, but this was the first time she's called, isn't it? Is she the one who mashed your fingers?"

He frowned. "You weren't supposed to notice."

"Oh, I didn't," she replied. "Just the swollen knuckles and the purple bruises and the fact that you dictated all your changes instead of penciling them yourself. Is she important? Special?''

"Both," he admitted.

"Is she pretty?"

Mark's grin was lopsided. "I'm biased."

"Are you in love with her?"

"You cut to the quick, don't you, Joyce?" He took a gulp of the fruit juice, then made a face when it dawned on him that it was prune.

"Mark," she said, taking his arm and steering him away from the tournament players. "I think of you like one of my sons. I have six, you know. And whenever one of them was in love, I always knew it." She patted his arm. "We've worked together for almost a year now, and this is the first time I've seen you so easily distracted from your work."

"Have you been covering for me?"

She laughed. "I've had to, because Bertha, Carrie and Hazel have been asking me if something was wrong. You know how observant they are. Joe and Peter have been pumping old Horace about you, but Horace is a true and loyal friend. He's kept as mum as the Sphinx."

"Good," Mark said, walking with her into the neatly pruned rose garden at the back of the yard. "If I were healthier and sure of my future, I'd ask Nancy Prentice to be my wife. It's as simple as that, but until I can prove to myself that I have a future, the situation is in limbo." He glanced down at her. "I'd appreciate your keeping this confidential."

She smiled. "You know me better than that, Mark. I don't talk about a client's affairs or my boss's personal life. But if you ever need a sounding board, I'm available."

"Thank you," he replied.

She crumpled her paper cup into a ball. "There's enough gossip running around this place to keep us all occupied for years, Mark. Fortunately it's harmless, but I've never fed it before and I don't intend to start now. So remember, I'm here if you need me." With that she spun him around, and they returned to the office to help another client in crisis.

NANCY REPLACED the receiver with the utmost care, as if it might snap at her. Mark's response to her call had knocked her off stride and undermined her confidence that their relationship was growing stronger by the week.

How could he be so unfair when he of all people should understand why she loved the law?

Before she could change her mind she grabbed the receiver and punched out the digits of his office in Peoria. "May I speak to Mark," she said politely when a woman answered.

"Sure, but he's with a client," the woman replied. "Would you like to hold?"

"I . . . yes."

"Is this Ms. Prentice?" the woman asked, her voice warming.

"Yes, I hate to bother Mark, but . . ."

"He was a bit upset after your previous call," the woman said. "My name is Joyce Adams. I've worked with him since he came to our center. We all love Mark dearly around here. He deserved a string of good luck for a change. He's a miracle worker to the men and women here."

"Mark is a very special man," Nancy replied, reluctant to say more to a woman she'd never met. "He enjoys his work."

"I hope he's doing the right thing by taking on this outside case," Joyce said. "He's working much harder than he's ever done before. His hours are long, and I worry about that. Has his physician given his approval for this change?"

"I...I leave that up to Mark," Nancy replied. "I do see a change in him. He's alive again, enthusiastic. I think the challenge is good for him."

"Perhaps."

"You think he's making a mistake?" Nancy asked, feeling her composure begin to crack.

"Time will tell, my dear," Joyce replied, her tone growing cooler. "He's made a marvelous recovery and I...we all want him to find happiness."

"That's what I want for him also," Nancy said. "Is he free yet? I could call back."

"They're just leaving. Please wait."

She found herself on hold for a few minutes, then the line opened again.

"Nan?" Mark's voice sent a shiver down her spine. "I'm glad you called back. I'm sorry. I'm just disappointed, that's all. I wanted to...discuss some aspects of the Burns case with you. But I'll work them out."

"Do you have a date set for the pretrial conference?" she asked, wishing she could attend as his associate.

"Two weeks from Monday," he replied. "I'm asking for depositions from Fischer and league officials. Fischer's attorney has already requested depositions from Sadie and her father, of course, as well as from the other girl and several of the male players on the team. He seems to be targeting your nephew Chuck.''

''Why?'' she asked, concerned for her nephew.

''The opposition may try to make an issue over a budding romance,'' Mark explained. ''You should see those two. I went over to Sadie's house, and Chuck was hanging around. It reminded me of those awful days of being sixteen, all the insecurities, the zits, every little problem becoming monumental.''

''I can't imagine you ever having a zit, Mark.''

He chuckled again. ''I had one the night of my senior prom when I wrangled a date with the homecoming queen. Justice prevailed. She had one, too.''

They laughed and the tension eased.

''Nan?''

''Yes, Mark?''

''I love you.''

She sighed deeply. ''And I love you.''

''You shouldn't have to put up with my crappy disposition.''

''Let me decide that,'' she replied. ''Mark? I have a meeting to go to and a brief to outline. I've got to go, but please don't ever get mad at me because of my work. Promise?''

He hesitated. ''I'll do my best.''

''I'll be back in a week. Wait for me?''

''Call me. If I'm not here, try the house. Sometimes I take off early and work at home. Belle says hi.''

She smiled. ''How is she? Oh, Mark, I've only seen the puppies twice since they were born.''

''They're eight-weeks-old now and ready to sell if I can bear to part with them, but having nine scampering dogs underfoot is too much. Even Belle is beginning to think so.''

"Nine? Did one die?" she asked.

"I sold one for three hundred dollars," he replied. "One goes to the owner of the male. I'm running an ad in Sunday's newspaper. By the time you get home, they may be all gone."

"Take care, Mark, and think of me?" she asked.

"Always."

CHAPTER FIFTEEN

MARK BRADFORD STOOD at the kitchen counter, staring at his vial of prescription medication. He reached for the can that contained the special cholesterol-reducing powder. He'd been instructed to mix a glass twice a day. He couldn't remember the last time he'd drunk a glass.

His chest tightened. *Psychosomatic,* he thought, rubbing the scar lightly with his fingertips. He picked up the plastic vial again and read the date. Normally he refilled it monthly, but the date on the vial was more than two months old. When he shook the container, it rattled with pills.

He couldn't possibly have forgotten to take his medication for more than a month. True, he'd become a little lax, skipping a day here and there, but a whole month? No, the pharmacist must have made a typographical error.

He mixed a glass of the powder and used the liquid to wash down one of the pills, vowing to be more careful in the future. The doorbell rang as he set the glass in the sink. He hoped it wasn't Horace. He enjoyed the older man's company, but not tonight. Nancy's plane was due in at six. He'd offered to meet her, but she'd insisted that she'd take a cab and go directly to her apartment and sleep. He didn't even expect a phone call until tomorrow.

When he jerked the door open, a flushed, incredibly beautiful Nancy Prentice stood on his doorstep, out of breath with excitement and teary-eyed with joy.

"May I come in?" she asked.

He grabbed her travel bag and small carry-on case, then stepped aside and waved her in, unable to suppress his pleasure. "I didn't expect you."

"I couldn't stay away," she replied. "I decided at the last minute to come here instead of going home. The taxi cost me a fortune, but I'm still on an expense account." She gazed at him and her eyes shimmered. "Oh, Mark, I missed you so much."

Still caught off guard by her unexpected appearance, he couldn't think of a word to say to her.

She tossed her purse onto a nearby chair and turned to him. "Do you think you could offer a little solace and comfort to an overworked colleague and devoted friend?"

He grinned. "Would a kiss and a hug do?"

"That'll do fine."

He drew her close, rejoicing in the soft comfort her body provided him and the tender, responsive kiss she gave him. "Hungry?" he asked.

"No, I ate on the plane over Colorado, but I could use a glass of lemonade and a slurpy kiss from Belle."

He pulled her close and walked her into the kitchen, where he poured the glass and watched her drink, savoring each little movement she made. She belonged here, in his home, in his kitchen. He knew that, but could he bring himself to ask her? And would she be receptive to his proposal? Now she had subsidized travel, gourmet meals on an expense account, rich clients and high-profile cases that could mean so much to her future.

He turned away, knowing he had no right to ask her to give all that up. Providing legal work to impoverished clients could hardly compete with what she already had.

She sat the glass down. "Can I see Belle and the puppies now?"

"Sure." He guided her outside, and they spent the next hour playing with the puppies.

"I've sold four more of them," he said. "They'll be leaving this weekend." He handed her a pup and watched while she played with it, holding it against her breast and nuzzling it cheek to cheek. *She'd make a wonderful mother,* he thought. *She deserves the chance.*

"What are you going to do with all the money you make on the puppies?" she asked.

"Put it into a building fund. Someday I want to add on to this place."

"How?" she asked, giggling when the puppy licked her nose.

"I don't know, but there's lots of space in the backyard for a room or two. If I build, I won't have so much to mow."

"Something practical, functional," she offered. "Maybe a second bathroom and another bedroom...or an office."

He nodded but let the subject drop. "I didn't expect you."

"I've been away too long," she said. "I came to reclaim my territory." She blushed. "I half expected you to have someone else to keep you company. I admit to being a tiny bit jealous at the prospect of competition."

He chuckled. "No one else could take your place, Nan. You're one of a kind. Tell me about the trip."

She hit the highlights, then inquired about the Burns trial.

"The pretrial conference is set for 10:00 a.m. on Monday," he told her. "It's been bumped twice. I've researched all the precedents and have my strategy laid out. Remember how you used to help me diagram the trials?"

"Do you still do that?" she asked, smiling fondly. "I do that sometimes, too, but did you know that most lawyers don't?"

"They should," he replied, reaching for her hand. "Sometimes I remember how well we worked together and wish I could offer you a partnership. Bradford and Prentice, how does that sound?"

"Why not Prentice and Bradford?"

"How about Bradford and Bradford?" His suggestion startled him as much as her.

"That sounds as if it might have possibilities . . . someday. But I thought we were going to take it easy and slow. The last time we discussed this you said you could barely afford a ring." Her cheeks paled as she put the puppy back with the others.

"I could get something with the proceeds of a dog sale."

She shook her head. "Save it for your building project. But thanks for suggesting the merger." She smiled across the puppies at him. "Someday, Mark, I'd consider it a privilege to practice with you as an associate, but let's table it for now. At the moment I'd like to have you hold me and kiss me and love me."

WHEN SHE AWOKE, Nancy rolled into Mark's arms, savoring the pleasure of being next to him. "You feel so good to wake up with," she murmured. "I never knew how wonderful it would be to simply lie in a man's arms, but not just any man. It had to be you. You make me feel so alive, yet at peace."

He mumbled against her hair, then placed a finger against her lips. "Quiet. We have fifteen minutes before the alarm goes off."

She pulled away. "Is that time enough to make love again?"

"Doubtful," he said, nuzzling her ear, "but we could try."

She pulled free. "On second thought let's wait." She gazed down at him. Her love for him grew with each hour they spent together, and when they were apart, she ached for him, not in a sexual way, but from deep in her emotional core. If their lives were threatened, she'd gladly give hers in order to save his. Was that obsession? No, she decided, it was unselfish love for another treasured human being.

"Meet me at my place at six," she suggested.

"Sounds great." He nibbled at her lips, then gave her a quick kiss. "It's good to have you back, Nan."

Reluctantly she slid from the bed. "I hate to run, but I've got to get home to shower and dress for work. It's back to the grind for this working gal. You busy today?"

"Some tax problems, a legal matter involving Supplemental Security benefits, and a deposition for the Burns trial," he said. "The league president, Mr. Al Glenn. I want to press him against the wall and make him squeal."

"Go get 'em, tiger," she purred.

He stood up, his body perfect except for the long incision. For a lingering moment she wanted to call in sick, but knew she couldn't risk it. "Go get dressed, handsome, before I change my mind and suggest we ravage each other again."

He grinned and covered himself playfully, then sailed into the shower.

"I'm leaving, Mark," she called through the closed bathroom door. "See you tonight."

"Yo," he called back.

With an aching heart she slipped from the house and drove to her apartment, resenting the intrusion of their daily lives.

"NANCY, THIS JUST CAME for you. It's from Mr. Jennings's office. Didn't you go with him and Kevin Scott to Chicago?" Her secretary, Louise Anderson, lingered near her desk. "Shall I wait?"

Nancy glanced up from the brief she was editing and accepted the envelope. "Mr. Jennings was in charge of everything back there. Kevin's a nice guy." She put down the envelope and continued her editing.

"Aren't you going to read it?" Louise asked.

"When I finish," Nancy replied absently. "Louise, I need you to start revising this brief just as soon as I finish. It was due yesterday, but isn't everything?"

An hour later she handed Louise the heavily notated document and started back to her desk, but decided to detour to the coffee corner.

Kevin Scott blocked her way when she turned to leave. "Did you get a memo?" he asked.

She gazed over the rim of her steaming mug at the black-haired man with brown eyes. "Yes, but I haven't read it yet."

He grinned like a Cheshire cat. "Maybe you should. We're about to take a step up the ladder."

Her eyes widened. "Really? Was it actually a—cripes, I don't really know the protocol for this kind of thing."

"I don't, either. The junior partners are tight-lipped about it. I asked around, and all one would say was that if we refuse to accept Jennings's offer, we may never get another one." Kevin extended his hand. "This may be a bit premature, but congratulations, Nancy. We've earned it."

Nancy hurried back to her office and closed the door. Could they really be considering her for a junior-level partnership position? She'd only been with the firm for a year and a half. Several of the men had been moved up, but no women. Yet Sylvester Jennings had seemed impressed with her work in Boston and Chicago.

Perhaps this was her lucky day. To wake up in Mark Bradford's arm and then get her first significant promotion, all in one day? *Too much to expect, but miracles can happen,* she thought, reaching for the sealed envelope.

Pulling out the single sheet of paper, she unfolded it, smoothed it out flat on her desk and, taking a deep breath, scanned the letter. Her heart sank.

"Dear Ms. Prentice," it began. *Not even a friendly "Dear Nancy"?* She stared at the first paragraph.

"During our stay in Chicago, you mentioned that you had a friend, Mark Bradford. I believe he used to be a junior partner at Burnside, Bailey, Summerset and Zorn. Please come see me regarding a favor I have to ask of you, this afternoon if possible." It was signed simply "Jennings."

Puzzled, she studied the letter again. Kevin Scott may have received a promotion offer, but she certainly hadn't. Sylvester Jennings was only curious about Mark. He obviously knew something about Mark, because he knew the name of his former firm. That being the case, Jennings probably also knew that Nancy had worked there for years before returning to law school.

What did the senior partner really want? she wondered. Did he want to feel her out as to Mark's willingness to return to full-time practice? Was he about to offer Mark a position in the firm? If so, would Mark be interested?

Swallowing her disappointment about the note's lack of promise regarding her own career, she took a sip of coffee, picked up a notepad and pen and headed toward the corner office. If Syl Jennings was about to feel her out regarding Mark's willingness to return to a prestigious firm, she was sure he'd be thrilled at the prospect, but she'd best suggest they contact him directly.

Syl Jennings's suite flaunted the disparity between the haves and have-nots within the firm, she thought. Elegantly paneled in walnut with antique furnishings that Nancy was hesitant even to sit on, the office did nothing to settle her nerves. It seemed aloof and much too formal to be hospitable to a mere mortal.

Syl Jennings's executive secretary, an older woman whom everyone called Swanson, glanced up. "Oh, Ms. Prentice, Mr. Jennings is waiting for you. I'll tell him you've arrived." She smiled, but it held no warmth, then murmured into the headset she wore. "You may go in now."

Cautiously Nancy turned the gold knob and eased the heavy door open. The cavernous inner office, with its two walls of glass that overlooked the north-central corridor of downtown Phoenix, was dimly lit with several lamps, but the paneling seemed to suck up the light and take away any warmth from the elegant room.

"Sit down, Ms. Prentice," Jennings said, getting to his feet and offering her a seat on the long brocade sofa that filled most of one paneled wall. "I've been waiting."

"I had to finish revisions on a brief so my secretary could get the corrections into the system, sir," she said. "I'm sorry if I've held you up."

"We need to discuss a matter that's rather... sensitive in nature." He waited until she found a comfortable position on the sofa before he sat down a few feet from her.

"I thought it might be about the case we're working on," she said. "Kevin said he—" She regretted revealing her conversation with the other attorney.

Jennings scowled. "Did...Mr. Scott discuss the memos?"

She shook her head. "No, of course not, just that he received one. I jumped to a conclusion." She smoothed the fabric of her suit skirt over her knees and willed her hand to stop trembling. "I was wrong in my assumption. What can I do for you, Mr. Jennings?"

"How well do you know Mark Prentice?" he asked.

"Quite...well," she admitted. "He's a good friend. He has been for years."

"Does he ever discuss his cases with you?"

She frowned. "He gave up his practice, other than a few simple cases," she said. "He does mostly tax work, counseling, things like that for senior citizens. He lives . . . he doesn't live in Phoenix anymore."

"Yes, I know. He has a home in Peoria." He chuckled. "I didn't think Peoria existed anymore."

She waited, growing leery of the man's motive.

"I knew of him from before his . . . little problem," Jennings explained. "Bob said he had a brilliant future ahead of him. Bob Summerset is a longtime associate of mine and we golf together. We've both grown up in the legal profession in this town and paid our dues before the boom days. A person should never forget those debts of gratitude from times gone by. He helped me once with a mutual friend."

"Who?" A cold chill raced through her.

"A man you probably don't know. Nate Weller was a businessman in town from the old days. We all grew up together, back when life was simpler. He had a legal problem and needed some good representation. Bob assigned the case to Bradford. Bradford never got to finish the trial, but old Nate was found innocent because of Bradford's enthusiastic presentation of the case. The jury was swayed by that young man, let me tell you. I sat in on the trial as much as I could, so I saw your friend in action."

He shook his balding head. When a long strand of dyed black hair slid down over one ear, he smoothed it into place again across his pate. "Too bad he left the firm. So, my girl, that's why I need you."

Nancy fidgeted on the sofa, easing away from the man.

"Recently he's taken a case that could prove embarrassing to a client of Bob's," he explained.

"Who's the client?"

"The client's name is confidential," he replied. "It's hardly the kind of case Bob can handle himself...you know him."

"I haven't seen or talked to Mr. Summerset since I resigned," she said. "That was over four years ago."

"Bob had a stroke last summer, and he's taking it easier," Jennings explained. "But he remembered that you and this Bradford fellow were, well, close. Bob and the other partners assumed you two were... involved, but that's neither here nor there, is it? You see, my dear, when a friend like Nate Weller—"

"*He's* the client?"

"No, but Bradford's handling of the Weller case is part of the problem." He smiled and draped his arm along the back of the sofa. "You see, my dear, the man still has this sterling reputation for winning cases. Bob has a client who is the son of a longtime friend, well, a friend of Bob's and myself and Nate's, too, actually. Our mutual friend went into salvaging and made a fortune, then upgraded his investments into a chain of do-it-yourself type lumber and hardware stores. You'd recognize the name, but I won't burden you with it. Now his son runs the operation, and Junior doesn't have quite the touch his father had."

She eased closer to the end of the sofa. "How does Mark Bradford fit into all this?"

Jennings's brown eyes narrowed, and he stared for several seconds into Nancy's. "Mr. Bradford is the attorney who represents the plaintiff in the matter."

Recognition clicked in her mind. "Are we talking about Fischer of the Fischer Home Centers? I never made the connection before. Stan Fischer is the owner of that chain of do-it-yourself stores? No wonder he can afford to donate to the league." She shook her head.

"Yes, yes, that's the company, and Stan Junior is the client. He's a fine man, who's done a lot of good for the community over the years. It's a ridiculous case, actually, nothing more than an irritation, but the girl and her father apparently want to make an issue out of it and publicly embarrass Stan Junior. Bob has assigned two junior partners to the case, but they want to avoid media attention."

Her premonition shifted to enlightenment. "So you actually know this Stanley Fischer? Maybe the case has merit."

He shook his head. "Sexual harassment can be so easily misconstrued." The wayward strand of hair slid down to lodge on the sidepiece of his glasses, and he smoothed it back into place. "I would never ask you to do this for one of our clients, but since Bob is my friend and he used to be your employer... Bob and I discussed it and felt you might be a likely subject to help us."

An unpleasant taste filled her mouth, and she fought to avoid letting her features reveal her dismay.

He mistook her silence for acceptance. "Talk to Bradford and find out his strategy," he continued. "See if he has a key witness he plans to spring on us." He held his hand up. "I know, I know, he'll have to reveal all his potential witnesses, but we want to be sure we can... excuse me... they can win the case, or better yet, have it thrown out during pretrial conference. The case has no merit."

"How do you know?"

"Few sexual harassment cases do," he replied blandly. "Frankly a girl has no business playing baseball at that age. She might get hurt. Then she'd sue."

"She's suing, anyway," Nancy reminded him.

"Whatever," he said, waving her remark aside. "Will you help us, my dear? It could mean a lot to me...and to your progress in this firm. You show promise, but there are a few dozen eager and bright males competing for the limited number of promotions to be handed out."

You bastard, she thought. *You want me to spy on Mark?*

"Ask him how the case is going and keep us informed," he said. "How often do you see the man?"

"Occasionally."

"Can you make it more frequent?"

She smiled, unable to hide the pleasant prospect of spending more time with Mark. "I can try."

"Good. Then it's settled. We'll expect a report by Friday. Action starts heating up on Monday." He got to his feet. "Thank you, young lady. You won't regret this."

"Mr. Jennings, I didn't promise."

"Now, now, all we're asking is that you do your best. Are you happy here?"

Surprised, she couldn't think of a reply.

"You *do* want a future with this firm, don't you? Something that's more lucrative than the entry level?"

"I'm already past that," she reminded him. Grabbing her pad and pen, she worked her way to the door. "No promises." She broke into a run once she closed his door behind her, and didn't stop until she found refuge in her own office.

THE BURNS CASE was postponed a week. Jennings has stuck his head into Nancy's office at midweek to let her know that she still had time to make her report. She ignored him.

All her days ended with time alone with Mark. The evenings and nights together had become special times for getting to know each other. They went for long walks and discussed the Burns case. If he'd taken on a particularly prickly case from the center, he'd used her as a sounding board, and she'd give him the name of someone within the court system she felt might be able to cut through the red tape.

Gradually they were laying down a foundation of trust and loyalty, and at work she seldom lingered after quitting time.

Now, on late Friday, she shoved some papers into her attaché case and made ready to leave. Louise knocked on the door and Nancy glanced up. "Come in."

"Jennings's secretary delivered this. Said it's important. What's all this secret memo business? Are you spying on the enemy for the boss?"

Nancy's head jerked up.

Louise laughed. "Just kidding. See you tomorrow, honey. Good to see you going home at a normal hour for a change. Is there a new man in your life?"

Nancy's mouth opened, then closed as she decided not to take the bait.

Louise left for the day, but Nancy lingered in her office and ripped the envelope open, curious about the contents of this latest missive from the powerful man in the corner office.

"Bring us Bradford's strategy on the Burns case and I, personally, promise to put in a few persuasive words in favor of your next promotion." Once again the note was signed "Jennings."

She shoved the letter and its envelope into her purse. Within minutes she was in her little red automobile and on her way home. Mark would be arriving at six. They'd go for a swim, then barbecue something on a tiny hibachi on her even tinier balcony.

WHEN MARK RANG her doorbell, he was twirling a pair of swim trunks in one hand and held a small bouquet of mixed summer flowers in the other.

She beamed. "You bought me flowers?"

He stepped inside and kicked the door shut with his heel. "They're from Horace Moore's flower garden. He said they're a thank-you for the wonderful chicken cacciatore you served him a few weeks ago."

"Tell him thank you," she replied, recalling the wonderful evening they had spent with his neighbor. Now it seemed so long ago. "Ready to swim?" she asked.

"Yep. If I kiss you once, we'll never get to the pool."

She grinned. "You're probably right. No touchy-feely until after we've eaten."

"What's on the menu?"

"I precooked chicken to barbecue on the grill and we can make vegetable shish kebabs," she said, pretending to lick her lips. "Add a tossed salad and some low-fat sherbert and, voilà, we have a scrumptious meal!"

She waved him to the bathroom to change and did the same near the bed, hoping he'd take long enough to allow her to switch. If he saw her naked, she'd probably come toward him, and he'd touch her, and she'd kiss him and slide into his arms, and they'd never get to the pool.

Two hours of playing and swimming were followed by twenty minutes in a Jacuzzi. Exhausted, they slowly strolled arm in arm back to her apartment. He lit the charcoal in the grill, and she dropped the pieces of chicken onto the rack once the coals were glowing. They laughed as they speared the various pieces of vegetables onto long metal rods and laid them on the grill.

"I wish we could eat out here, but it's still pretty hot," she said. "I'll go set the table and pour the drinks. Can you have wine tonight? Everything else is so healthy."

"Tonight is special," he said, glancing toward her. "Tonight calls for wine and flowers and kisses . . ."

"And loving and holding and touching?" she asked.

His smile was answer enough.

MARK LAY ON HIS BACK, staring at the ceiling. Nancy lay curled on her side, sleeping soundly.

Still suffering from lingering jet lag, she'd apologized for her continual yawning, but had encouraged his lovemaking, not only responding to his every caress, but at times taking the initiative herself. Afterward, as they'd lain in each other's arms, he'd told her about his progress on Sadie Burns's case.

When she asked about Fischer's counsel, he'd chuckled. "Our old firm, Burnside, Bailey, Summerset and whoever. They assigned it to two of their underlings who are so cocky and arrogant that I'll consider it a pleasure to knock them off. If the judge is fair and the jury isn't biased, there's no way we'll lose this one.''

He'd planned to give her the ring he'd bought earlier in the day, but between making love and discussing legal matters, he hadn't found the right time or mood. He'd missed his first chance right after they finished dinner. The wine had given them both a glow, and he'd considered retrieving it from the pocket of his jeans, but she'd kissed him, and then one thing had led to another... Now she was asleep.

He'd give it to her over breakfast.

An hour passed and still he couldn't sleep. He got up and removed the small velvet case from his jeans and opened it. As he stared down at the plain gold band, he wished he'd been able to swing something more elaborate.

Maybe someday he'd give her a diamond to go with it. He hoped she'd understand. He put the box on the nightstand and lay back down.

His chest felt heavy tonight. He decided it was tension. He'd been tense all day about the ring, wondering if was rushing her, if she'd think him silly, or if she'd throw her arms around his neck and kiss him wildly.

He got up again and went to the bathroom. Maybe if he read for a while, he could sleep. He sat down at her desk and scanned the books on a shelf above it.

Her purse blocked part of the shelf and, pushing it out of the way, he retrieved a nonfiction volume about the history of British common law. *So I suppose this is your leisure time reading, right, Nan?* Smiling, he glanced over his shoulder at her sleeping form, her bare arm stretched across her pillow, the sheet barely covering her breasts. He found her irresistible asleep or awake.

He slipped the book back into place and scanned for a different subject. Her purse blocked his way again, and he moved it once more. The clasp fell open, and as he tried to close it, an envelope and a folded piece of stationary popped up as if it had been crammed into the purse haphazardly.

The return address on the envelope read Staley, Jennings and Kaufman. It was addressed to Nancy but didn't have a mailing address or a stamp. He frowned, recalling that when he asked about her day, she'd hedged and changed the subject. Was this the reason? Did this crumpled letter contain upsetting news? A promotion? That wouldn't upset her. She'd be bursting with pride and would have told him. Surely not a dismissal.

Curiosity got the better of him, and he slid the paper from the purse, knowing he had no right to read it.

He unfolded the sheet and smoothed it out. As he read, his heart sank into the pit of his stomach. "Bring us Bradford's strategy on the Burns case and I, personally, promise to put in a few persuasive words in favor of your next promotion." It was signed by a man named Jennings, the first name listed on the left column of the letterhead.

You're stepping in with high-powered company, Nan, he thought. *How did you get to be so important so quickly?* He read the message again, then slowly turned to stare at the woman asleep several feet from him. *Bring us Bradford's strategy?* Is that why she'd let him do most of the talking? Was she willing to break the bond between them to get ahead in her work? *Unethical, Nan.*

Hadn't they talked about ethics and morality and conscience and the price a person paid for violating his principles? Of course they had.

Disappointment made his temples pound. He'd told her everything, spilled it all in his eagerness to share his strategy with her. But how was Stan Fischer's legal counsel involved with Staley, Jennings and Kaufman? Did a relationship exist between the two firms? He'd check around.

He refused to let a novice attorney, even one as sharp as Nancy Prentice, wreck his case, not after all the hard work and long hours he'd put into it.

He had to get out of Nancy's stifling single-room apartment and get a breath of air before...before what? The knowledge that she'd betrayed him after all that had happened between them sickened him, bringing a pain from deep within his body.

His arm ached, and he stopped dressing in order to massage it, but no relief came. He snapped the fastener on his jeans and returned to the desk. Running a hand through his rumpled hair, he fought the urge to scream and shout, to wake her, demanding to know why she'd committed such a mortal sin against him. But as he took deep breaths, fighting to keep his composure, he knew why. It was simply a matter of priorities.

He'd let Nancy sway him from his course, coax him back into the practice of law, and then she'd turned the tables on him once she'd gotten what she'd wanted—a step up the corporate ladder in one of the largest legal firms in the greater Phoenix area.

He grabbed a pen and wrote across the face of the letter: "Take it. You won't get a better offer. It's more than I could ever give you."

He couldn't bring himself to sign his note more than "M. Bradford." He glanced at the bed one last time. He should have known she had some ulterior motive for getting involved with a cripple like himself. He'd been a fool. But no more.

CHAPTER SIXTEEN

ALL THE WAY HOME Mark could feel his heart thumping harder and harder. If he didn't get himself under control and settle down, he'd have to give Dr. John Merrick a call for some help.

He couldn't remember ever being so incensed, but the pain that encircled him as he drove the old truck into his driveway was more than simple anger. Nancy had used him, and he couldn't forgive her for that.

He didn't want to see her ever again, or hear from her, or listen to her pleading for forgiveness. But then she was a proud woman, and he doubted she'd ever ask for his forgiveness or his understanding. What was there to understand? What she'd done was ethically and legally wrong.

He let himself into the quiet house and gazed around. He'd expected to feel solace and security, but only loneliness and isolation greeted him.

He slid his hand into his pant pocket to retrieve the jewelry box with the gold ring. He'd wasted his last umpiring check on the damn thing. His fingers came out empty, and he realized he'd left it on Nancy's nightstand. He ran his hand through his hair in frustration. There would be no chance to retrieve it now. Oh, God, why hadn't he grabbed it before he'd charged out of the place?

In his bedroom he stripped down to a pair of jogging shorts and a faded gray sweatshirt. When he
yanked on the laces of his running shoes, one broke
and he cursed beneath his breath as he tied the frayed
ends into a clumsy knot.

He grabbed the leash and went into the backyard,
whistling softly to Belle. "Want a break from those
kids, old girl?"

Belle wagged her tail as if to thank him for rescuing
her. Three nine-week-old puppies yapped excitedly,
scampering up to him and standing on their hind legs,
their paws perched on his bare calves. All three had
been sold to out-of-town owners who would be picking them up within the week. "Not this time, boys,"
Mark said softly.

He eased the pups aside and let Belle slip through
the narrow opening into the house, then followed her
out the front door and into the predawn darkness.

He lost track of the miles and time until he spied the
neon sign of the old café a mile from the ballpark.

He glanced at his watch. Five-thirty. Still well before the customary breakfast crowd. Only a few in-
somniacs were inside at this hour, taking their first
dose of caffeine for the day.

The manager waved to Mark and Belle, motioning
them to a back booth. Belle crawled beneath the table
and circled before lying down almost out of sight.

"How ya doin', Mark?" the gray-haired owner
asked, pouring him a cup of decaffeinated coffee.
"The usual?"

Mark shrugged, but when the Egg Beater omelet
arrived, he picked at it, finally leaving half of it on his
plate.

An hour and a half later Mark was home again. The walk had failed to revitalize him. After a shower, he dressed in brown slacks, a tan short-sleeved dress shirt and a colorless new tie his sister had sent him. The shower hadn't done anything to energize him, either. He often walked to the senior citizens center, but today he didn't think he could make it.

He climbed into his battered blue truck and, once at the center, busied himself reading through the three legal pads of questions and answers he'd collected from his four star witnesses: Sadie Burns, her teammates Chuck Andrews and Amber Todd, and Sadie's father, Sam Burns.

The first of several pretrial conference sessions would take place early in the coming week, and he didn't want any surprises. Last week he'd deposed Stan Fischer, and the three other league officials and a perturbed regional official who had expressed his dismay over the local problem.

The man's expert testimony as to the overall goals and objectives of the worldwide program reassured Mark that Stan Fischer was an aberration. He felt confident about the strength of his case.

Sadie Burns had been denied her civil rights and suffered sexual discrimination and harassment, but thank God there was no sign of anything worse. Mark felt confident that a jury would be swayed by the facts of the case, and within two weeks they should be in the courtroom selecting that jury.

He glanced at his watch. Nancy would be up by now, possibly holding the box with the ring. More likely she'd find his note telling her to go ahead and spill the beans to Jennings.

An image flashed through his mind—Nancy's blue eyes shimmering with disbelief, Nancy racing to the telephone to call him and plead for his forgiveness. He shook his head. There had been a time when that might be what she'd do, but she'd hardened since earning her degree and stepping into the legal world. She'd only pretended to be the same sweet little Nancy Prentice whose smile could make his pulse pound.

His secretary Joyce arrived. "How long have you been here?"

"From about eight," he admitted.

"You okay?" she asked. "You don't look so good."

"I couldn't sleep."

She peered at him. "Work can be good for a troubled soul."

He chose to ignore her remark. "Hold all my calls, please."

"Even if Ms. Prent—"

"Especially if Ms. Prentice calls."

She squinted at him. "You hiding out from her, boss?"

"I'm busy, and so are you if you know what's good for you." He picked up his pen again and tried to concentrate on the chicken scratches on his legal pad.

"Well, *excuse* me," she said, putting her hands on her ample hips. "Are you looking for trouble, young man, or have you already found it?"

He sat at his desk, staring stonily at the yellow pads.

"You've had a lover's spat," she guessed.

"Leave it be," he warned.

"Touchy this morning, aren't you? Well, I don't care what the reason is. There's no reason to take your frustration out on me. I came to help."

He took a deep breath. This woman was one of the finest secretaries he'd ever worked with, but at times her bluntness grated. "I'm sorry. You're right, Joyce. I've got too much on my mind these days. Please take calls so I can get some work done. Okay?"

Joyce grinned. "Sure thing. And if Ms. Prentice does call, I'll make an excuse. She's always pleasant to talk to. I'm sure she's very nice and—"

"Enough, Joyce." He began to make careful notations down the left column of the first pad, pretending to ignore the older woman's curious gaze.

She gave up her effort to cheer him up and turned to leave. "Anyway, whatever's gone wrong, I think you should apologize. What do you have to lose?"

"My self-respect," he mumbled.

"Mark Bradford, you sound like a priggish snob. It's not like you at all." She leaned over his desk. "What's really wrong? Maybe I can help."

He leaned back in his chair. "She screwed up and I screwed up," he admitted. "It's probably for the best."

She patted his hand. "Time heals all wounds, my dear. Give her time to realize how wonderful you are and she'll come around."

He chuckled cynically. "I'm not so wonderful sometimes. Now if you'll get out of here, maybe I can get some work done. And you're right. Time heals all wounds, so let's let time start its job. Could you get me a cup of decaf?"

NANCY PRENTICE DOUBTED there was a living nerve left in her body. When she found Mark's terse note scratched across the face of Jennings's memo, she'd stared at it for a full minute before the reality of its meaning sank in.

She'd staggered back to the bed and then her gaze had fallen on the shiny gold ring. When she picked up the velvet box and stared at it, her heart broke. If he loved her enough to buy a wedding ring, why didn't he care enough to let her explain the meaning of the memo?

Gradually her pain and disbelief slid into anger— anger at herself for not destroying the memo and anger at Mark for prying into her personal affairs. Why had he opened her purse, and why had he pawed through its contents and found the letter with its damning words?

And why had Mr. Jennings stooped so low as to suggest that she compromise her own principles in order to help another firm's case? A case involving a man who'd proven his own guilt without a doubt?

All the while she'd been in the shower she'd mulled over how best to deal with the problem. Obviously Mark had drawn wrong conclusions, and all she had to do was explain . . . if he'd give her a chance. He'd always been overly principled. That was one reason why she'd admired him all these years. Surely he would listen to her explanation.

She dressed and gave Mark a call at his home. Five minutes after eight on her watch. He usually didn't go to the center until 10:00 a.m. She dialed the center and let the phone ring a dozen times, but no one answered. It didn't officially open until nine, anyway.

Maybe he'd gone out to breakfast or next door to Horace's house for a cup of coffee. Pride prevented her from calling the older gentleman.

She folded the letter carefully and slipped it back into her purse where she'd thought she'd put it the previous night. How he'd found it still troubled her. Surely he hadn't rummaged through her purse? He didn't have a right to do that, regardless of how close they'd become. Not close enough, she thought, locking her apartment and walking slowly to the parking lot.

At the office she sought refuge in her cases. She called the center twice, but both times his secretary, Joyce, said Mark was in conference. Later the excuse changed to a business appointment. Nancy had the uneasy feeling Mark was merely avoiding her.

Jennings's offer had been just that—an offer. Why in the world would Mark think she'd stoop to such a low trick as to rat on him? Surely he knew she had more strength of character than that. If he didn't, then it was his problem, not hers.

The day dragged on.

She spent the next day in court. "Any messages?" she asked when she returned.

"Several," her secretary replied, handing her a stack of pink slips.

Nancy scanned them, but none was from Mark Bradford.

Another week passed. She spent three days in court and the other two working late. No messages from Mark. The knife he had plunged deep into her heart was twisted at the end of each day by his silence.

Jennings called her in for a brief meeting. "What have you learned from your friend?" he asked.

"I . . . haven't seen him lately," she replied. "Mr. Jennings, I don't think this is ethical."

"This isn't a matter of ethics, my dear," he said. "We're not representing either of the parties. If we can assist an associate in need, we should. Bob Summerset is my friend, your former employer. We have an obligation to help if we can. However, the case has been postponed another week, so you still have time. You can submit a written report on plain paper. Why don't you skip a signature and don't address it to me."

He smoothed a long strand back into place over his bald spot. "We wouldn't want anyone to jump to the wrong conclusion, would we? I'll pass it on to Bob and that will be that. We play a few rounds of golf tomorrow. Can you have it ready by then?"

She stared at him. Had he been that positive that she'd cave into his demand? "Mr. Jennings, I can't."

"What others don't know won't hurt anyone," he murmured, giving her an oily smile that made her feel dirty.

"It would hurt Mark Bradford and his client," she said.

"A little girl and a has-been lawyer?"

"A talented young player and a fine attorney," she countered. "They both deserve fair play."

"A nuisance case, nothing more. It's not worth the time we're spending on it."

"Then why involve me?" she asked.

"It's the simplest solution we could think of. Summerset says that Bradford was the sharpest young lawyer ever to come into the firm. Damn shame that he had to get so sick. Frankly Summerset thought he'd become permanently disabled. What brought him back to life?"

I did, she thought. She edged away from the sofa. "Mr. Jennings, I can't tell you a thing about Mark

Bradford or the case. We aren't seeing each other anymore, so I can't help you.''

"Too bad," Jennings murmured. "You could have profited greatly if you'd cooperated. Under the circumstances . . . too bad.''

A LIGHT TAP SOUNDED at her door, and Nancy glanced up from her desk to find Kevin Scott leaning against her doorjamb, grinning like a cat who'd just swallowed a goldfish.

"Did you hear about the promotions?" he asked. "You were gone all day, so I wasn't sure. Did you get your official notice yet? I never expected the senior partners to loosen up the purse strings and give us newcomers bonuses like—anyway, I know where mine's going. I've got my eye on a nifty little silver BMW, and now I can swing a cash offer. How about you?''

She tore her gaze from his beaming face. "I don't discuss my personal affairs with fellow employees, Kevin. Now I've got work to do. I'll be working late as it is. Okay?''

Puzzlement swept across his face, then disappeared. "Sure, Nancy. I didn't mean to pry, but all the others are boasting openly. I'm surprised you aren't, unless you . . . didn't—''

"Good night, Kevin," she insisted.

She waited another half hour after Kevin Scott left the office. Obviously she hadn't been one of the chosen few. Had she been excluded because of her refusal to cooperate? She had to know.

Jennings was still in his office reading a legal journal, and she tapped on the doorjamb to get his attention. He looked up and resettled a long strand of lacquered hair over his head.

"There's a lot of talk going around the firm this afternoon," she said.

He snickered. "Yes, I suppose it's hard for some of those Young Turks to keep things to themselves."

"Kevin Scott and Barney Rivers started the same day I did," she said, remaining by the door.

"Yes, and they're bright, eager young men, aren't they?"

"Brighter than I am?" she asked, not caring about diplomacy.

"Shall we say...*wiser?* Better sense of judgment?"

"Thank you," she said, straightening to leave. "I just needed to confirm it wasn't my performance, at least my legal performance."

"There's always another time, another way," he suggested, letting his gaze flicker over her body.

His remark didn't deserve a reply, she decided. Marching back to her office, she gathered her papers and shoved them into her attaché case and left the building.

NANCY SAT CURLED in a chair, staring at the flickering television screen. Two weeks had passed since she'd been rejected by the man she loved. Now she'd been rejected by the very man who had brought about the first rejection.

She'd given the firm her all since joining it a year and a half earlier. It seemed, though, that getting ahead didn't depend on talent and hard work, but on bending the rules or sleeping with the boss.

Her sister Linda called to invite her to Nichole's birthday party on the weekend, but Nancy begged off.

"Bring your umpire friend," Linda suggested.

"Maybe."

"Are you two still seeing each other?" Linda asked. "You missed a ton of fascinating gossip when he turned out to be an attorney and sued Fischer. The entire league, except for the president, is rooting for the Burns girl. Al Glenn just wants to avoid controversy. I hope they're both gone next year."

"How did the Braves end their season?" Nancy asked.

"They won six and lost six. Not bad considering," Linda said. "Nichole got a trophy for good sportsmanship at the league picnic. Remember? I invited you to that, too, but you didn't show up."

"Sorry."

"What's the matter, sis?"

"Just overworked," Nancy said, refusing to divulge her problems with Mark.

"Well, tell your good-looking ump hello from all of us and give him a kiss. We all loved him for the short while we had his services."

"Let's talk about something more cheerful," Nancy said. "How's the new baby?"

"Mary Beth is the best baby I've ever had," Linda purred.

Nancy chuckled. "You say that about all your babies. And Layne? How's her baby boy? I'm ashamed to admit that I haven't been over to see them yet."

"She's noticed, I'm sure, but she's so busy with her brood she hasn't had time to fret," Linda replied. "Send little Jeremy a couple of dozen diapers and Layne a handful of good paperback novels to read.

She says Jeremy hasn't learned to sleep much, so she's up around the clock.''

"Five children must be a handful," Nancy said, wondering if she would ever get a chance to experience motherhood. "Tell her I'm sorry and I'll get over there next week for sure. I'm busy, terribly busy."

"Nancy, Nancy, learn to take time to smell the roses, or you'll find yourself a lonely, embittered old woman before you know it." Linda added a few more choice words, leaving Nancy dejected with herself.

"I've got to go," she replied, hanging up seconds before she broke into uncontrollable sobbing. She turned off the television and went to bed, but sleep wouldn't come.

He has no right to treat me like this, Nancy decided. Tomorrow she'd confront him. Thanksgiving weekend was approaching. He'd be alone. Maybe she could offer to cook a turkey and they could spend the long weekend mending fences.

She shoved the idea aside. Horace would invite him over. If not Horace, then friends from the center. He could call her just as easily as she could call him.

Was he asleep right now? She rolled over onto her side and stared at the black silhouette of the telephone on her nightstand. Maybe she'd call him and let it ring just three times.

She turned on the night lamp and reached for the telephone, then stopped abruptly when her gaze fell on the blue velvet box. She opened it, removed the gold ring and slid it onto the third finger of her left hand. *Oh, for the dreams that might have been.* If she'd torn the letter up and thrown it away, and if he'd given her the ring, would they be husband and wife right now?

No, silly, it's only been two weeks. She tugged the ring off and put it back into the box. If she'd had any sense at all, she would have packaged it up and mailed it back to him. Then he'd know how she felt about his walking out. But as she turned out the light again and tried to sleep, she knew the most important thing in her life was to reestablish a relationship with Mark, regardless of the cost to her pride.

MARK SCOWLED across the desk at the two white-haired women who had insisted on seeing him.

"We don't care if Joyce says you're busy or not," Bertha Cashmore insisted. "You've not been your usual self, and we want to know what's wrong."

"Yes," her friend added. "We used to bring you cookies, and you'd at least show your appreciation, but now you don't even pretend to enjoy them. The last oatmeal cookies I brought you turned moldy and Joyce threw them out. What's wrong?"

"Ladies," Mark said, holding up his hands in supplication, "I'm sorry, but I haven't been . . . I've been busy."

"You're not feeling well," Bertha said.

"I'm fine," he insisted. If they knew how fatigued he'd felt lately, how heavy his chest became with the slightest exertion, how his left arm had begun to ache again, they'd have a fit and probably call an ambulance. Maybe that wouldn't be a bad idea, he conceded, but kept his thoughts to himself.

"I know the signs," Bertha insisted. "My George had three heart attacks."

He narrowed his gaze at the persistent woman. "And what are my signs?"

"You're gray unless you're flushed," she argued. "My George said you couldn't even finish a game of shuffleboard the other day. He told me right then and there to keep an eye on you."

Mark suppressed a grin. "Give George my thanks."

"You've lost your... zest! That's what it is, your zest." Bertha smiled, thoroughly satisfied at having put her finger on his problem.

"Unless it's a woman," her friend suggested. "Mark Bradford, are you having girlfriend troubles? Tell us the truth. Joyce is as closemouthed as a saint."

He chuckled. "Good for her."

"No, Hazel, it's not a girlfriend," Bertha said, putting her hand on her friend's forearm. "This is more serious. Mark, promise us you'll call your doctor and tell him how you feel. An ounce of prevention, you know."

"Can be a pound of cure," Hazel concluded.

"Yes, ladies, I promise," Mark said. "Now, unless you have a tax matter or a legal problem to discuss, I really do have work to do."

He watched as they fussed their way out of his office. Much of the time both women seemed scatterbrained, yet they had seen through his attempts to hide his condition. In addition to feeling beat each evening he'd been toiling with the problem of Nancy Prentice. He couldn't get her out of his thoughts.

At night he longed for her beside him. If she were there, he could share his concerns. In the past two days they'd become more than concerns. But when the pain went away he'd been able to convince himself that he'd imagined it all.

He'd finally gotten his prescriptions refilled, only to learn that he'd skipped more than two months' worth of the medication. Could that have caused his discomfort?

The telephone rang, and he reached for the receiver, but a twisting stab that started in his middle and shot up to lodge beneath his left shoulder blade sucked his breath away and doubled him over, making him feel as if a huge elephant were stomping on his chest. The telephone rang twice before Joyce answered it. Numbing fear immobilized him as he stared at the glowing light on the telephone and waited for it to go out.

He needed Joyce. He wasn't sure what she could do for him, yet when he tried to reach for the button to page her, his arm wouldn't respond. The scenario held an eerie sense of déjà vu for him. At least this time he was alone and wouldn't make a public spectacle. But ignorance had been bliss the last time. Now he knew the consequence of these messages his body was sending to his brain.

"I don't want to die," he murmured aloud. "Nancy, I'm sorry." He needed to call her, hear her voice, explain his mistake. He had no proof that she'd run back to Jennings and told everything. He was thirty-seven years old, and he didn't want to die until he'd had a chance to tell Nancy he loved her and to try to explain that he'd made a gross mistake in walking out on her. *Nancy, I need you.*

His pride took control. *But not like this. Wait until I know what's wrong. Wait until I'm well again.*

But would he ever be? What about the case pending? He couldn't let Sam and Sadie Burns down, not when they could taste victory. At times he could actually smell its powerful scent. But how sweet would a victory be if he couldn't share it with Nancy?

The door opened and Joyce came in. One glance at him and she ran to the desk. "You're ill."

"Think so," he gasped.

"Shall I call an ambulance?"

"No, but phone Dr. John Merrick and tell him I need to see him." He took a deep breath but found it painful to exhale. Perspiration popped out on his forehead. "Tell him to meet me at the hospital."

"Are you sure it's that serious?" she asked, the color draining from her face.

"I've been down this road before," he replied, clutching his chest as he waited while she placed the call.

"His nurse says he'll meet you there and not to fool around," Joyce said. "She also said to hurry and to take a nitro, several if you need them."

He grimaced. "In my pocket." With Joyce's help he took two nitros, but they didn't seem to help.

"Oh, Mark, I'm frightened for you," Joyce said.

Slowly he got to his feet, angry at his own weakness. "I was going to drive myself but...could you call a cab?"

"Don't be silly. I'll drive you," she said, sliding her arm around his middle. "Jacob, Horace," she shouted as they reached the lobby. "We have an emergency here. Help us!"

The two men grabbed Mark and half carried him to Joyce's automobile through a swirl of concerned seniors. In a blur of pain Mark caught the irony of the moment. It wasn't supposed to be this way, he thought, with two men in their eighties assisting a thirty-seven-year-old heart attack patient to an emergency room.

"I'm going with you," Horace insisted, leaping into the back seat as Joyce started the car and pressed the accelerator to the floor.

"A WOMAN NAMED JOYCE is on the phone," Nancy's secretary said, sticking her head in the doorway. "She says it's important."

"Joyce?" Nancy couldn't think of anyone she'd met named Joyce except for Mark's secretary. "Is she from the Peoria Senior Center?"

Louise glanced down at the pink note in her hand. "Yes, she said she's the receptionist and secretary there. Are they a new client?"

Nancy's heart lurched. "What does she want?"

"She said she has to talk to you, that it's *critically* important. She refused to explain. Want me to say you're in conference?"

If this was about Mark, why hadn't he simply called her himself? she wondered. "I'll take it. Thanks." She swallowed twice and tried to regain her composure before she reached for the receiver. "This is Nancy Prentice. May I help you?"

Silence greeted her for a few seconds. Then she heard the rush of an exhalation before the woman spoke. "I work part-time as Mark Bradford's secretary."

"Yes, yes, Mark has spoken highly of you," Nancy said, tensing at the tone in the other woman's voice.

"Yes, well, Mark had . . . he developed . . . a problem. He's going to be unavailable for several days. He's concerned about the Burns case and he requested that I get in touch with you."

"Problem? What kind of problem?" Images of him struck down again knocked her off balance. "Is he ill?" she asked, half rising from her chair.

"No, no, just a... personal problem," Joyce insisted.

Relieved, Nancy dropped back into the chair and leaned forward. "Has he had to leave town?"

"Uh, yes. The important thing is that he find someone to take over the Burns case," Joyce explained. "It's in the final phase of the pretrial conference. We expect the judge to rule next week, but now Mark won't be able to be there on Monday."

"Couldn't he ask for a postponement?" Nancy asked, more puzzled than ever at the direction of the conversation.

"It's been postponed too many times already," Joyce explained. "Under the circumstances he'd prefer the case be handled by someone he trusts."

"Someone he trusts? Me? You must be mistaken," Nancy said. "I haven't seen or heard from him for weeks and..." She hated the trembling in her voice. "I'm sure you misunderstood his request. He would never want me to handle—"

"Ms. Prentice...may I call you Nancy?" The other woman didn't wait for a reply. "Nancy, Mark was insistent I get in touch with you and no one else regarding this case. I know it's a holiday weekend coming up, but could you stop by the center this evening?"

"I suppose so, but are you sure?"

"You can use Mark's desk, and I'll help you gather the files," Joyce said. "He needs the reassurance that you've agreed to help. If I'm not here when you arrive, I'll leave the back door unlocked. Please go on in and . . . oh, God, please help us. He doesn't need this to worry about at a time like this."

"Where is he?" Nancy asked, her growing concern overshadowing her resentment at the woman's mysterious behavior.

"I think the world of Mark, and he asked that I respect his desire to keep this problem private," Joyce said, as if she had practiced the statement repeatedly. "He suggested you ask for a leave of absence for a few weeks to carry the case through trial. I'm at your disposal. If there's a conflict of interest, he suggested you . . ." The woman rattled off several alternatives, but Nancy had stopped listening.

Mark wanted her to work with him? Was this his way of apologizing for walking out on her? Did he still love her? Could they possibly become friends again, even lovers? Her heart raced as her thoughts leaped ahead to wonderful scenarios of working side by side with him for years to come.

"I need to get back to him, Nancy," Joyce said. "He'll weather this little problem much better if he knows his legal affairs are in good hands. He says you're a brilliant researcher and attorney."

Nancy's grip tightened on the receiver. "He said that? I thought he hated me."

Joyce chuckled softly. "I seriously doubt that he hates you, my dear. Quite the contrary. He talked about you all the way to the—"

To the airport? Nancy wondered. "Did he have to fly somewhere? Was this an emergency?"

"In a manner of speaking," Joyce hedged. "Can I tell him you'll take over the case?"

"Of course."

CHAPTER SEVENTEEN

"AM I HAVING another heart attack, or am I dying from something else?" Mark asked, trying to stay alert in spite of the pain-relief medication he'd been given.

"Hmm," Dr. Merrick said.

"Would you mind being more specific?"

Dr. Merrick studied the results of the EKG done shortly after Mark's arrival at the Arizona Heart Institute, comparing it with the results of the angiogram completed a few hours later. "A moderate...no, make that a *mild* myocardial infarction." He glanced down at Mark. "This is nothing like that first one. This is a .22 rifle blast compared to the hydrogen bomb before."

"People die from .22s," Mark said, fighting the old cynicism that had swept his hopes and dreams away before.

"You've developed some new blockage," Dr. Merrick continued. "Your blood pressure was climbing through the roof when you came in, but it's dropped significantly." He scowled at his patient. "I'm concerned about the blockage. Have you been taking your medication?"

Mark stared out the window. "Most of the time, but recently I've been under...I've had some distractions."

"Stressful?" Dr. Merrick asked.

"More than usual," Mark admitted.

"Have you skipped many doses?"

"About two months' worth. I don't know how it happened. I got sidetracked on this case and..." He hurt too much even to shrug. "The time slipped by."

"You were due for a checkup last month," the physician said. "My secretary forgot to send you a reminder. My God, young man, do we have to baby-sit all you heart patients? Can't you take responsibility for your daily lives?" He stepped closer to Mark's bed and peered down. "What case?"

Mark described the Burns lawsuit in brief but concise terms.

"When did you start taking on cases like that?" Dr. Merrick asked. "I thought you'd agreed to be retired."

"I was, but when I met Nancy, this woman I used to know—I told you about her. We started to make plans, at least I did. Is it so unthinkable that I plan for a future? Just one case, that's all I needed to prove I could—"

"Kill yourself?"

Mark glanced away. "You said I didn't have much of an attack."

"All heart attacks are serious, Mark. Have you forgotten all we've discussed? This one barely registers, but you're getting ready to have another major one," Dr. Merrick warned.

The pallor on Mark's cheeks increased. "When?"

Dr. Merrick arched a brow. "You want me to give you the date and time?"

"No, but I need to get back into practice," Mark insisted. "We have plans, important plans, but without a means of support, I can't expect her to—" He turned away. "I was grabbing for a brass ring that wasn't there."

Dr. Merrick pulled a chair up close to the bed. "Mark, listen to me. You've had a mild attack. Your rhythm is unstable. Have you been troubled with angina?"

Mark nodded but didn't say a word.

Dr. Merrick listened to Mark's chest again. "This is a blessing in disguise," he said at last. "The angiogram shows two new areas of blockage on the back side of your heart. We need to open them up before they cause serious damage."

"Open-heart surgery?" Mark closed his eyes. "I don't think I could go through that again. Thanks, but no thanks." He listened to the sounds in the room, the bleeping of the monitor, the soft bubbling of the oxygen as it passed through water, voices coming from the hallway.

"There are other alternatives," Dr. Merrick said.

Mark's thoughts slipped back to those terrible days when he awakened in the cardiac care unit with all the invasive tubes and the pain, most of all the unforgettable pain.

"Anything but opening me up," he said, wishing he could recapture the control he'd once had over his body, travel back to a better place and time. Who was he trying to fool? He'd lived for three and a half decades under a delusion. The heaviness in his chest persisted, gnawing at him as a constant reminder of his mortality.

"We have some new laser techniques, but for you, I recommend an old-fashioned angioplasty," Dr. Merrick said. He described the procedures to Mark, how a small incision was made in the groin area to allow a flexible wand to be inserted with a balloon on its tip to be inflated at the proper spot.

"We belong to the same union as do our cousins, the Rotor Rooter fellows," he explained, "but we squash the plaque against the sides of your pipes instead of reaming them out. I've scheduled it for this evening. They'll come for you about six. I'm afraid you'll be missing supper tonight."

"I'm not hungry," Mark mumbled.

"Do you want me to get in touch with this Nancy woman?" the physician asked. "You should have someone with you when you come back to your room. Give me her number. I'll phone and explain the procedure, and I'm sure she'll be here in a flash."

"No," Mark replied. "I made it alone the last time. I can get through it again."

"You weren't alone," Dr. Merrick reminded him. "You had your family with you. Would you rather we notify your parents or your sister?"

"No."

"What is Nancy's last name?"

"No tricks, please," Mark said. "I'll get in touch with her after I'm out of here. She doesn't need to see me like this."

Dr. Merrick busied himself with the equipment monitoring Mark's condition. "Does she love you?"

"I think so," Mark said, grimacing as he tried to shift his position in the bed.

"Do you love her?"

"Yes," Mark replied.

"Then she would want to be here," Dr. Merrick insisted.

"No, we had a misunderstanding. I made a perfect ass of myself." Mark forced himself to grin.

"I'm not surprised at that," Dr. Merrick replied, chuckling. "I suspect whenever you do anything, you do it with perfection."

This time Mark's grin was genuine. "That's no way to talk to your patient. Now tell me more about the angioplasty. Will there be any complications? You remember I had several the last time."

"You could walk out of here on Monday," Dr. Merrick said, "but we'll keep you here an extra day or two. I could call Nancy to come get you."

"I'll take a cab," Mark insisted.

NANCY ARRIVED at the center at eight o'clock, but the building was dark and the door locked. Puzzled, she walked around the building, checking the other entrances. She found a rear door unlocked just as Joyce had promised.

Inside, she turned on the lights, hurried past three large pool tables and a Ping-Pong table, past two craft rooms and a library, to the front of the building. The facility had been partitioned into a card-playing area and a cozy conversational area. A third of the room had been set aside as a reception and office space.

A wood-grained name plaque on a door leading off this area read: Marcus Bradford, C.P.A., LL.D., Financial and Legal Services.

Her vision blurred. He was such a brilliant man, one of the most caring persons she'd ever known. "Oh, God, he's a truly good person," she prayed aloud. "Help us to work out our differences."

She closed her eyes, allowing her thoughts to center on Mark for several minutes and continuing to ask for divine guidance and help for them both, but especially for him. "Not me, Lord, but him. Help him to understand that I love him no matter how he makes a living or how healthy he is."

A sense of guilt settled around her. Had she pressured him into accepting the Burns case? Where was he now? Why hadn't he spoken to her directly? "Forgive me, Lord, if I've hurt him. Give me a second chance."

She opened the door into Mark's office and surveyed the small room, recalling his spacious office at Burnside, Bailey, Summerset and Zorn. There could be no room for a sofa in this tiny room, only a scarred desk and chair and two folding metal chairs for clients. How different his world had become.

Touching his chair seemed to bring him closer. The brief he'd been reading lay open in the center of his desk, as if he'd been called away suddenly and unexpectedly and planned to return momentarily.

She sat down in his chair, feeling imaginary arms surround her as she ran her fingers over his notes.

His handwriting had always been crisp and easy to read. Quickly she absorbed the strategy of his pretrial presentation and was struck by the direction he'd been taking. *He has no intention of allowing this case to reach a jury,* she realized.

The facts had been collected and laid out in such a forceful manner that a defense attorney would be a fool to let such damaging evidence against his client be revealed in a public courtroom.

If she had Stan Fischer for a client, she'd convince him to admit his guilt and settle immediately. Nodding her satisfaction with Mark's handling of the case, she began to gather the files up in a stack at the corner of his desk.

Mark, my darling, we'll win this case, she thought, *and when you come back, we'll sit down and talk.*

Taking the files with her, pausing only long enough to write Joyce a note about what she'd taken, Nancy exited the building and headed home.

On Thursday morning, when Linda called to remind her that Thanksgiving dinner would be served at 2:00 p.m., she begged off with a splitting headache. Her adrenaline was pumping overtime, and she didn't want to lose her momentum.

That night, when she finally put aside her notes and went to bed, her thoughts were filled with images of young Sadie Burns and her friend and all the discrimination they'd been forced to accept with no adult but her father willing to risk the wrath of a manager like Stan Fischer.

She awoke several times during the night thinking of Mark, wondering where he might be and what had caused him to abandon the case that was so close to a conclusion.

On Friday she wrote and revised her argument. "I need a break," she murmured to herself, and went for a swim. But within an hour she was back at the table, verifying facts, validating testimony, making sure she hadn't taken anything out of context.

She woke up on Saturday with a throbbing headache. Two aspirin gave her relief, and she returned to the table. During the night, she'd awakened with an idea concerning Sam Burns's deposition, but when she searched the table for his folder, she couldn't find it.

She checked the list of files she'd taken from Mark's office. Sam's folder hadn't been one of them. Had she missed it? Doubtful, she decided. Perhaps it was at Mark's home.

A tiny smile lifted the corners of her mouth. Perhaps Mark had returned from his trip earlier than he'd expected and was home now. Would this be a good excuse to confront him? But confrontation wasn't what she wanted. She wanted to feel his arms around her, pulling her close, assuring her that all was well between them.

She stopped at a fast-food restaurant and purchased a hamburger, fries and a thick chocolate shake. As she sat at a table enjoying the food, she thought of Mark and his special diet. She took another bite of her hamburger, feeling guilty that she could eat such items.

Her appetite vanished, and she tossed the remainder of her meal into the trash receptacle. Would the center be open on Saturday? she wondered. She decided to chance it, and when she arrived, she found several cars parked near the side entrance.

A dozen gray-haired men were arguing over a game of shuffleboard on an outdoor court, but when she inquired about Joyce, she was told the woman seldom worked weekends.

"Now that young Mark is out of commission for a few weeks she might not be back for days," one balding man said.

"Out of commission?" she asked. "Why?"

The men exchanged glances and shrugged, closing ranks and making it clear they considered her an outsider. She knew she'd be wasting her time to press them.

Returning to her car, she drove to Mark's, her pulse leaping when she saw his blue truck parked in the driveway. *He's here!* She ran from her car to the front door but received no response when she rang the bell and pounded on the door. Several minutes later she gave up and walked dejectedly away.

Apparently he had flown out of town, after all. Someone had to be caring for Belle, though. She doubted Mark could afford a kennel. She glanced toward Horace Moore's small yellow house. Surely he knew Mark's whereabouts. Would he tell her?

Nothing ventured, she thought, walking across the lawn. She looked from Mark's lawn to Horace's. Both had been freshly mowed, but by whom? Mark? She remembered he'd mentioned that occasionally he did the old man's lawn.

She glanced up to find Horace Moore standing at his open doorway, staring at her. "Good morning, Mr. Moore, I was hoping to find Mark here."

"He's in the—" Horace scowled. "You don't know?"

She stepped onto his porch. "He's where? Horace, no one will tell me a thing. All I know is that his secretary asked me to take over the Burns case and I agreed. But now I need a file and—" Fear tore at her when she saw the expression on Horace's weathered face. "Horace, where is he?" Her throat tightened. "Is he...hurt? Sick? Oh, no, has he had another—?"

Horace turned away. "Come on in." In the kitchen he poured two cups of coffee and sat down. "He's at the Arizona Heart Institute."

"Oh, God, no. Is he...how bad is he? Is he...going to die? Oh, my God, I've got to go to him. I've got to see him!" She bolted from her chair. "What's the address? I don't know where the institute is. Oh, please, Horace, help me."

Horace grabbed her hand and pulled her back into her chair. "Listen to me, Nancy," he said, continuing to hold her hand. "I went to see him last night."

His face shimmered before her. "Is he...conscious?"

"Yes, but he's had a complication," Horace said.

"From what? What did they do to him?" She tried to stand up again, but he restrained her.

"He had a little bitty heart attack, and the doc gave him an angioplasty to open two arteries," Horace explained. "Mark's been working too hard. Didn't he tell you he had to take it easy? He has to pace himself, and he stopped doing that. Even worse, I reckon he let himself get a little sidetracked and forgot some of his medication, and that aggravated his condition. The lawsuit he filed for that little girl didn't help, either."

"But he wanted to take the case," she insisted.

Horace shook his head slowly and swallowed a long sip of coffee. "I reckon he tried to be his old self again just to please you, but he can't do that, not even for you."

Her cheeks burned. "Are you saying I did this to him?" Her eyes widened. "I'd never hurt him."

Horace shook his head. "Didn't you push him into taking the Burns case?"

The truth of his accusation struck her with the force of a lightning bolt. "I...didn't mean...I suggested he get a second opinion. Was that wrong?"

"For him, yes." Horace took a sip of his coffee and studied her. "He loves you, you know, maybe too much."

She blinked, and a tear trickled down her cheek. "How could he love me too much?"

"He was willing to risk his life for you."

More tears flowed. "I never asked him to do that. I'd never want him to... all I said was..." She wiped her cheeks but couldn't bring herself to meet his gaze. "I love him very much, Mr. Moore. I never meant him harm. You've got to understand that. What can I do now?"

He pulled his hands away from hers. "Maybe leave him be?"

A huge lump formed in her throat as they stared at each other. "No," she whispered. "Why? I could never—"

"Even if it meant his survival?" Horace asked. "I've grown to love that young man like my own son, and I've seen him change since meeting you. At first the change was good. It was as if he had discovered something powerful and intoxicating. He had a reason to get up each day. But he became compulsive, obsessed about the case and earning enough damn money to ask you—oh, damn it all."

"He bought a ring," she murmured.

He held up his hand. "Yes, he showed me the ring. Frankly I thought he was jumping the gun, but I didn't say anything. When a man's in love, he's in no mood to listen to logic. *Was* he jumping the gun?"

"Not if he'd been willing to resolve a misunderstanding," she said. "But I don't need a ring. I just want him to get well and stay well." She got to her feet. "If I have to stay out of his life in order for him to have that, I will." She lifted her chin. "I love him enough to let him go. But I must see him, at least once. Please tell me the location of the hospital."

As NANCY DROVE to the hospital, Horace Moore's accusing words played over and over in her mind. He was right. It was her fault that Mark had pushed himself beyond his limits. She would apologize for her insensitive actions, even though her motivations had been well intended.

But why had Mark kept this new problem a secret? If he loved her as he claimed, he'd know she'd be worried sick. Did he think she didn't care? Why did he insist on excluding her from his life? Did he think she only wanted to be with him when he was well? Was he ashamed? There was no reason. How dare he exclude her?

She parked and hurried to the information desk to get his room number. Taking the elevator to the fifth floor, she stepped out into an airy lobby with a nursing station in the center.

"Room 521?" she asked the uniformed woman behind the bank of computer monitors. The woman pointed down a hallway and returned her attention to the monitors. What would she say when she confronted Mark? Should she throw her arms around him and tell him she loved him no matter what his condition? Apologize, then threw her arms around him? Give him a sedate kiss?

Horace Moore's harsh words swept in again, bringing guilt with them, and she hesitated at the closed door of Mark's room. Was he alone? Conscious? Bedridden? She wasn't sure she could handle that. Maybe he wouldn't want to see her. Obviously he didn't. Otherwise he would have contacted her.

She eased the door open and slipped inside. Mark's blond hair contrasted darkly against the stark white pillow. His eyes were closed, but his coloring looked good, she decided. Yet there was something unnatural in the way he lay so still. He looked too strong, too masculine. He should be up and about, playing ball, umpiring a game, walking with her and holding her hand. Laughing and putting his arm around her.

Instead, he lay in a hospital bed. And it was her fault.

He shifted beneath the sheet and light spread, bringing his bare leg from beneath the covers. When he tried to bend his knee, he groaned and eased it down again. He brushed the sheet aside, exposing his thigh, and she gasped. His leg, from where it surfaced from beneath the sheet to his knee, looked as purple as a piece of raw liver, and the limb was twice its normal size.

Nausea churned in her stomach. She swallowed and tried to accept his condition.

He shifted his head on the pillow and reached for the control panel along the inside of the guardrail, bringing his head and torso up several inches.

She walked closer, her heels clicking on the tiled floor.

His eyes opened. "Nan?"

She edged closer. "Horace told me you were here. Mark, your leg. What happened?"

He held out his hand, and she took it, rejoicing in his warm clasp, but concerned about his lack of strength.

"I have a little hemorrhage," he said, his voice low but steady. "It happened the last time, too. It's the blood thinner. You should have seen it yesterday. It was twice this size. I have this thing about fat thighs, especially when they're my own."

Tears burned her eyelids. "How *dare* you not tell me you were here."

"I didn't want to bother you," he said, glancing away.

"That's a shabby thing to say." She clung to his hand, hugging it against her body. "Mark?" She waited until he met her gaze. "I never told Jennings a single bit of information about the Burns case, not a bit. And I never intended to. It cost me a promotion, but I don't care. If I can't live with myself, why would I want to practice law?"

"You may never become a success in this business with that attitude," he warned, squeezing her hand.

She edged closer to the bed. "How are you? Horace said . . . well, he said a lot of things."

He reached out and brushed a tear from her cheek. "Don't cry, Nan. I can't bear to see you cry."

His touch sent a shiver of guilt through her. "Did I do this to you?" she asked, fearing his answer. "Did I make you so sick? Horace said—"

"Horace talks too much. I did it to myself."

She doubted that. "If I'd known what it would do to you, I would never have even suggested you take on the Burns case. Oh, Mark, I feel so responsible."

She reached out, needing to touch his face. As her hand caressed his cheek, she could feel the slight stubble of his blond beard against her palm. She bit her lip, trying to keep her self-control. No use. Sobbing, she buried her face against his throat, desperately wanting to turn back the clock.

He stroked her hair, clutching her against his chest while soothing her with his words. "It's okay, sweetheart. It's going to be okay. You'll see. Give me a few

more days and I'll be up and about as good as before.''

She sobbed against him, unaware of the creak of the
door opening and closing behind them. "I love you so
much," she cried. "It breaks my heart to see what I've
done to you."

"Shush, sweetheart," he murmured, kissing her
rumpled hair. "Did you find the ring?"

She nodded but stayed pressed against him.

"Do you still have it?"

She nodded again.

"You didn't flush it down the toilet or throw it out
in the trash?"

She giggled nervously. "I could never do that."

"Then keep it," he whispered. Taking her chin in
his hand, he eased her close enough to kiss her lips.
"I'm glad you came. Will you come see me again?"

"I'll try," she choked.

"Want to talk legal strategy?" he asked.

His remark reminded her of the Burns case and how
her insistence that he try it had brought him here. "I'll
keep you posted on the case, but maybe you can't afford to have me as a friend, Mark. I'm harmful to
your health."

"Good morning," a strange man's voice sounded,
and she whirled around to find a tall, slender, gray-
haired man leaning against the far wall, wearing a
heavy scowl. "I'm Dr. John Merrick. And
you're...Nancy?"

"Yes." She chafed under the man's intimidating
expression.

"You're the one who coaxed my patient back into
the profession that almost killed him once before?"

Shocked by the doctor's accusation, Nancy bolted from the room.

DR. JOHN MERRICK WANTED to follow the hysterical woman who had left the room in tears, but his primary concern was for Mark, who was struggling to get out of bed. "Lie still, Mark."

"I've got to go after her," Mark said, his eyes wild with concern. "Let me up. Help me, please. Get these damn things off me."

The monitor line turned flat as one by one he tore the electrodes from his chest. Before his foot touched the floor two nurses charged through the door, followed by a male orderly.

"Keep him here!" Dr. Merrick shouted. "Keep him in bed and get him hooked up again. Restrain him any way you have to. Dr. Brewer is on the floor if you need him. I'm going after that woman."

He turned to Mark, who had dropped back onto the sheets. "Listen to me, Mark, no woman is worth dying for, not even this one, but I'm going to find her and reason with her. Now rest." He glanced at the nurse practitioner. "I'll be back. It may take a while, so one of you please stay with him."

The physician ran from the room in time to see the flash of the woman's blue dress as she stepped onto the elevator. He took the stairs two at a time, guessing that she'd go directly to her car and try to drive away.

He'd seen this behavior before, and convincing her that she needn't shoulder the entire guilt for his patient's condition wouldn't be easy, especially when he knew she'd persuaded Mark to return to an undesirable profession and life-style. He hadn't helped the situation any with his insensitive remark, but he'd found himself angry at Mark's relapse. Perhaps he should shoulder some guilt himself.

Outside the building he spotted the woman halfway across the parking lot. He broke into a run again and caught her as she slid a key into the door of a late-model red compact.

"Nancy, wait," he called. When she ignored him, he grabbed her elbow. "Take the key out," he said, using his most authoritative voice. She obeyed but refused to look at him. "You're upset," he said. "You have reason to be, but we need to talk . . . about Mark and you and how I'd like to help you both. Mark's welfare may hinge on this. Please give me a chance."

She stiffened and looked directly at him. Her ashen cheeks contrasted with her bright blue eyes, now swollen from tears that had spiked her dark lashes. Under more pleasant circumstances she was probably a beautiful woman, but today she seemed prematurely aged with worry and guilt.

"Let's sit down," he said, taking her elbow and guiding her across the manicured lawn to a picnic table used by the staff. When she hesitated, he pulled her down onto the bench and straddled it himself. "Don't try to run away. You've got to face this and work it through."

"I almost killed him," she sobbed.

"Maybe, but I doubt it." Dr. Merrick told Nancy about Mark's first heart attack, how he'd managed to start Mark's heart again twice. "And that doesn't count when I stopped it myself in order to do the bypass," Dr. Merrick added.

Her hands trembled, and she tore the dampened tissue into shreds as she listened. "When Mark and I met again, he was a very angry man," she said at last. "Did you know that?"

Dr. Merrick leaned against the table, resting his chin on a fist. "I suspected as much. Mark gave me the answers he thought I wanted to hear, but I had my wife look up newspaper accounts of some of his trials. I knew he had lost his chance at a great future in law and I tried to help him adjust...but without much success. Maybe I'm responsible for all this, too."

She shook her head. "You saved him. I talked him into going right back to what caused his..." She wiped a tear from her cheek. "If I hadn't pressured him, he would have been content to stay at the center and be satisfied with half-time work. But I brought his discontent back to life and stirred him up enough to... It's my fault."

He chuckled. "I can see how you could stir him up, but I suspect that was good for him. He recaptured his virility with you. Don't be embarrassed. We talked about it once. Give him a few weeks and he'll be virile again. Some cardiac medication makes a man impotent, but not the kind I'll put Mark on. He just needs time to regain his strength."

"The best medication for Mark is for me to stay out of his life," Nancy insisted. "We had plans once, but no longer. I know Mark can't have children, and that's okay with me, but still... I have a busy career. I'm hyperactive. I like to get things done. I'd be a bad influence on Mark. He needs to slow down and I can't."

Dr. Merrick reached out and took her hands in his. "First of all, it sounds to me as if you and Mark are perfect for each other. The best thing you have going for you is love. Secondly Mark can father children if he chooses to."

"But he says—"

"If you marry him, the two of you should receive genetic counseling so you know the odds. If your love is strong enough, you can overcome great obstacles. The biggest one is Mark's health."

"And that's terrible," she conceded.

"Not really," he countered. "Any one of us could be hit by the proverbial beer truck and die tomorrow. Mark has a condition that can be life-threatening, but we've discovered it in time."

"But you couldn't stop him from getting sick again." She looked uncertain.

He took advantage of her confusion. "Skipping his medication was his biggest mistake, but now I know to keep closer contact with him. You can help me."

"Me? How?" she asked.

"Together we must make sure he abides by the rules that will preserve his health and extend his longevity. Equal rights aside, my dear, it tends to be the wife who keeps an eye on a husband's health. If you helped each other, you could have decades of happiness together."

She pulled her hands free and got to her feet. "Dr. Merrick, you make it sound so easy, but the reality is Mark is lying in a bed in this hospital, and I put him there. You tell him that I'll win his case for him. I owe him that much and more. The *more* as far as I'm concerned, is my promise to leave him alone so he can live."

CHAPTER EIGHTEEN

"I WANT TO TAKE a leave of absence or else have time off without pay," Nancy said, standing inside the closed office door of Sylvester Jennings.

He chuckled. "We don't dock our attorneys for a few days of rest and relaxation. Go ahead as long as your calendar is clear."

"It involves a legal matter."

"Your own? We provide free counsel to our employees." He smoothed a six-inch wayward strand of hair. "In some trouble?"

She took a deep breath and charged ahead. "An attorney friend needs someone to take over a case," she explained. "He's been hospitalized, and I promised him I'd see it to its conclusion. It shouldn't take more than three or four days."

"And you're positive you can settle the matter that quickly?" he asked, his wrinkled squint reflecting his doubt.

"It's a strong case." She debated the ethics of her situation. "Sir, I'm filling in for Mark Bradford on the Burns discrimination case. I want you to know up front."

"That little girl and . . . Stan Fischer, Junior?" Jennings's scowl deepened. "You're willing to take on your old firm?"

"With vigor," she admitted.

"So you think you can win?" he asked, coming around the desk. "That would be something. A young upstart female lawyer beating one of Bob's over-priced youngsters? Doubtful, Ms. Prentice, very doubtful."

She glanced at her watch again. "Do I have your permission to take the time off?"

He shrugged. "Keep your secretary informed of your whereabouts in case we need to contact you, but be aware, Ms. Prentice, this may have an adverse effect on your future with us. Is this matter worth that risk?"

Nancy visualized her financial future slipping away, but the image of Mark in his hospital bed and depending on her stiffened her resolve. "Yes, sir, it is."

His mouth tightened into a hard, narrow line. "When do you want to start your leave?"

She glanced at her watch. "This morning in about...an hour? No, make that fifteen minutes. I plan to walk to the Superior Court building. I talked to Louise yesterday, and she's rescheduling my appointments. Thank you for the time off, and I'll be back on Thursday or before." She extended her hand, but he turned his back on her.

She hurried to her office, gave Louise a victorious smile as she scooped up a volume of revised statutes in case she needed to refer to it, then headed toward the elevator.

An hour later she sat at the end of a long conference table surveying the people around it. "Some of you know me personally," she said. "I'm Nancy Prentice. I've been working with Mr. Bradford on this matter from the beginning. My associate has been hospitalized and will be unable to continue. I spoke to Mr. Carpenter yesterday, as well as our clients."

Sam Burns nodded. "Hate to hear about Bradford, but we know you'll be as good."

She smiled confidently at the nervous client. "I'm as familiar with the case as Mr. Bradford is. We researched the precedents together. I have his full support and cooperation."

She turned to Stan Fischer and his attorney, who were whispering to each other. "Mr. Carpenter, shall we begin?"

George Carpenter, a short, rotund man in his thirties, smiled in a condescending manner. "Sure, Ms. Prentice. Didn't you used to be a legal assistant at Burnside, Bailey, Summerset and Zorn?"

"Yes, for ten years." She didn't have to justify or explain her qualifications. "I'm sure we'll bring this case to a speedy conclusion. Now then, may I have a few minutes with you, Mr. Carpenter? Privately?"

Only the twitching muscle in his jaw revealed his surprise. "Sure. Stan, why don't you go smoke a cigarette outside?"

After the others filed from the room, Carpenter leaned over the table and grinned. "Want to strike a deal, Counselor?"

"Exactly," she replied. "According to the deposition you took from Sadie Burns, her testimony clearly shows that your client conducted himself in a bigoted, insensitive and illegal manner that deprived my client, Sarah Burns, of her civil right to play baseball on the Pony League Cubs team."

"But my client's testimony in his deposition taken by your associate—what's his name?"

"Bradford, Mark Bradford. I think you remember his name. His skills are amazing, don't you think? He was able to get your client to admit his biases, to his dislike and prejudices toward girls in sports. He admitted having no intention of letting the two girls on his team ever reach the batting box. As you'll note on page seven of Fischer's deposition, he states..."

She took time to retrieve the deposition and flip through the pages, although she'd memorized the man's statement. "He states, 'Broads don't belong on baseball teams. They distract the boys, get them all hot and bothered. Boys are horny at that age, and boys will be boys, so I did them a favor and kept those damn girls benched or doing trash patrol. Girls are good at that. You know, keep 'em doing little domestic chores. It comes natural to them.'"

She glanced up at Carpenter. "Can you imagine a man being that prejudiced in this day and age?"

Carpenter frowned.

She flipped several pages deeper into the Fischer deposition. "He admits here on page eighteen." She waited for Carpenter to find the page. "He admits to being aroused by the girls wearing shorts to practice. Mr. Bradford himself observed Mr. Fischer looking down the front of Sadie's shirt during a game when he demanded she bend over and pick up a coin."

Carpenter shrugged. "So the man was turned on. That isn't criminal."

Nancy smiled and closed the file. "In this case I believe it is, Mr. Carpenter, and I believe a judge or members of a jury will agree. Your client admits to being aroused by a fourteen-year-old girl. He admits to talking to his male players about their sexual feeling toward having two girls on the team. I'm prepared to prove that he encouraged the boys' sexual responses by putting the girls in positions that fostered those reactions.''

She leaned back, smoothing the lapels of her gray woolen blend jacket, and studied the other attorney. She'd give him a chance to respond before pressing him for a settlement.

''So he's easy to turn on,'' Carpenter replied. ''We both know that's not criminal. If it were, we'd be in criminal court. This is a civil case. Let's keep it that way. We wouldn't want to confuse the members of the jury, would we?''

She smiled, knowing she was on the right track. ''I have to present evidence that shows your client's preponderance toward discrimination. If I were you, I'd be concerned about Sadie and her teammates telling their experiences with Mr. Fischer during this last baseball season. When the men and women of the jury begin to think about their own daughters or nieces, even the little girl down the street in their neighborhood, coming into contact with men like Stan Fischer, they'll begin to see him in a most unsavory light.''

''My client won't be taking the stand,'' Carpenter said.

''A wise decision,'' she replied. ''I doubt he would impress a jury with his blatant bigotry.''

Carpenter left his chair to pace the room. After several circles around the perimeter, he stopped directly behind her chair. ''My client can be persuaded to be reasonable.''

She whirled around on the chair's swivel base. ''Another wise decision. It would avoid an unpleasant and embarrassing trial.''

''Could be,'' Carpenter admitted.

"Will be," Nancy promised. "I can guarantee a public trial will prove grossly embarrassing to your client. Why, I wouldn't be surprised if fathers began to avoid Fischer Home Centers for fear their daughters might come into contact with... unsavory clerks or managers. See how his reputation could spread?"

He frowned. "It would never get that bad."

She shook her head as if in sympathy for his client. "I don't understand why any man would want to let the world know what a lecherous old man he is. He'll be the laughingstock of the entire valley. Does he really want that? He'll also bring shame to the Little League program."

Carpenter held up his hand. "If my client agrees to settle, would you be willing to drop the other suit against the league officials?"

She stood up to equalize their negotiation. "I think so, but of course I'll have to discuss it with the Burns family."

He squinted at her. She realized she was taller than he was. When he straightened, she knew he was conscious of the disparity.

"Why don't we take our seats again and get down to business?" she suggested.

"Fine," he said, sliding into a chair halfway down the long table. She settled into the chair directly across from him.

"My associate had a call last week," she said, wanting to knock the opposing attorney further off stride. "A reporter from Channel Five wanted an interview. Then a few days later a reporter from the *Arizona Republic* called to verify the basis of the suit." She shook her head. "Not good publicity for a program designed to foster good sportsmanship for children. Devastating for Fischer's business, too.''

He nodded. ''If your clients will drop the suit against the league officials, my client will admit to his misconduct and agree to a cash settlement. He has ample business and personal liability coverage.''

''We have no intentions of ruining him financially, but Fischer and men like him must stay out of sports unless they can conduct themselves in a fair, unbiased and legal manner. Without much effort I could convince a jury that Fischer's intent might be more than sexual harassment and sexual bias. His remarks about being turned on imply...well, I doubt I have to be graphic. Juries have vivid imaginations, as do most parents when it comes to the safety and well-being of their children.''

Carpenter flushed. ''How much?''

She began a mental calculation of Mark's share of the settlement. If she could get an adequate settlement for the Burnses, she could also ensure Mark's financial security for a few years. He'd hinted they would settle for as little as a hundred thousand dollars. Would Carpenter go for two hundred thousand dollars? Mark would get a third. How much? Don't get greedy.

Before she could voice an offer Carpenter wrote a figure on his yellow legal pad and shoved it across the table.

''No higher,'' he warned. ''We won't settle for a dollar more than four hundred thou.''

She kept her features blank. ''I don't know. Maybe we should go to trial, after all. A man like Fischer deserves his fifteen minutes in the limelight.''

"Four hundred and fifty thousand," he countered. "Our last offer and the other suit is dropped."

"Fischer must give the two girls and their parents personal apologies," she added.

"He refuses to make a public apology," Carpenter said. "He's adamant about that."

"We agree. There's no reason to make a public display out of our settlement, but the girls deserve an apology from that terrible man, as do their parents. I've witnessed his conduct, and it's despicable."

Carpenter sighed. "I know. He's a first-class son of a bitch."

She smiled her acknowledgment. "Shall we present our negotiated settlement to our respective clients?"

"We agree on the amount and the apologies, but we want one more condition. Fischer insists he meant well, and he doesn't want the league to suffer from this action. He wants an agreement in writing that you won't sue the league officials at a later date."

"Agreed," she replied, "on condition the league officials run an article in the newspaper declaring their policy of fair and equitable treatment of all children, regardless of sex. It must run before next year's registration begins. We've already discussed this with the regional officials, and they'll write the statements."

They shook hands.

Carpenter nodded. "I'll find Fischer outside. He's a chain-smoker. He said that's the worst thing about being a manager. They won't allow smoking on the field. He can't smoke in this building, either. He considers it discrimination."

She shook her head in amazement. "I'll present your proposal to the Burns family, and if they agree, we'll prepare the papers. It'll take a few days."

"I have a set already drawn up," he admitted. "All we need to do is insert the amount, the conditions and the date. I can get a clerk to do that. Fair enough?"

"It's a deal," she replied, extending her hand to seal the agreement, then went to find Sadie and her parents.

NANCY HURRIED through the crowded restaurant to the reserved private room for the celebration already in progress. They had held off on the dinner until Mark was back at work in the Peoria Senior Center and the settlement check had been received, cleared the bank and the proceeds distributed.

Nancy had returned the stack of folders to Mark's office on Tuesday after the settlement, met Joyce for the first time in person and announced the results.

"That's so wonderful, but we were willing to settle for much less," Joyce said. "How did the amount get so high?"

"Legal strategy and a good bluff," Nancy explained. "I felt as if I were in a high-stakes poker game. Maybe I was. But Carpenter told me later that the board believed Mark would be asking for a million."

Joyce laughed. "At least Mark won't have to worry where the money will come from to pay the utility bill or buy that new set of law books he's been wanting. And Mark had planned to donate some of the proceeds to the center. Do you think he still might?"

"You'll have to ask him," She rose from his chair. "Well, I've done what he asked, so I'll be leaving. Do you expect him back at work soon?"

Joyce frowned. "Didn't he tell you? He'll be in on Monday. That wonderful Dr. Merrick insisted he take a week off and he agreed. Oh, my, haven't you told him about the settlement?''

Nancy glanced away. "You can do that. I kept my promise.''

"But...what about the check? When will it come? What about your fee? Without your help none of this would have happened.''

"I want nothing,'' Nancy said.

Joyce's features revealed her surprise. "Surely you get a portion. You deserve it.''

Nancy shook her head. "Please tell Mark to apply my portion toward his practice. I owe him that.''

How could she have explained to the woman that the award settlement didn't begin to ease her sense of guilt for bringing Mark to death's door again. If the money would provide him financial security for a few years, then he'd have time to adjust to a slower paced life-style again. This time it would be without her to bring complications.

Now, as she reached the entrance to the private dining room, she paused, listening to the voices. Sadie's giggling, Sam Burns's boisterous laughter, Joyce repeating the amount of the settlement. Then she heard Mark's voice, confident and steady, as if the group was celebrating nothing more significant than a family birthday. She knew her sisters had been invited, along with the other girl's family, the Todds.

Although she'd planned to skip the dinner entirely, Mark had called her and personally invited her. It had been the only time they'd spoken since their few brief moments in the hospital.

"Excuse us, ma'am."

Nancy turned to find two waitresses with heavily laden trays standing behind her. She opened the door and slipped inside, hoping everyone would be distracted by the arrival of their dinners and not notice her sliding into a chair.

To her dismay the only empty chair was next to Mark's at the head of the table. Trapped, she felt all eyes turn toward her as she walked stiffly to the chair.

"Sorry I'm late," she murmured.

She felt his gaze on her and reluctantly looked up, her heart bursting with love for him. She hoped he'd find peace and happiness now that his financial worries had been solved.

"Thank you for coming," he said.

She wanted him to reach out and touch her, but if he did, she feared she might flee from the room, or worse, throw her arms around his neck and ask him to forgive her. She tore her attention from him and concentrated on the others gathered around the table, accepting their greetings and comments.

A glass of champagne appeared in front of her, and several rounds of toasting followed. Glancing toward Mark out of the corner of her eye, she noted that he took an occasional sip of his drink, ate a portion of broiled lobster and had dribbled French dressing on a tossed salad.

Smiling, she looked up to find him studying her. "This isn't your usual diet," she said.

"Tonight we celebrate, thanks to you." He reached for his glass of champagne. "A toast to the woman who made this all possible." They lifted their glasses to Nancy.

She shook her head. "The credit all belongs to Mark. And to Sadie Burns. Without her willingness to pursue Fischer through the legal system, we wouldn't be sitting here tonight. To Sadie."

She held up her glass, and the others joined her.

"You're both too modest," Sam Burns declared, and he proposed a toast to Mark *and* Nancy.

"You haven't ordered," Mark said, leaning close in order for her to hear above the noise. He waved the waitress to their end of the table.

"No, no, I don't want anything," Nancy said. "I can't stay long. I have another appointment."

Mark straightened. "Where?" His voice grew cool. "With a client?"

She looked away. "It's personal."

He stayed silent for several minutes, and when he spoke again, it was as if the exchange had never taken place. "Sadie, are you looking forward to next year's baseball season now that you're guaranteed playing time?" he asked.

Sadie turned her liquid blue eyes toward Nancy's nephew, Chuck Andrews, who sat beside her. "I want to thank you, Nancy, and you, Mr. Bradford, for all you've done for us." She smiled at Chuck, who grinned back, clearly infatuated with the pretty teenager.

"Please understand, I loved playing ball," Sadie continued. "My grandmother always encouraged me to play my best. It was like a family heritage for me to play baseball. But I talked it over with Grandma Burns and she understands. Mr. Fischer was the worst man I've ever known, but it's not because of him that I'm retiring officially from league baseball. It's because I'm not a kid anymore."

Chuck nodded. "She's already fifteen."

She smiled back at him. "Chuckie is playing American Legion ball next year. Their games are on the same nights as ours." She sighed dramatically. "I couldn't bear to miss a single game Chuckie plays, and when he's not playing, we want to go to the games together, don't we, Chuckie?''

"Yeah," he said, grinning as he winked at her. "And Mr. Bradford is going back into umpiring, aren't you, sir?"

"That's true," Mark replied. "They've asked me to do a sportsmanship workshop before the season starts. It'll be mandatory for all managers and coaches. It'll include a discussion of legal issues."

Nancy's eyes widened. "They'd let you back in after what you did to them?"

"Don't forget that we let the league off the hook, Nan. I had no trouble getting them to support the training workshop. Murray Harper is the new president. He says he's been asking for this for years, but Fischer and Glenn always voted it down."

"Will you have time for all that?" she asked.

"I'm back to half days at the center," he replied, "so I've got time to do a lot of things. For one, I'm remodeling my house." His gaze lingered on Nancy. "And we're starting a fund-raiser for the center so we can expand the facility. We're getting crowded."

Nancy took a sip of her champagne. "It sounds as if your life is back to normal yet still exciting and full."

"There's room for you."

She couldn't resist looking at him. "You're doing so well without me."

Before he could reply Chuck tapped his glass of cola. "Sadie gets to be part of Mr. Bradford's workshop," he boasted. "She gets to talk about how to work with girls. I'm helping her this winter. She'll be terrific."

Sadie laid her head on his shoulder. "Isn't he radical?" she asked everyone.

Laughter broke out, and everyone seemed to start talking at once. Nancy's gaze jerked from one animated face to the next, but her heart grew heavier as the minutes ticked away.

Mark reached out and covered her hand. "Can we go somewhere and talk?" he whispered. "Couldn't you contact the person you're meeting and reschedule?"

"I don't know." She eased her hand from his. "How are you feeling?"

"Almost like new. Dr. Merrick says if I follow orders, I should be good for another year or two."

"Please don't say that," she said, her voice trembling. "You'll be fine now. I hope you put the fee you earned to good use or invest it wisely. I . . . need to . . . please excuse me."

He grabbed her hand. "Nan, I want you to come back."

"No, I'm harmful to your health."

He shook his head. "That's crazy. I love you."

"You're much better off without me, Mark. Even Dr. Merrick thinks so."

He squeezed her hand. "I won't give up on us that easily, Nan. I'll be thinking of you. Remember that. I want you in my life. It's empty without you, but it's got to be on mutual terms. I'll wait until the time is right."

Nancy's eight-year-old nephew Larry worked his way to the head of the table. "Mr. Bradford, will you show me where the boy's bathroom is? I can't find it and my dad won't stop eating long enough to go with me."

Mark stood up. "Sure, Larry. Excuse me, folks. Nan, please stay until I get back. I need to talk to you."

As he walked toward the exit to the main dining, Nancy watched his every move. He'd lost weight again. His shoulders seemed broader than she remembered, his jacket hanging on his tall frame. His trousers, too, seemed to hang loosely on his lean hips, as if his clothes needed to be sized down. But with proper nutrition he'd regain his strength and stature.

The image of his body formed in her mind, lean and muscular, a body that she'd loved so passionately and that had brought her great ecstasy and fulfillment. But her love went deeper than passion. Now she loved him enough to walk out of his life forever and let him live.

She retrieved her purse from the floor and excused herself, slipping out through the lounge entrance rather than risk meeting him again.

Once safely back in her small apartment, she turned on her answering machine and went to bed, curling up into a ball and willing herself to sleep.

But sleep never came. Each time she tossed and turned she found an imaginary Mark Bradford haunting her, beckoning to her, shouting at her, insisting that she join him. Maybe she was going crazy, she thought. He had no right to make her life so miserable, not when she'd done all she could to make his better.

A WEEK LATER Mark Bradford sat in his office, staring down at the official notice from the national organization called Foundation for Legal Access. In spite of the intense effort he and Joyce had put into the application, the award of a fifty-thousand-dollar operating grant did nothing to lift his spirits.

Joyce fidged in a nearby chair. "We didn't get it. I can tell by your face. Oh, Mark, I'm so sorry. We worked for weeks on gathering all that data."

"But we did get it," he said.

"Then why do you look so sad?"

He leaned back in his chair, mulling over his dilemma. "I'm going to take some of my fee from the Burns case and donate it to the center," he said. "I don't need it all. We can hire an assistant, and I'll have fewer cases to handle. I've already placed some ads. We won't be in a money crunch for a few years."

"That's wonderful," she replied.

"I want to ask Nancy Prentice to come into our operation," he said half to himself.

"Then ask her."

"She'll turn us down."

She came around the desk and gave him an impulsive hug. "You leave it to me, Mark, my boy. We'll get her here by hook or by crook. God works in mysterious ways, and I have a direct line of communication, so expect the unexpected."

CHAPTER NINETEEN

"DID YOU HEAR about Thompson?" Kevin Scott asked, sticking his head through Nancy's open doorway.

"I suppose he got a promotion," she said, not interested in hearing about the success of those around her. Since leaving the dinner and Mark Bradford, she'd concentrated on her pending cases, winning most of them, settling out of court on a few and losing enough to keep her humble. Her billable hours had kept pace with her colleagues, but she'd been passed over for promotion again.

Although policy made discussion of salaries and promotions taboo, few could keep their good news to themselves. By the time official announcements were made, the story was usually old news.

Kevin gazed thoughtfully at her. "Your time will come. It's got to. Hey, did you hear about that Peoria lawyer who has a poor man's practice with seniors? He's running ads in the *Arizona Legal Review* for an assistant. Can you imagine anyone accepting the position when it only pays twenty thousand dollars plus expenses? The guy must be crazy."

"He means well, I'm sure," she replied. "Legal assistance for the underprivileged seldom pays well."

"Geez, but who could exist on a pittance like that?" Kevin scratched his temple. "The guys were talking about him at lunch. Andrew Leake says he's the same guy who had a heart attack right in the courtroom a few years ago and then disappeared.''

Nancy bristled. ''Stories like that are best dropped unless you know all the facts, Kevin.''

''He probably got a big enough payoff to live comfortably. So why come back doing good deeds like that? Beats all, doesn't it? I mean, why would a sharp lawyer like Bradford get out of the fast track and show up in Peoria of all places?''

When she didn't reply, Kevin gave up and left.

Later that afternoon she called Mark's office. ''Everyone's talking about your advertisement,'' she said, being careful to keep her tone casual. ''Have you had many applicants?''

''Two,'' he said, ''both young law school grads who failed to pass the state bar exam. Not quite the caliber I'm looking for.''

''Can you afford to increase the salary?'' she asked. ''Some of the guys around here were commenting about the amount you were willing to pay. They weren't impressed.''

''Then I wouldn't be impressed with them, either,'' he said. ''How are you?''

''Fine. Busy. The days pass.''

''Well, I have a phone call waiting. I should go.'' He paused, as if he wanted to say something, but didn't.

''Bye, Mark.''

MARK CALLED HER a few days later about a detail of the Burns case. ''I needed to make sure before I closed the file.''

She gave him the answer and told him where he could find the supporting document.

"Thanks," he said. "Sorry to bother you."

"Have you hired an assisant?" she asked.

"No, so I've decided to upgrade the position to an associate and upped the ante to twenty-five thou."

"Can you afford the increase?"

He told her about the operating grant they'd been awarded. "We'll run out of funds a bit quicker. But if that's what it takes to get someone, we'll have to do it."

"The associate will probably be making more than the boss," she commented.

He didn't reply.

"Good luck," she said, knowing she was stalling.

"Want to be interviewed for the position, Nan?"

She wished she had the courage to challenge him with an acceptance. "I already have a good job, Mark, and now I only owe two thousand dollars on my student loans. Before long I'll be debt-free except for the car."

"And then what will you do? Get a bigger apartment, trade up for a fancier vehicle? Buy a new wardrobe? Maybe invest in a home? Make it a good one, Nan. You deserve a nice place. Remember years ago when you told me someday you'd have the good life? I'm pleased for you. Go for it while the getting is good, especially if that's what's important to you."

"Mark, you're wrong. Do you know so little about me?" Her intercom rang with two lines flashing at once. "Mark, I've got to go. Call me back."

The minute she hung up Louise entered, waving a pink slip. "Old Jennings may be on the warpath," she warned. "His secretary and I took our breaks outside. She says the partners' meeting was all about billing hours. His secretary says he's calling in all the lower-level attorneys and raking them over the coals, some for no reason.''

"And now it's my turn?'' Nancy asked, not relishing another confrontation with Jennings.

"No, this one is from Randall Staley,'' Louise replied. "He wants to see in you in his office at four.''

"Mr. Staley?'' Nancy glanced from the note to her secretary. "He's equal to Jennings and a lot more pleasant to deal with. Maybe I'm not being fired, after all. And I won't have to watch Jennings fuss with that strand of dyed hair of his all the time. Why doesn't someone snip it off while he's dozing in his chair?''

Louise chuckled. "His secretary plans to do it the day she retires.''

"GOOD AFTERNOON, Ms. Prentice. Please sit down,'' Randall Staley said, waving his hand to two chairs near the spacious window of his airy office.

This corner suite, decorated in soft pale blues and dusky roses, reflected the pleasant disposition of its occupant. How Staley and Jennings had remained partners in the same firm for three decades was a mystery, Nancy thought. Perhaps the fact that they'd inherited the firm from their respective fathers accounted for the long-lasting relationship.

Staley smiled and nodded his full head of white hair toward the view from his window. "Amazing to see what's happened to this city, isn't it? Frankly I long for the good old days.''

She returned his smile. "It's been this way since I was a child,'' she said, then hoped he wouldn't take offense to her age reference. "You wanted to see me?'' she asked.

"Yes, I wanted to talk to you before we placed the announcements in tomorrow's business section of the *Arizona Republic*," he said. "We've made some decisions about our junior-level people."

She sighed. "And I've been passed over again. I'm not surprised. Who gets the honors this time? And why am I being given this privileged information?"

"Because you're one of the chosen few," he said. "If you accept, you'll become a probationary beginning partner in our firm. You've proven your worth, and frankly, anyone who can step in and win a case over my old rivals at Burnside, Bailey, Summerset and Zorn gets my support."

She rose from her chair. "You didn't pass me by this time? I thought I'd killed my chances when I asked for the leave and took that case."

"Sit down, please," Staley said, now smiling broadly. "Now we have your salary to negotiate. We were thinking about a twenty percent increase, with another in a year if your billable hours stay up."

Mentally she calculated the gross salary he was offering her. The amount brought a lump to her throat. She'd be able to pay off her debts with a month's salary.

"We have lots of confidence in your future within this firm," Staley said.

"We? Mr Jennings said..." She straightened in the comfortable chair. "I feel as if I'm being jerked around, Mr. Staley. Mr. Jennings made it very clear that I'd made a fatal mistake by helping Mr. Bradford."

Randall Staley nodded his understanding. "Syl Jennings has decided to retire. I've convinced him that he and Bob Summerset can enjoy life on the golf course as much as in this building. Bob's stroke last year has troubled Syl. I also know he's become rather crotchety these past several months. So you needn't worry about Syl Jennings."

"So he had nothing to do with this offer?" she asked.

"It's my decision," Staley said. "Within five years, if your performance stays on course, I'm sure you'll be offered a most lucrative partnership. I can guarantee that."

She eased back into her chair. "How can you be so sure of the future?" she asked, thinking of all Mark's plans. Where would Mark be five years from now? Still able to work only part-time? An invalid? Gone?

She rose to her feet again. "Mr. Staley, thank you for recognizing my abilities, but I must decline your generous promotion. I'm resigning. I'm taking a position with Mark Bradford. It'll start right after Christmas."

"Bradford? I'm sure we could match his offer," Staley said.

She smiled. "I'm sure you could."

"SHE'S HERE, MARK," Joyce said. "I saw her drive up."

Marks features were immobile as he adjusted his burgundy tie. "You can leave as soon as you show her in. Say a prayer for me, Joyce. I need all the help I can get on this one."

"She cared enough to call," Joyce reminded him. "I recognized her voice the minute she spoke. She took our bait. Now you turn on the charm."

He rose and stretched, knowing the next hour wouldn't be easy for either of them. "You make it sound so simple."

"Love is never simple, but the rewards are worth the agony, don't you think?"

He grinned, sat back down and waited.

A few minutes later Nancy rushed into the office. Joyce motioned her into Mark's office and waved. "See you two tomorrow. Good luck to both of you."

Nancy brushed several curls from her temple, then slid out of her full-length blue quilted car coat. *She's as nervous as I am,* Mark thought.

"Is it cold outside?" he asked, admiring her wind-blown curls and the flush on her pale cheeks.

She smiled and tossed her coat and purse onto an empty chair. "The weatherman says a cold snap has blown in. It's windy. I'm sure there's snow in the north country."

An image of them together, playing in the snow, came to Mark, and he smiled back at her. *Maybe someday.* "Sit down please," he said.

She slid into the chair, keeping her legs primly together and smoothing the skirt of her tailored suit over her knees. Her black pumps made her calves extra shapely. He'd always thought she had beautiful legs.

He tried to concentrate on the interview at hand. She seemed harried, unsettled, as if she found herself in a quandary about...what? Her career? Had something happened? Was she here to make up or to ask seriously for the job? And why would she be willing to take a major step down from her prestigious firm and her high salary?

"Do you want to hear about the position?" he asked.

"Please, yes." Her fingers intertwined in her lap, and he could tell she was fighting to keep them motionless.

God, she's in a worse state than I am, he thought.

He described the duties and hours, the salary and benefits, then told her again about the grant they'd received. "It's not full-time," he admitted. "I can't afford full-time help, not for the long haul, but you'll have your own office."

She glanced around the crowded room. "Where?"

He chuckled. "I donated forty thousand dollars to the center. The board of directors thanked me, then promptly launched a building program and included space for a second office and another secretary. We'll be doing the center's books and office work, so we'll need a clerk, too. We'll hire from a pool of older adults who are interested. There's a lot of wisdom and experience in this area."

"They love you," she said. "They want to keep you here."

They sat across from each other, each absorbing the essence of the other.

"How's Belle?" she asked, twisting her hands.

"She's fine," he replied. "I sold all the puppies. I was tempted to keep one but decided against it. I used the money to replace the kitchen range and put in a dishwasher. I bought a microwave, too." Why had he told her that? He tried to keep his thoughts from drifting to personal matters.

"I know you're not really interested in this job," he said. "You've got a great position at Staley, Jennings and Kaufman, and I can't compete with their salary. We *can* offer health insurance now, though. We found a medical policy that we could afford. It'll cover all

employees but me. My preexisting condition pre-
cludes—"

"I understand," she replied. "I'm unemployed. I
resigned from Staley, Jennings and Kaufman today, a
few hours ago actually. Randall Staley offered me a
promotion, but I turned him down. The money no
longer matters. If you turn me down, I'll start looking elsewhere."

"You quit a great job like that? Why?"

She brushed a tear from the corner of her eye.
"Mark, I want to be here with you. In spite of everything I . . . money doesn't matter as long as . . . I can
work with you. You know we make a good team."

He eased his center drawer open and glanced inside. No, he decided, the time wasn't right yet. He
closed it and looked across the desk again. "We need
to clear the air," he said. "First, this albatross you've
been carrying around about being responsible for my
relapse. It wasn't your fault. It was mine."

"Then you forgive me?" she asked, wiping a tear
that trickled down her cheek.

"There's nothing to forgive, but if it makes you feel
better, yes, I forgive you. But, Nan, can you forgive
yourself? I don't want you here because of some mis-
directed guilty conscience. I want you with me because we love each other."

"I phoned Dr. Merrick," she confessed. "He says
I've been acting irrational." She smiled across the desk
at Mark, making his heart race. "Now he says I've
come to my senses. He agrees that I can keep a better
eye on you if we live together." Her forlorn expression tore at his heart.

"I won't want us just to live together." He reached
into the drawer again and slid the ring into his palm.

"I've always wanted a partnership, but the name has to be Bradford and Bradford. I can order the sign tomorrow."

"Bradford and Bradford?" She rubbed her temples again.

"Yeah, a husband-and-wife partnership."

She wiped her cheeks again. "Bradford and Bradford? Just the two of us?"

"I'm asking you to marry me." He came around the desk and took her hand, pulling her to her feet. "Can we forget this mess we've gotten ourselves into, Nan? I love you so much. I've missed you like hell. Will you marry me?"

"I never expected this...."

He pulled her against him. "I've been so lost without you. I want to wake up with you in my arms. I want to hear you laugh and watch you play with Belle. I want to go for long walks with you so we can talk. I want to make love to you again and again."

"Oh, yes, Mark," she cried. "I want all that, too."

He stroked her cheek, then slid his finger along her jawline. "I want a peaceful life and happiness and being with someone I love. Those are the things that are important to me, more important than money. I've finally learned that. It's wealth of a different kind. Could you be satisfied with that?"

"Oh, Mark, I love you," she whispered, stretching to reach his mouth. "If we're together, that's all that matters. Yes, I'll marry you, and together we'll make the best partnership you could ever imagine."

"Do you still have that little gold wedding band?" he asked.

"Of course. It's in my purse. I carry it with me wherever I go," she admitted. "It makes me feel as if you're close."

"A wedding ring alone looks incomplete," he said, kissing her lightly. "When Joyce told me you were coming in, I went out and bought this to keep it company." He retrieved a small diamond ring from his pocket and slid it onto her finger. "It's not very large."

"It doesn't matter," she replied. "It's the most beautiful ring I've ever seen. When can I put on its mate?"

He glanced at the calendar on the wall. "Blood tests, the license and a three-day wait. We should be able to get a justice of the peace to give us a Christmas wedding...unless you want something more complicated. Would you settle for a new husband for Christmas?"

"That would be the best gift I can imagine," she said, seeking his lips.

When she eased back and gazed up at him, her eyes were dilated. "So what do we do until Christmas?"

"We can go home and make up for lost time," he said, grabbing her coat and draping it over her shoulders as he guided her out the door. "I don't have any etchings but I could show you my new microwave."

"I can think of more imaginative activities than that to fill the time," she replied.

EPILOGUE

MARK BRADFORD SAT comfortably in the lawn chair, his long legs stretched out in front of him as he stared at the miracle squirming restlessly on his lap.

"Today's Easter, huh, Daddy?"

"Yes, Amy," Mark replied for the third time, tugging playfully at the straw hat she wore.

She giggled. "But it's your birthday, too, huh, Daddy?"

"Yes, sweetheart, it's my birthday."

"Grandma Bradford says you're forty-three years old." She held out a quilted fabric basket Nancy had made for her. "Want a jelly bean, Daddy?" She held out a red candy, and he opened his mouth so she could toss it in. "You caught it!"

He chuckled. "We've practiced all morning, silly."

She glanced over her shoulder toward the house. "Mama says Dr. Merrick is coming and Grandma and Grandpa Prentice and all my cousins." She shook her head. "I sure like having lotsa cousins."

"Me, too, babe."

"Is forty-three old?" she asked. "I'm only this many." She held up four fingers. "How did you get to be so old, Daddy?"

He gazed at the intense blue-green eyes staring back at him. "It's a miracle, honey. I used to live in the fast lane until I got sick. Then I met your mother again." They'd gone through this routine hundreds of times.

She laid her soft hand against his mouth. "And then you decided you loved her, but she got mad, and then you kissed her." She clapped her hands excitedly. "Your turn now. This is the best part."

He inhaled deeply and slowly let it out. "And then we got married and—"

She bounded on his lap. "I want to finish it."

He pretended to scowl. "I'll bet you forgot how it goes."

She grinned, and he recognized a dimple identical to his own on her cheek. "I never forget. Uncle Horace says so. After you and Mommy got married, I was born!" She grew solemn. "And now I gotta learn a new part, huh?"

He glanced toward the house and could see shadowy heads inside. "Yes, the story is going on."

"Will I have a little brother or a little sister?" she asked.

"The doctor did some tests, and he says it's a baby boy," Mark said, thinking of the series of diagnostic tests that had been conducted to determine the genetic makeup of the fetus. Their son appeared to be healthy. *Two home runs,* he thought. So far they'd beaten the odds.

"It sure takes a long time to make a baby, doesn't it?"

Only seconds, he was tempted to reply, but knowing his daughter's uncanny ability to remember everything she heard and share it with her two sets of grandparents and all her cousins, he decided against it. "It takes nine months. We have two more months to go, so be nice to your mother. She gets tired."

Amy looked aghast. "I'm always nice to Mama, and I'm always good, too. Uncle Horace says so."

"He's biased where you're concerned," Mark countered. "Just do your best."

"I always do my best," she said, puffing out her small chest a bit.

That would be one of the problem areas in the future, he feared, recognizing the traits that could send her rushing headlong into the fast lane of society.

"Daddy, how did you and Mama make me?" she asked, cocking her head thoughtfully.

Mark swallowed and tried to think of an appropriate answer for a four-year-old. "Well, your mother and I...we...came together in a special way...and you started to grow in your mother's tummy." He studied his daughter as she considered his explanation.

"And then you came together anudder time and made anudder baby?" she asked, playing with the buttons on his shirt.

More like thousands of times, he thought, thinking of the depth and intensity of their relationship over the years. "Yes, honey, we did."

"Mmm." She frowned and pursed her pink lips. "Why did you want to make me?"

"That, my precious, is easy to answer." He pulled her closer and kissed the tip of her tiny nose. "We knew we'd love you."

"Even before you saw me?"

"You better believe it. We talked it over with Dr. Merrick, and the three of us decided it would be a good idea." He tickled her tummy. "And it was. Any more questions?"

Amy shook her head, knocking her straw hat askew. "No, Daddy." He adjusted her hat and she smiled. "Uncle Horace is coming over, too," she said, offering him another jelly bean. "He says that old hospital is no place to be on Easter."

"He's right, honey," Mark replied, recalling the events that had saved his neighbor's life. "And he has you to thank for finding him in time."

Amy Bradford had disobeyed her parents' rules and gone next door to show her beloved "uncle" the new dress her mother had sewn for her for the upcoming Easter holiday. In minutes she'd come racing back to tell her mother that Horace was sleeping on the floor and wouldn't wake up.

Nancy had called 911, then raced next door to stay with Horace until the ambulance came. He'd had a stroke, but was recovering nicely, and was now home with a live-in housekeeper who had training in physical therapy. Mark had done the paperwork to get funding to cover the expense.

Since he'd married Nancy, he'd become known as the "West Side Legal Advocate" and had been asked to appear before the legislature several times to testify for legislation for the forgotten segments of the population.

A month earlier, when Nancy decided to take a few years off from practice, he'd received word that the center had been awarded a five-year grant for operations, and now he could hire two assistants.

He leaned his head back and gazed up at the pale blue sky. It had been seven years ago today that he'd been struck down with his first heart attack. Finding Nancy again had turned him around and given him new incentive to live each day to the fullest. They had been married quietly on Christmas Day.

A year and a half later she had presented him with this miraculous child sitting on his lap.

Amy giggled and crawled closer, then slid her arms around his neck. "I love you, Daddy," she whispered in his ear, then kissed his cheek before jumping to the grass.

"I love you, too, Amy."

He watched her disappear into the house, then leaned back in the chair and closed his eyes. The spring sun warmed his body as the love surrounding him warmed his heart. Amy was only one of a string of miracles he'd experienced since meeting Nancy Prentice again.

"Got room on your lap for another woman?"

He glanced up to find his wife standing next to the lawn chair. "I always have time for you, Nan. How did you get out of the kitchen?"

"They chased me out," she admitted, adjusting the billowing top around her midsection. "They love the addition you've built on. They didn't know you were an accomplished carpenter."

He put his open palm on her belly and smiled when he felt the responding kick from his son.

"You like that, don't you?" she murmured.

"You get to carry him, but I get to communicate with him," he explained.

She kissed him. "I knew you'd be a wonderful father."

"No more suggestions about moving to a larger place in a better neighborhood?" he asked.

She shook her head. "I finally convinced them all that we were happy here. Reminding them that the house is paid for strengthened my argument."

"Nan, do you ever wonder how your financial affairs would be today if you'd never come to that ball game and brought me that root beer? If you'd stayed with Staley, Jennings and Kaufman? You'd have a lucrative practice, probably be a junior partner by now." She leaned quietly against him and didn't speak. "Be honest with me, Nan. I love you more than life, but sometimes I wonder."

A tinge of the old fear and uncertainty began to churn. He hated the feeling, wondering if he would ever be entirely sure.

Her hand crept up his shirtfront to settle on his neck. "Mark Bradford, you make me very angry when you talk like this. No amount of money would ever equal what I have now, because I have happiness, true happiness, and I'm very proud of our accomplishments. And don't you get too independent about working without me. Give me a few years to get these kids into school full-time, then I'll come back and work part-time."

"I could bring my work home and you could help me," he hinted. "After supper when the kids are in bed."

She grinned. "After the kids are in bed, we'll have other things to concentrate on. Dr. Merrick says having sex is like jogging ten miles, so I figure it keeps us both in good shape."

"God bless Dr. Merrick," Mark said, reaching out to caress her cheek. "And his report on Amy reaffirms the first tests."

She caught his hand in hers, and when he looked into her eyes, they were shimmering with tears, making them sparkle like wet sapphires. "She's not even a carrier of the gene. We gambled and won, didn't we?"

"Let's hope our string of miracles continues with number two," he said. "Dr. Merrick says there's no sign of trouble, but I worry about it, anyway."

Her fingers trailed the opening of his shirt. "Dr. Merrick also says they're developing new drugs and procedures. If our son does carry the gene, his treatment would start immediately. No surprises like you had. Your family kept it a secret. We won't."

"End of sermon?" he asked.

She blushed, then slid from his lap and stood up, holding out her hands to him. When he joined her, she put her arms around his neck. "I wish I could get closer."

"You'll always be close to me, my love," he whispered, pulling her as close as her rounded body would allow. "You're the beginning and the end of my string of miracles. You hold it together like a necklace of fine pearls."

When his mouth covered her lips, her mouth opened, inviting his entry. The kiss deepened and lingered until he knew she could feel his predictable reaction to having her in his arms.

"You'll have to be satisfied with just kissing for now," she murmured, locking her hands behind his neck. "I know several anxious children who are dying to come out here and start hunting for eggs and candy. I threatened them with canceling Easter if they came out before I gave the signal."

Mark glanced toward the house. "What's the signal?"

"The fourth long, stand-up kiss," she said, her voice soft and seductive. "They think we kiss a lot."

He grinned. "Perceptive relatives," he said, but didn't make an attempt to kiss her.

"Aren't you going to start?" she asked. "Amy is beside herself with excitement."

He suppressed a groan when she smiled and ran her tongue slowly along her lower lip and made a soft, kissing motion.

"We've got three more to go," Nancy murmured.

"Then let's get on with it," he said, pulling her into his arms. "We don't want to disappoint our audience."

HARLEQUIN SUPERROMANCE®

CELEBRATE THE SEASON
with Harlequin Superromance

Christmastime is truly a Season of Joy. This holiday season,
Harlequin Superromance is pleased to bring you two very special
stories.

#528 SEASON OF LIGHT by Lorna Michaels
Home in Cincinnati for the holidays, Jill Levin was tormented
by thoughts of the baby she'd given up years ago. Ben
Abrams had only the eight days of Chanukah to prove to her
that the holiday season could be truly a time for healing,
reconciliation . . . and miracles.

#529 KEEPING CHRISTMAS by Marisa Carroll
Jacob Owens was shocked when Katie Moran and her baby
son, Kyle, appeared on his doorstep in a snowstorm only
weeks before Christmas. Katie was obviously running from
someone, though she wouldn't say who. Jacob vowed to keep
Katie and Kyle safe with him—at least until Christmas.

HAVE A HOLIDAY SEASON TO REMEMBER—
WITH HARLEQUIN SUPERROMANCE
On sale in December wherever Superromance books are sold.

HSCTS

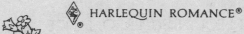

HARLEQUIN ROMANCE®

**Harlequin Romance
has love in
store for you!**

Don't miss next
month's title in

THE BRIDAL COLLECTION

A WHOLESALE ARRANGEMENT
by Day Leclaire

THE BRIDE *needed* the Groom.
THE GROOM *wanted* the Bride.
BUT THE WEDDING was *more* than
a convenient solution!

Available this month in
The Bridal Collection
Only Make-Believe
by Bethany Campbell
Harlequin Romance #3230

Available wherever Harlequin books are sold.

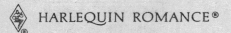

HE CROSSED TIME FOR HER

Captain Richard Colter rode the high seas, brandished a sword and pillaged treasure ships. A swashbuckling privateer, he was a man with voracious appetites and a lust for living. And in the eighteenth century, any woman swooned at his feet for the favor of his wild passion. History had it that Captain Richard Colter went down with his ship, the *Black Cutter,* in a dazzling sea battle off the Florida coast in 1792.

Then what was he doing washed ashore on a Key West beach in 1992—alive?

MARGARET ST. GEORGE brings you an extraspecial love story this month, about an extraordinary man who would do anything for the woman he loved:

#462 THE PIRATE AND HIS LADY
by Margaret St. George

When love is meant to be, nothing can stand in its way . . . not even time.

Don't miss American Romance
#462 THE PIRATE AND HIS LADY.
It's a love story you'll never forget.

PAL-